FOUND

Also by Shelley Shepard Gray

Sisters of the Heart series
HIDDEN
WANTED
FORGIVEN
GRACE

Seasons of Sugarcreek series
WINTER'S AWAKENING
SPRING'S RENEWAL
AUTUMN'S PROMISE
CHRISTMAS IN SUGARCREEK

Families of Honor
THE CAREGIVER
THE PROTECTOR
THE SURVIVOR

The Secrets of Crittenden County
MISSING
THE SEARCH

FOUND

The Secrets of Crittenden County

BOOK THREE

SHELLEY SHEPARD GRAY

AVON

INSPIRE

An Imprint of HarperCollins*Publishers*

FOUND. Copyright © 2012 by Shelley Shepard Gray. Excerpt from *Daybreak* © 2012 by Shelley Shepard Gray. All rights reserved. Printed in the United States of America. No part of this book may be used or reproduced in any manner whatsoever without written permission except in the case of brief quotations embodied in critical articles and reviews. For information address HarperCollins Publishers, 10 East 53rd Street, New York, NY 10022.

HarperCollins books may be purchased for educational, business, or sales promotional use. For information please write: Special Markets Department, HarperCollins Publishers, 10 East 53rd Street, New York, NY 10022.

FIRST EDITION

Library of Congress Cataloging-in-Publication Data has been applied for.

ISBN 978-0-06-208975-5

12 13 14 15 16   OV/RRD   10 9 8 7 6 5 4 3 2 1

In loving memory of my mother, Barbara Galloway

Those who look to him for help will be radiant
with joy; no shadow of shame will darken their
faces.

Psalm 35:5

It is better to look ahead and prepare than to look
back with regret.

Amish Proverb

Prologue

Jacob Schrock knew how to keep a secret. It was the way he had been raised.

His parents ran Schrock's Variety, which was in a lot of ways the center of their community.

Since he was his parents' only child, he'd always known he would take over the business. Even when he was small, sitting by his parents' side at the front counter, he felt a part of things. He also learned that selling merchandise to most of their friends and neighbors meant being privy to a lot of information they'd just as soon keep private.

"It's not our place to comment on purchases, Jacob," his father had told him all his life. "We offer things for them to buy, not gossip about."

By the time he was six or seven, he had taken that advice to heart. He became adept at going about his business with only half an ear to the private conversations floating around him.

Now, though, he wished he hadn't gotten so good at hiding his emotions.

"Are you sure you don't want to come over tomorrow night?" Lydia Plank asked. "My *mamm*'s going to make popcorn and hot chocolate."

"And probably another hundred things," Frannie Eicher said. "Your mother is a wonderful-*gut* cook."

As Jacob sat, listening to his friends chatter, he felt the iron grip with which he'd held himself tight slowly lessen. He'd missed this. He missed this . . . normality.

He and a group of his friends—Lydia, Walker Anderson, Beth Byler, and Frannie—sat on the store's porch, some in rockers, some sitting on the porch railing, drinking hot apple cider, eating day-old donuts, and basically doing what people his age did when they could: gossiping about life.

This slice of normal was just what he needed.

He craved it after what had happened during his last argument with Perry.

Still talking food, Lydia grinned. "My mother has a reason for making so many treats for me and my friends. She knows if everyone's there, she'll be able to know what we're doing."

"We are all over eighteen," Beth said. Looking around, she added, "Most of us are over twenty. Your *mamm* shouldn't care what we do anymore."

Frannie grabbed another donut and scoffed. "Parents always care, Beth."

"My *mamm* is interested, but she'll stay out of the way, I promise," Lydia said. "It will be fun."

"Sounds exciting," Walker Anderson said sarcastically, though not in a mean way. Just because he was English didn't mean he was stuck up like that. But he didn't hang out with them much.

Jacob considered accepting Lydia's invitation, but only for a minute. If he went, the conversation inevitably would turn to talk of Perry, of his recent exploits, his new friends, and of how Jacob's father had fired him.

Jacob definitely didn't want to go down that rabbit hole. "I don't think I can make it, but thanks for asking," he said.

Ever since his father had fired Perry Borntrager for stealing money out of the cashbox, Jacob had been feeling more and more out of sorts. Perry had been angry and hurt that Jacob had never warned him that he was going to be let go.

And though his *daed* had been right, and Jacob had been mad at Perry about the thefts, it had been uncomfortable. After all, he and Perry had been friends all their lives.

To make matters worse, everyone in the county seemed to know what had happened. And Jacob, used to keeping others' secrets, had been having a difficult time dealing with how everyone knew one of his.

Now, a few weeks later, things hadn't gotten much easier. Perry lurked around the store with new *Englischers*. Sometimes even wearing fancy sunglasses, of all things, even when it was dark outside.

The two of them, once close friends, had become distant. There was a lot of anger pulsing between them. Misplaced on Perry's part—he never was one to take responsibility for his actions.

And as Jacob watched his father struggle with firing a boy he'd practically help raise, Jacob's resentment grew. He was so angry that Perry had taken advantage of his family, of their friendship.

He'd never even apologized.

Lydia shrugged, bringing Jacob back to the present.

"All right, Jacob. But if you change your mind . . ."

"If I change my mind, I'll let you know," he replied. He breathed deep, desperate to push away his dark thoughts. Desperate to concentrate on the friends he still had.

But then one glance over Lydia's shoulder proved that goal

was going to be impossible. "I can't believe he had the nerve to come around here," he muttered.

Of course, his barely suppressed anger brought everyone else to their feet and turning around. Perry was walking toward the store with his sister, Deborah, at his side.

As if any of them would want to talk to the Borntragers.

Lydia closed her eyes and sighed at the sight of her ex-boyfriend.

"You don't have to talk to him, Lydia," Jacob blurted. He knew breaking up with Perry had broken her heart. "We should go inside and ignore them both." In two seconds, all of them could be inside and pretend the Borntragers weren't a stone's throw away.

"You want to ignore Deborah?" Frannie asked, her tone horrified. "Jacob, we can't do that. It wouldn't be right. Deborah's never done anything wrong."

Still more concerned with Lydia, who had tears in her eyes and, selfishly, himself, he said, "I don't want to talk to them."

But Beth, being Beth, couldn't seem to let it go. "That don't make sense, Jacob. You can't blame Deborah for her brother's actions."

Sure he could. He'd always taken responsibility for his family and their actions. He expected the same of others. Plus, he'd watched enough people in the store to know that most family members were aware of what other people in their homes did even if they pretended to turn a blind eye.

There was no doubt in his mind that Deborah had known that Perry was stealing from the store. For that matter, she'd probably known all along and had been protecting Perry.

"Don't make a big deal out of nothing, Jacob," Walker said.

"It's still a free country. You can't expect Perry to never walk on your store's sidewalk."

Jacob knew Walker was probably right. And when he spied Deborah casting a quick, longing glance their way, he knew Beth was probably right, too. It was wrong to shun Perry's sister for his crimes.

But just because he knew what the right thing to do was, it didn't mean he had to do it. So instead of relaxing, he rose and stood near the door to the store. Watching and glaring. Waiting for them to walk by. In just a few minutes, they'd be gone. Then they could relax and pretend that they'd never seen Perry and Deborah.

But Frannie ruined everything. She rushed down the steps. "Hi, Deborah. Hey, uh . . . Perry."

The siblings stopped and looked at her warily.

Beside Jacob, Walker groaned.

Jacob held his breath, hating that he had no control over the situation.

He felt completely ineffectual as Frannie barreled on. "Deborah, you want to join us?"

Both siblings looked startled by the invitation. "Well, I don't know," Deborah said, looking at Perry.

Jacob gritted his teeth. He ached to tell Frannie to take back the invitation. Or to just leave with Perry and Deborah.

After a split second, Perry turned his head. Met Jacob's gaze. Jacob stared right back, daring Perry to approach him.

"Go ahead, Deb," Perry finally murmured. "I don't care."

After another pause she nodded. "Okay, then, *danke*."

Frannie hooked her arm around Deborah's elbow and guided her onto the porch. Almost immediately, Beth walked over and hugged the girl.

All the while, Perry stood off to the side. Watching. To Jacob's surprise, Walker brushed passed him, walked down the steps, and spoke to Perry for a minute or two. Then, with an annoyed shake of his head, Walker rejoined the others on the porch. More cider was poured, more snacks consumed. Their conversation was inane and forced, not a one of them glancing Perry's way.

Jacob knew they were trying to pretend everything was just fine, but Jacob thought their actions were stupid. Perry was standing right there. On his property. He'd stolen money from his parents, he'd sold drugs to other kids in their community.

He was bad news, he was trouble and he deserved nothing. Not even to be ignored.

How could his friends look past that?

When another minute passed and Perry still stood on the sidewalk, Jacob walked down the steps. "What are you still doing here? You know you're not wanted, don't you?"

"I know. You've made sure of that, Jacob." Laughing softly, Perry added, "I don't think I would be welcome to even buy a stick of butter in your store."

"You'd be right."

A look of pain flashed through Perry's eyes, surprising Jacob. And, for an instant, making him feel guilty.

Though he sensed his friends behind him were listening—and maybe didn't even completely approve of the way he was acting—Jacob didn't give up. "You need to go. I don't want you here."

Perry walked closer. Now only a few feet separated them.

Perry was at least thirty pounds heavier than Jacob, and had a good two inches on him, too. A prickly sense of fear inched up Jacob's spine.

With a hard glare, Perry said, "So is it now against the law to stand here?"

"I don't know if it's against the law or not. It don't matter, though. My father doesn't want to see you ever again," he retorted. Even though his father had never said that. "I sure don't."

An expression flew across Perry's face. Perhaps it was disdain? Maybe more like disappointment?

After another second, Jacob added, "If Deborah wants to stay without you, I'll make sure she gets home safely."

Jacob waited for Perry to argue. To refuse to budge. But instead, he just shrugged and walked away, his shoulders drooping slightly.

Almost as if he had been the one with a reason to be hurt.

Again, Jacob felt guilty. Maybe he shouldn't have been so mean? Maybe there could've been a better way to remind Perry that he'd been the one to ruin their friendship?

His mind on that, he turned around and walked back up the steps. But when he looked at Deborah, sitting calmly there on his family's front porch . . . just like her family had done nothing wrong . . . his anger and frustration got the best of him again.

"Listen, I'm going to start locking up. If y'all want to hang out together, you're going to need to do it someplace else."

Walker stood up to him. "Jacob, I know you've got a grudge against Perry, but you need to settle down. I don't understand why you're acting so crazy."

Walker didn't understand. None of them did. And, maybe he was acting a little crazy.

Actually, he probably was. As he grabbed a plate of

donuts and strode into the dark store, he fought to control his temper.

Prayed for guidance.

Because one thing was sure. If he didn't find a way to control his temper very soon . . . he would do something he would regret.

Chapter 1

"Most folks don't know this, but Perry was afraid of the dark."
DEBORAH BORNTRAGER

"It is better to look ahead than to look back and regret."

Deborah Borntrager gazed at the Amish saying that her grandmother had neatly stitched as a sampler years and years ago and tried to embrace the notion.

But, as always, the pithy statement seemed far too corny to say and far too difficult to adopt. She'd always thought the simple saying was a little too "simple." Especially since, lately, all she was doing was looking back with regrets.

But was that the reason her mother had hung the sampler on Deborah's bedroom wall when she was a little girl? Looking backward instead of forward had long been her flaw.

After neatly securing her dark brown hair, pinning her *kapp* on her head, then placing her black bonnet, she walked past Perry's old room and paused for a moment in his doorway.

Her gaze swept past his unmade bed, the dust gathered on his bureau, the cobwebs in the corners of the room. The police hadn't been in his room since the day he disappeared, yet her mother had steadfastly refused to change a thing.

Not even when his lifeless body had been found at the bottom of a well.

It wasn't the way of the Amish to dwell on death, but for her family, it was hard to let Perry go. Often, Deborah heard her mother enter his room late at night, but she never sat on the bed or touched anything. Instead, she'd just stand in the room and cry.

Deborah wrapped her arms around herself, felt her grief drape her like a cloak. Swallowing hard, she backed out of the doorway and continued down the narrow hallway, past the washroom and the closed door of her parents' room, and trotted down the stairs, her shoes clicking softly on the wooden steps.

Once again, her father had left the house early for the fields, leaving the kitchen to her mother.

And once again, her mother hadn't gotten out of bed.

In the weeks since Abby Anderson had found Perry's body at the bottom of a well, her mother's health had steadily declined. She'd become weak and listless, and even tonics didn't seem to help much.

Deborah supposed she couldn't blame her mother. No woman wanted to outlive her son. And no woman ever wanted to hear that her child had been murdered.

Instead of making coffee and breakfast for her mother like she usually did, Deborah fastened her cloak and left the house as quickly as possible. She was going to find a job today.

She had to. No longer could she spend her days at home, worrying about her parents, mourning her brother, and wishing she could redo the past.

Yes, getting a job would be such a blessing in many ways. She could earn some money, have more independence, and finally have more in common with her girlfriends. Lydia Plank worked at her parents' greenhouse, Beth babysat and had a day-care service for *Englischers*. And Frannie Eicher? Frannie owned her own bed and breakfast!

Yes, her friends seemed to know exactly what they were doing in their lives. And each of them had experienced a bit of romance lately as well.

Lydia and Walker Anderson had begun courting. Frannie and Luke Reynolds, the city detective investigating Perry's death, were now seeing each other, too. And while Beth didn't have a sweetheart, she'd confided to Deborah that she'd developed a little crush on one of the men who'd stayed at the inn while Frannie was in the hospital a few weeks ago.

All of her friends had felt that first tingling sense of interest from a man. She, on the other hand, had only gotten a good taste of disdain.

Pushing her doubts away, Deborah walked quickly through the woods and popped out near Stanton Park. It was a busy place today. Several mothers and their children were out, enjoying the sunny, warm morning. When one waved to her, Deborah waved back, then continued on to the first place she had in mind: an antique dealer.

Walking inside a garage, the home of Esther's Antiques, she greeted the owner. "I'm looking for a job, Esther. Do you need some help?"

The older lady, dressed as usual in a thick black dress and apron, shook her head. "I'm sorry, Deborah, but I don't."

As usual, the store was overcrowded, smelling musty and

damp. She ran a finger along an old oak dresser. "Are you sure? I could dust and clean for you."

Esther frowned at the dirt on Deborah's fingertip, but still shook her head. "Everything could use a good cleanin', that is true. But I can't afford the help. Business has been slow. I am sorry."

Her heart sinking, Deborah nodded. "That's okay." After saying her goodbyes, she moved on to another shop—this one a woodworking store about a half mile away.

But the owner didn't need help, either. And neither did the folks at the Amish bakery, or at three of the nurseries in town.

By noon, she felt her spirits sink as her only other option for employment loomed up the hill and in the distance just like a circling hawk or some other bird of prey: Schrock's Variety Store.

What was she going to do?

Unbidden, the earnest words written on the sampler surfaced. *Don't look back, look forward.*

But did she dare?

Of all the times to take Amish wisdom to heart!

As she continued to walk, it seemed as if her feet were functioning on their own. No matter how much her mind and heart tried to beckon her body in a different direction, her feet just kept walking down the sidewalk.

Right to the Schrock's door.

She didn't want to go in. And she really didn't want to see Jacob Schrock again.

"Deborah? You're ruining my traffic flow, child," Mr. Schrock's loud voice rumbled through the thin door. "Walk in or move to the side."

She opened the door and stepped inside.

Mr. Schrock had on reading glasses and his face was screwed up as he stared at an invoice sheet. "Do you need help? If so, be quick about it; I've got too much to do today for lollygaggers."

His terse tone made her shoulders tighten. She swallowed hard, gathered up all her courage, and said, "I, uh, came to see if you needed some help."

His head popped up as his eyes narrowed over the tops of his wire frames. "With what?"

"In the store," she said, stating the obvious. Self-consciously, she pulled her shoulders back and lifted her chin. The last thing she wanted him to see was that she was a nervous wreck. "I am looking for a job."

"Are you, now?" Slowly, he folded up the invoice he'd been studying and gave her his full attention. She felt his gaze look her over . . . just like she, too, was full of numbers that didn't quite match up.

She squirmed under his gaze. This had been a mistake. "Do you need any help?" she asked quickly. Ready to get the embarrassment over with. "If not, it's all right."

"Why is it all right? Do you need a job or don't you?"

Oh, why had she come here? Why would they hire her after what Perry'd done? Almost everyone in Crittenden County looked at her differently now. She was sure they felt differently about her, too.

"I do," she finally answered.

She stood still while he walked around the counter and inspected her again. "Hmph," he said.

She stepped backward. What was she thinking, coming into the store, asking for a job in such a weak way. If only she could just disappear . . .

"How do you feel about kittens?" he asked.

Stunned, she mumbled, "Kittens?"

He nodded. *"Jah."* With a bit of amusement in his eyes, he added, "You know . . . baby cats?"

She felt her cheeks flush at his gentle teasing. "I like them fine." *Why on earth was he talking about kittens?*

"Do cats or kittens make you sneeze? You wouldn't believe how many folks seem to be allergic to the little monsters."

Monsters? "Nee. I am not allergic to cats, Mr. Schrock."

He smiled. "Then you have got yourself a job. I haven't had a female helper here in ages. You might be a nice change of pace. Especially if you're real fond of cats."

Deborah almost pointed out that she'd never said she was fond of cats. She'd only admitted that they didn't make her sneeze. But she held her tongue.

"You can add numbers and such, yes?" he asked.

"Yes, sir."

Mr. Schrock thrust out the invoice sheet he'd been studying when she'd come inside. *"Wunderbaar!* Here's your first job, Deborah Borntrager. Match the invoice numbers to the items I just unpacked in this box. Check them off one by one. Understand?"

It sounded simple enough. "I understand."

"Gut. Now, I'm going to find you more things to do." And with that, he wandered down the center aisle, opened the door that led into the storage area and office, and closed it behind him.

Leaving her essentially in charge of the front of the shop.

Well, this wasn't how she'd thought she'd spend her first day at work, she mused. But she supposed it made sense. Mr. Schrock had never been a man to do things in a predictable way.

Thinking it was time to do what he asked, she shrugged out of her cape and hung it on a peg near the shop's front door. As she headed back to the counter, she took a good look around, noticing everything seemed as it always did—packed with neatly organized merchandise on one side and filled to the brim with freshly baked goods on the other. In the back was a small dairy case filled with milk and cheese.

Picking up a pencil, she leaned on the counter, figured out what she was supposed to be counting, then picked up some boxes of muffin mixes and started looking for the item numbers. After locating the first set of numbers, she relaxed a bit.

This was certainly an easy enough task. And it did, indeed, feel mighty good to be out of the house. To be doing something productive instead of worrying about her mother.

Yes, coming to Schrock's Variety certainly had been the right decision. She checked off the numbers and scanned the invoice for the next set of numbers.

"Out of all the places in Crittenden County, you decided to get a job here? Really?"

She turned to the voice and pretended the words didn't make her heart break. Jacob stood in the doorway to the back storage room. Deborah turned back to her task. "I didn't think my being here would upset you, Jacob." But of course that was a lie. She'd known he wouldn't want her in the store. After all, he hated her. Hated her whole family.

As a moment passed, Jacob's eyes narrowed. Then, his expression turned blank. "You being here doesn't upset me. I've learned to never think about you at all."

"If that were true, why are you so angry?"

"I'm not angry. I just don't care to see you."

"Jacob!" his father said sternly as he walked in from the back of the store to join them. "You apologize now."

"I will not. I'm done pretending to be okay with things that aren't." Folding his arms across his chest, Jacob looked down at her from his almost six-foot height. "Deborah shouldn't be here, and you shouldn't have hired her, Daed. You owed me that at the very least."

"This ain't your concern, Jacob."

Surprise and true hurt filled Jacob's gaze before he turned on his heel and stormed out.

Watching the interplay and feeling frozen by the strength of Jacob's anger, Deborah desperately tried to regain her composure. "Mr. Schrock, do you want me to leave?"

"Of course not, child," he said. But his expression was wary and his shoulders were half slumped, revealing just how much his son's anger had taken a toll on him. "Look, you go back to those invoices now. And try not to worry. Jacob will come around. He's just . . . ah, having a bad day."

There was a whole lot more going on than a bad day, but Deborah wanted the job. She needed it as much as Perry had needed his independence . . . and his drugs.

So because of that, she smiled wanly as Mr. Schrock walked back to the storage room.

When she was alone, Deborah looked at the door that Jacob had stormed through and felt a fresh wave of sadness. So much had changed over the last year.

Once, Jacob had been one of her brother's best friends. Once they'd all been friends. Once, she'd had a childish crush on Jacob.

Now none of that was true.

Chapter 2

"Perry and I have the same hazel eyes. That's where our similarities ended, I'm afraid.

DEBORAH BORNTRAGER

"Luke, you've been working with Mose all morning. Surely you need a break for supper?" Frannie asked as she walked into Mose's cramped office. In her arms was a basket filled with a variety of containers and what looked to be a plate, napkin, and silverware.

With a smile, he looked at his girlfriend and couldn't believe how lucky he was. Since arriving in Crittenden County, he'd not only strengthened his relationship with Mose Kramer, but he'd fallen in love, too.

God really was good. Ever since he'd gotten shot and put on leave from the Cincinnati Police Department, his life had changed in innumerable ways.

First his old buddy Mose had asked if he'd help him with a murder investigation in southwestern Kentucky. Then, little by little, he'd begun to feel at ease in the mostly Amish county. Finally, he'd met Frannie and felt a spark between them that was unlike anything he'd experienced.

If fate hadn't stepped in, Luke knew he'd still be limping around Cincinnati, Ohio, counting the days until he could work twelve-hour shifts.

And trying to figure out his life. He'd still be struggling with balancing his work, his free time—and wondering if he'd ever find a partner in life, someone he could trust completely.

Getting to his feet, he took the basket from her hands and set it on his desk. "Frannie, what did you make? It smells so good."

"Just bean-and-ham soup. And cornbread, seven-layer salad, and blond brownies."

She was such a good cook, Luke felt like the luckiest guy on earth. "Only all of that, hmm?" he teased. "In that case, I think I might be persuaded to take a break. If you stay here and eat with me."

As he hoped, she blushed prettily. "I would enjoy that, but I'm afraid I cannot get away that long. I've guests coming in this afternoon. I need to get back and wait for them."

"Do you know who they are?" Whenever he thought about the men who'd come to her inn, armed and danger-ous, he felt sick. "Do you want me to go to the inn and wait with you?"

Her eyebrows rose. "I most certainly do not. I'll be fine."

"But you'll call me as soon as they arrive?"

She wrinkled her nose, illustrating yet again what she thought about the cell phone he insisted she keep on hand in case of emergencies. "I don't think I'll be in any danger, Luke. My guests are a group of ten ladies."

His concern flip-flopped from concern for her safety to his mental health. "Ten? You only have four guest rooms."

"They are sharing rooms. And bringing some kind of blow-up mattress! They are having a 'girls' weekend'."

Already, he could imagine what Frannie's inn would be like, filled to capacity with that many chatty women. "How long do they plan to stay there?"

"Until Sunday, of course." She chuckled. "Oh, Luke. You should see your face! You looked scared!"

Ten women out for a weekend's worth of good times sounded noisy. And he'd likely get no time alone with Frannie if she was going to be bustling around, tending to their needs.

But he didn't want to upset her, of course. She looked so happy and proud. More than once she'd relayed to him how much she wanted the inn to be a success. "Congratulations. Having the inn filled to overflowing is a true accomplishment."

"*Danke.* My bank account is going to be mighty pleased with their checks, for sure." Stepping closer, she said, "I know you're working hard, but don't forget to eat. The soup is hot, and I made sure to give you plenty of brownies to share with Mose."

"You're too good to me, Frannie."

Smiling brightly, she met his gaze for a moment, then ducked her head and left.

He watched her walk briskly down the sidewalk in front of the sheriff's office, located in a trailer next to a bank building. Frannie's bright blue dress and apron fluttered with her stride, and the black bonnet strings covering her prim white *kapp* floated around her neck and shoulders.

How had he ever imagined that she was bossy? She was simply confident. And a hard worker.

But there was a softer side to her, too. Underneath her chatty exterior was a vulnerable woman who needed someone to believe in her.

"Mooning again?" Mose said from the doorway.

"A little," Luke allowed. "I can't help it—I'm in love."

Mose rolled his eyes as he approached and picked up the basket. "At least you're not about to go hungry."

"She made enough for two. Want some?"

"Of course! But first, I think we need to talk about our case. Do you really think you have enough to close it?"

Pushing aside Frannie's basket, Luke studied his latest typed set of notes. "I had hoped we had enough evidence, but I don't think the D.A. will accept the case as it is without a confession. We've got to dig deeper, Mose."

Mose rocked back on his heels. "Is it time to bring him in? No lawyer can fault us for bringing a suspect here for questioning."

Luke considered the idea, but ultimately dismissed it. "It's your call, but I don't think we're ready to press yet. I'd like to do another round of interviews with a couple of people. I need to speak with Deborah Borntrager, and maybe the Millers again. They're not going to like it, but it can't be helped."

"I want this case sealed up tighter than an icebox in July, Luke. We can wait another few days to make sure we have everything we need." Turning away, Mose stared out the front window. "I tell you, when we first found Perry, I didn't think anything worse could tear this community apart. But I'm afraid the news of who killed him might do more damage."

Luke had to agree. It was one thing when a loved member of a community was found murdered.

It was a whole different story when one of their own was discovered to be a murderer.

Chapter 3

"I guess we'll never know if Perry regretted his choices or not. I choose to think that he did."

BETH ANNE BORNTRAGER

From the moment his father had walked into Jacob's room, it was obvious his father had something important on his mind.

First his *daed* had fussed with the brush and spare change on the dresser; then he'd thumbed through the pair of *Sports Illustrated* magazines on his bedside table—and hadn't made a single comment about how Jacob shouldn't be indulging in such foolish fantasies.

Sitting in the recliner by the window, Jacob had watched and waited as patiently as he could. After all, he'd learned the hard way that it did no good to rush his father. All rushing did was bring on a lecture about being respectful.

But he had to get to the store soon, and he wanted to finish getting ready in private, not with his father looking on. When another minute passed, Jacob couldn't take it anymore. "Daed, was there a reason you came in here? Besides, you know, reading about the latest statistics on the football teams?"

His father turned sharply and glared. "Jacob—"

Knowing where he was headed, Jacob cut off the lecture before it started. "I'm sorry, Daed. I don't mean to be disrespectful, but it is obvious that you have something on your mind. We might as well get it over with."

With a sigh, his father sat down on the desk chair. The old wood creaked slightly under his weight. At last he spoke. "Jacob, there's no beating around the bush with this. The fact is, you are not being a good and decent person to Deborah Borntrager."

Jacob looked at his dad and immediately regretted the conversational push he'd just given. Deborah was the last person in the world he wanted to talk about.

Especially with his father.

Picking up a pencil, his father tapped the end of it on the desk. "You know how we raised you. To value forgiveness. To not hold grievances. We may not always be the best examples"—his father shifted uncomfortably—"but, Jacob? Talk to me about this. You must have something to say about how you've been treating Deborah."

"I really don't." Studying the line between his father's eyebrows, Jacob wished he had the nerve to talk back to him. There was a whole set of excuses for his behavior spinning around in his mind, all of which he felt to be true.

But because he took honoring his father and mother to heart, he kept his silence. Telling his parents the truth would only lead to more uncomfortable conversations.

Slowly his father shook his head. "Jacob. I know what you are doing, and holding your tongue ain't an option. I came in here to talk, and talk we will do."

Practically feeling his father's glare burning his skin, Jacob looked away. "I hear you, Father," he said finally. "I know I've been rude to her." He ached to add that he couldn't help himself. That every time he saw her, he was reminded of just how messed up his life had become.

But how could he tell his dad that without revealing his own insecurities?

"And?"

"And nothing, Father."

With a sigh, his father got up from the uncomfortable desk chair, walked to the side of the bed that faced Jacob, and sat down. To Jacob's surprise, his feet were only clad in thick wool socks. Glancing at his father's feet, how wide and solid they were, Jacob decided they were a perfect symbol for his father. If nothing else, his father was a robust, sturdy man. Usually his feet were planted solidly on the ground, and his will was just as unshakable.

"Jacob, I know it is hard, but you need to give your anger to the Lord. Vengeance is His, don't you remember? There is nothing that happened that can't be fixed."

He didn't want to be flip, but he couldn't even begin to imagine how anything could be fixed. Too much had happened. Their once idyllic life had been shattered the moment Perry decided to welcome drugs into their world. "Daed, Perry died," he said baldly.

"Ach. I know that. I mourn the loss, as well. But I'm sorry to say that there's nothing we can do about that. We can't bring him back to life." He sighed, flexing his feet a bit, then added, "I don't think Deborah could have done anything about her brother's actions either. Perry was a strong-willed man. Don't hold her responsible."

Jacob bit the inside of his cheek in order to keep his silence.

Because seeing Deborah reminded him of Perry. Because Perry was dead, and therefore unable to pay for the consequences of his actions. Because, even though he'd never wanted to admit it, he'd always felt that she was meant for him.

But now there was no way he could ever fall in love with a woman who's brother had hurt him so much.

"I don't know, Daed," he said instead of speaking the truth.

His father narrowed his eyes, looked like he wanted to say a great many things, but then got to his feet and padded to the door. "Things will get better, Jacob. I promise you that. Why, sometimes I think they already have! But please take a care with Deborah. Perry's actions are not her doing and she truly needs some friends right now. You mustn't forget, she's lost a brother. And that is a mighty sad thing."

"I'll try and do better," he promised. And he would. Just as soon as looking at her didn't remind him of all that had happened.

Besides, his father was wrong.

No matter how much a person might want to deny it, the fact was you couldn't change the past. What had been done was done.

A person needed to accept that. And then, of course, learn to live with the consequences.

Lydia loved being in Walker Anderson's arms. But as the windows in his truck fogged up and their kisses became too passionate, she knew that once again, they needed to say good night.

Pulling out of his embrace, she scooted to her side of the bench seat. "Oh, Walker. That's enough for now, I think."

He immediately let her go, but his hand still reached for her own. "You sure?" His voice was a little husky, and a little out of breath.

She almost smiled. He sounded the way she felt inside. But someone had to keep a clear head. "I am sure, Walker."

He sat up straighter and ran a hand through his blond hair, kicking up the golden strands this way and that, like he did when he was agitated. "Sorry. I know you're right."

She was right . . . but she still missed being in his arms. "We have to be careful, you know."

"I know. But . . . Lydia, we've also got to decide what we're going to do about our future."

She didn't even try to pretend that she didn't understand what he was talking about. Ever since they'd fallen in love, they'd put the practical sides of their lives on hold. It had been so much easier to stay in the sweet haze of a new romance.

After all, who wanted to dwell on all they were going through? First, they'd been suspects in Perry's murder investigation. And then she'd found out that she'd been adopted. There was also the matter of grieving for Perry. For most of the last few years, she'd been sure she'd marry Perry. So even though they'd broken up long before he died, a portion of her heart had been his.

And she'd grieved for the boy he used to be.

But now she and Walker were in a quandary. She was Amish and he was not. She wanted to remain faithful to her church and her upbringing, while Walker didn't seem to have any desire to become Amish. These were mighty big problems that should have kept them apart from each other.

But they were in love, armed with feelings that were far from passing fancies.

When she looked at Walker, she felt like she'd finally come home. She was comfortable with Walker, more comfortable and happier than with any other person in her life. He understood her, and she understood him. She was proud of him, and proud of all the things he believed in.

But being proud of someone and loving them didn't necessarily mean that all their problems went away. Or that they had a hope of an easy, trouble-free future.

Taking a chance, she said, "Walker, what do you think we should do?"

"I don't know. It seems like there're only two choices. Either you leave your faith or I become Amish." He chuckled then, letting Lydia know that the last "choice" he mentioned wasn't really an option as far as he was concerned.

Perhaps it was the woman's place in a relationship to do all the changing? And granted, she'd been so torn about whether her birth mom had been Amish or English, she would've thought that she'd have easily given up living Plain.

But something had happened when everything in her life had turned upside down. In the middle of figuring out who her birth parents were, she'd figured out who she was.

And her heart was telling her that she was Amish.

"There is one other choice, I suppose," she said quietly.

"Yeah? What's that?"

She cleared her throat. "We could break up."

He pulled his hands away and clenched them on his lap. "Really? You're actually thinking like that?" His voice was hoarse and thick. Almost as if he was fighting back tears.

"*Nee,*" she said in a rush. "But, well, it's true, don'tcha think? Some relationships aren't meant to be."

"Not meant to be? Huh." Silence descended on them as a

raccoon skittered across the dead-end street, his striped tail illuminated in the glow of the midnight moon.

Lydia's hands began to tremble in the ominous quiet between them. She began to regret her words, especially when he turned on the ignition and without another word pulled out into the dark, windy street.

She gazed at him, watching the muscle in his cheek pulse every time the shadows switched and the moon's glow hit his face just right. He was mad, and hurt.

Lydia didn't blame Walker. If the conversation had been reversed, and if he had been the one to bring it up, she would have been upset, too.

But she didn't attempt to take back her words. Someone had to be practical. When they were almost at her house, he turned her way and finally spoke. "Do you want to break up, Lydia?"

"Not at all," she replied, so quickly that her words were practically stumbling over each other. "Walker, I wouldn't have kissed you like I did if I didn't love you. You know that, yes?"

After he pulled into her driveway and parked, he spoke again. "I know you love me. And I love you, too, Lydia." When he gazed at her, his brown eyes piercing in the night, he said, "Don't give up on us. Not yet. I know things are hard, and that we're still trying to get used to each other's lifestyles. But we'll figure something out. I promise, we will."

"I won't give up, Walker." Lifting her chin, she said, "I'm going to start praying really hard. The Lord has to have a solution for us, don'tcha think? I just need to pray more often and ask for His guidance."

His gaze softened. For a moment, she worried that he was

going to tease her—after all, *Englischers* didn't always embrace the total faith in the Lord that the Amish did.

"That was a good reminder, Lydia," he finally said. "You are exactly right. I'll pray harder, too." Looking beyond her, he smiled. "You'd best go on inside. I think your mom is waiting up for you. She's probably ready to go to sleep."

Reaching out, she squeezed his hand quickly, then opened her door and stepped out. "Good night, Walker. Sleep well."

" 'Night, Lydia. I'll see you tomorrow."

She stayed on the front porch until he drove out of sight. Then quietly, she opened the front door and slipped inside.

From inside her parents' bedroom doorway, she saw her mother's shadow.

"Thank you for watching for me, but I am home safe."

"I'm glad of that."

Lydia ached to rush to her mother's arms and confide everything. To share how wonderful-*gut* it felt to be in Walker's arms. To share all the sweet things he said to her, and how she was sure they were meant to be together.

But she was anxious to begin her prayers, and now wasn't the right time, anyway. Her mother was tired, and would be shocked to learn all that Lydia was contemplating.

"*Gut naught*, Mamm," she said simply as she went to her room. The moment she closed her door, she fell to her knees and began to pray.

Only after her knees had gone numb and she climbed in bed did she even think about what she would do if God didn't give her prayers some answers.

Being alone all over again was going to be a very terrible place to be.

Chapter 4

"I never understood why Perry got second and third and fourth chances, but I never did."

DEBORAH BORNTRAGER

"So good to see ya today, Deborah!" Mr. Schrock said when he walked toward the front of the store. "The missus says you've settled right in like a duck to water."

When Deborah arrived for her second day on the job, Mrs. Schrock had given her the task of cleaning out the dairy cases. That meant everything needed to be taken out, the cases carefully cleaned with watered-down bleach, all products carefully examined for expiration dates, then put back.

It was not an easy job.

And despite Mr. Schrock's encouraging words, Deborah was afraid she had not taken to it that easily. First she'd forgotten to put on gloves, making the paper cut on her hand sting when it had come in contact with the bleach.

Then, of course, she'd splashed some of the solution all over her dress. Now there was a great white stain smack in the middle of her black apron.

Added to that, she had six more hours to go. It was anyone's guess what trouble she'd get into next.

But of course that didn't mean she should share any of that with Mr. Schrock. "*Danke*. I'm happy to be here."

He stepped closer, peering over her shoulder. "How's the cleaning going?"

"It is fine. I should finish by two or three." With God's help.

"*Gut!* Mind the bleach now, it can be a tricky thing to clean with."

Yes, she had certainly found that out. "I will, *danke*."

Clasping his hands together, he smiled. "All righty. Mrs. Schrock and I are going to pay a visit to the Millers for bit, but Jacob will be here to keep you company."

And . . . that meant her "great" day was now complete. "I'll look for him, then," she said. "I'm sure I'll be just fine." His lips pursed, making Deborah stand up straight. It looked like he had something he wanted to say. When he paused, she thought she'd nudge him along, "Yes, Mr. Schrock?"

"I . . . I, uh, I wanted to tell ya . . ."

"Yes?"

"Mind the kittens, wouldja? Take them out and cuddle them once an hour or so. All God's creatures need some love and affection every now and then."

Glancing to the corner of the store, to where a pair of kittens lay contentedly curled up next to each other in a pen, she smiled. "I will enjoy that job."

He laughed. "See? Some folks don't think I should sell animals here, but it's a *gut* thing. Everyone needs something to love, and pets love you back. Even when you don't always deserve it, you know?"

Forcing herself to ignore the sharp pang of sadness that his words brought her—because she absolutely did not have anyone to love—Deborah chuckled about the kittens as she got back to work.

Behind her, she heard Mr. Schrock's booming voice chatting with his wife. Then she heard the door open and shut.

Then, almost stealthily, new footsteps approached.

Vigilantly, she kept her back to the noise. It had to be Jacob, and the longer she delayed seeing him, the better. She picked up a dry rag and began wiping down the excess water from the glass shelf. The footsteps came closer.

Her shoulders bunched up. Almost as if she expected a blow.

But then the footsteps stopped. The hairs on the back of her neck stood up as total awareness fell over her.

She had no choice but to turn around . . . and see that her hunch was correct. Jacob Schrock was behind her, his gaze solemn and piercing. "Jacob. Good day."

He nodded silently.

For a moment, she boldly stared right back at him. Bracing herself for another tirade to spew from his lips. Especially now that they were alone, there would be nothing stopping him from lashing out at her.

But instead of his usual anger, he looked uncomfortable. Finally, he said, "So it looks like you got dairy duty today."

It sounded almost like an olive branch. Anxious for things to be smoothed out, she nodded. "Indeed, I do."

He pointed to her apron. "You got some bleach on your apron."

"I know." To cover her embarrassment, she shrugged like the spot didn't matter. "It's ruined, for sure."

"That's too bad."

"Yes, but it's nothing to worry over. I can make a new apron easily, and I'll make a quilt with the scraps from this one."

The topic of her apron now discussed to death, he stepped back. "I'll be over at the counter. It usually gets pretty busy around noon or so." He cleared his throat. "If it does . . . I might need your help."

"All right." Well, at least he wasn't yelling at her. There was that, at least.

Deborah turned back to her chore, feeling strangely at a loss for words. She didn't want to work with him like this, with all this tension. But what else could she do?

"Hey. Uh, Deborah?"

"Yes?" she said to the dairy case. No way was she going to face him again.

"My *daed* says I should apologize. He said that I've been rude to you."

The words were stilted and choppy. And in Deborah's opinion, it was a pretty sorry apology. Surely even a child could speak from his heart!

She knew she should accept it gracefully and move on. But she was tired of his rudeness. And so tired of pretending her feelings didn't matter. "And what do you think? Do you want to apologize?"

"I think that he might be right."

She couldn't help it, she slowly turned to face him again. "You do?"

He bit his bottom lip, then spoke. "I do." Exhaling, he said, "I am sorry for taking out my anger toward Perry on you. He and I had some rough times, as I'm sure you know. And, well, every time I think about how you're his sister, how the two of you are related, it makes me want to take my frustrations out on you."

"I was his sister, not his master, Jacob. I had no control over what he did, or if he hurt your feelings."

"I realize that. Now. It wasn't right. I know that."

She ached to remind Jacob that she'd felt betrayed, too; and she was grieving. That she, too, was feeling confused and hurt and scared. After all, she had lost a brother. And more than that, he hadn't died of natural causes. Someone had murdered him.

And that even though Perry had made mistakes, and had hurt a great many people, he'd had no chance to repent or ask forgiveness. Someone had taken that opportunity from him.

But even telling Jacob what was on her mind wouldn't make anything better. It wouldn't make the hurt go away, or ease her loss.

"Thank you for the apology," she said woodenly. "I appreciate it."

"Do you think you'll be able to forgive me?"

His eyes were wide and honest. And against everything warring inside her, she felt herself melt. No good would come from holding on to her anger.

"Of course I forgive you," she said.

His shoulders relaxed and his lips curved slightly. "I'm grateful. Thank you, Deborah." He bit his lip. "Maybe we could start over, the two of us?"

How could they do that? She'd known him all her life, but she'd never honestly considered them close. Their relationship had been more of an extension of his friendship with Perry. Could years of stilted conversations ever change into something else?

Surely she could try.

"I'd like for us to be friends," she said at last. "I could, ah, use all the friends I can get right now."

"I know the feeling."

As if their honest words had startled them, they once again shared a sweet smile. The way they used to, back when the three of them used to walk to school together.

"Well, I better get back to the bleach," she quipped, trying to make her words seem light and almost impersonal. It would never do if Jacob discovered how much she used to like him. Before he could spy a hint of that in her face, she quickly turned back to the dairy shelf.

She heard him turn and walk away, greet a pair of ladies who entered the store.

But standing there in front of the dairy case, Deborah felt her face flush. Once again her silly, betraying heart had begun to imagine life with Jacob Schrock. Life as friends—and so much more than that.

The idea made her almost tremble with frustration. Oh, when would she ever get a clue? Getting close to Jacob would only bring her more heartache.

Because she'd never be able to forget Jacob's note to Perry. The one he'd sent just before Perry went missing.

The note Perry had hidden in his bedside drawer.

The note she'd found and had done her best to hide ever since.

Well, that had been easy—about as easy as getting a tooth pulled! Jacob thought as he walked back to the front counter after greeting the women who'd just entered the store.

Deborah had accepted his apology. But she'd been notice-ably cooler than usual. And instead of just hurt and pain flooding her gaze, he had spied something else, too—a deep, simmering anger.

He felt bad that he'd been the cause of it.

Thankfully, the bells at the front door chimed, signaling a new customer. "May I help ya?" he asked, wheeling around to see who entered.

"Yeah! You can get me fifty pounds of flour and bird seed," Walker Anderson joked as he walked through the doors. Coming closer, he chuckled. "What's with you, Jacob? Since when do you ask if I need any help with anything?"

"Sorry, I was trying to take my mind off something, I guess."

Walker's smile dimmed. "Is everything okay?"

"Yeah, sure. What are you doing here, anyway? I thought you swore off this place on your days off."

"I did. But then my sister talked to my grandma, who asked if I could bring her a couple of things from the store."

"Francis and James?"

"Yeah." Walker shrugged. "I guess my grandpa is feeling under the weather." His frown deepened. "My dad is driving him to the doctor today."

"I hope it's nothing too serious. Walker, you want to grab the flour or the seed?"

"You don't need to get either. I'll do it."

"I can help. I'm not busy. I'm just standing here, watching Deborah work."

Walker's head swung to the right. "Deborah? Oh, hey, Deb!"

To Jacob's surprise, Deborah waved one slim hand. "Hiya, Walker. How goes it?"

"Well enough." His smile grew. "Hey, you look great over there, scrubbing."

One of her eyebrows rose. "And why is that?"

"Because that means I'm not doing it," he teased with an even broader grin.

"Whatever I can do to make your job easier pleases me greatly, Walker Anderson."

Feeling like the odd man out, Jacob glanced from Walker to Deborah and back again. Had they always been so comfortable around each other? And he called her 'Deb'? When had that come about?

"Walker, I'll go get the seed from the back. You get the flour," Jacob said.

"All right, sure," he said. "As soon as I go say hi to Deborah."

Feeling cranky all over again, Jacob walked to the back of the store. Why did he care if Walker and Deborah got along so well?

Was it because he'd been rude to her for days and she hadn't melted at his awkward apology? Or, was it something else?

Looking her way, for the first time Jacob noticed that her eyes were pretty—not just the same shade as her mother's and her brother's. And that she really was a petite woman. Why, the top of her head barely reached his shoulder.

And her brown hair was dark, the color of darkly brewed coffee. Or perhaps it was mahogany? Whatever the color, it made her pink cheeks look pretty. And her hazel eyes shine bright.

With a bit of surprise, he realized that none of these things took him completely by surprise. He'd noticed her beauty before. He shook his head. If Deborah ever found out what he'd done to her brother, she would certainly hate him all her life.

And there was a very good chance that she'd make sure everyone else in Crittenden County hated him, too.

Chapter 5

"Although I never knew Perry, I can't help but feel sorry for him. It's never easy to change a person's perception of you. Sometimes it stays with you forever."

LUKE REYNOLDS

Sitting at his desk in the back of Mose's dusty office, Luke Reynolds read over his notes, and then read them over again. Everything on the assorted sheets pointed to one person. And though he didn't like the direction the facts had taken, they had to be right. If there was one thing he'd learned after a decade in law enforcement, it was that facts didn't lie.

Leaning forward, he braced his elbows on the imitation wood of the ancient metal desk. Flipping back a few pages in his notebook, he reread the interviews he'd conducted with Lydia Plank and Walker Anderson. With Perry's parents and sister.

With Frannie and the Millers, and Abby Anderson and her girlfriends. Yep, he had to be on the right track. But what was going to be the best way to prove it?

Mose rapped his knuckles on the desk as he entered the office. "When are you going to start helping me out with the rest of the work around here? Every time I go out on a call, I leave you here hunched over your notebook like an old miser."

Luke sat up, the muscles in his back sending shock waves of distress as he did so. "An old miser, Mose?"

"You know what I mean. You're hunched over when I leave, and still in the same position when I get back."

After slowly getting to his feet, Luke stretched. "I'll start answering more calls when my boss hires me on for real."

Looking troubled, Mose scratched his head. "You know these things take time. Got to get the funding approved, ya know."

"I'm teasing you. I went and talked to the department over in Paducah. I think there might be a spot for me on their force."

"Is that what you want?"

"It's close enough to what I want." What he wanted at the moment was to hang out at Frannie's inn and relax. But since their wedding was going to be put on hold until Frannie's father got used to the idea, Luke made do with working as many hours as he could.

Plus, until the right person was tried and convicted for Perry Borntrager's death, his work wasn't done. "Paducah is a whole lot smaller than Cincinnati, but they've got their share of city problems. Because that's what I'm used to, I think it will be a good fit. Plus, it's only thirty miles away."

"I can see how you might feel more at home in a city environment."

Now that the subject of his future employment was settled, Luke motioned to Mose's chair. "Have a seat and look at these notes, would you? I've drawn some conclusions, but I need your brain. Tell me what you think, would you?"

Mose settled into his own chair, and after taking time to clean his reading glasses with a bandanna he retrieved from his pocket, he slipped them on and picked up the report. As he flipped back and forth through the notes, his posture changed.

"Jacob Schrock, huh? I know we agreed on this, but it still breaks my heart. I wish everything didn't point to him."

"It's got to be him. Right?"

"I've known Jacob a long time, Luke. He's seemed to be a caring, likable sort. I wouldn't have thought that young man was capable of killing another person."

"I think we are all capable, given the right circumstances."

"And you think he was motivated enough? Your reasons don't seem quite strong enough for Jacob to commit murder."

Luke sighed. He'd been thinking the same thing. He knew Jacob had been angry with Perry for lying to his father, and for stealing from the family business. He also knew that Jacob had been very upset that Perry had still been hanging around the store after he'd been fired.

Jacob seemed to distrust Perry enough to publicly shun him. But there was a big difference between not liking someone and wanting them dead.

"That's why I need to go talk with him some more." Leaning forward, he showed Mose the notes he'd made while conducting his interviews. "I want to go visit with Deborah Borntrager, too."

"I agree with you there. Both of them left soon after Perry's body was discovered. Their trips seemed a little too coincidental to me."

Luke sighed in relief. Talking over the case was restoring his confidence. "I'm going to go talk with her tonight."

"Sounds good. Listen, when you go visiting to the Schrocks,

I think I should go with you. Aaron Schrock is a good man, but he has a tendency to guard Jacob like a mother bear."

"I was hoping you'd offer to come with me. I have no problem interrogating suspects, but everything's changed now . . ."

"Because of your relationship with Frannie," Mose said.

"Yeah." Feeling a little sheepish, he said, "Mose, I can't believe I was so full of myself when I first got here. I really thought you needed my help because you were inexperienced."

"It is true we don't get a lot of murders around here—"

"But that wasn't it, was it? It's because these people here, they grow on you, don't they? You don't want to expect the worst of them."

Mose shrugged. "I needed you here and you came, Luke. That's all that matters to me. When do you want to visit tomorrow?"

"In the morning?" he suggested. "We might have a better chance of talking to him for a while in private before the store gets too busy."

"He's an adult, Luke. We can bring him here without his parents' permission."

Mose was right. But Luke also had a lot of experience with scared kids in interrogation rooms. Sometimes the change in environment rattled them so much, getting a confession was near impossible. "I hear what you're saying, but I don't want to push hard. Not yet, anyway."

Mose scanned the report again, then for a moment seemed to scan Luke with the same intensity. "I'll trust your judgment," he said. "So, before you go find Deborah, want to go get something to eat?"

"Maybe. Where are thinking?"

Mose smiled slyly. "Mary King's?"

"Done," he said, getting to his feet. Now that he was settling into the rhythm of the county, he was realizing two things. First, never to push hard when pushing gently would achieve the same results.

And two? Never pass up a chance to eat at Mary's.

"I'm really glad you came with me, Lydia," Walker said as he pulled into the parking lot of the community college he'd been attending. "I wanted you to see the campus."

Lydia looked at the gray office building with a wave of apprehension. She'd thought they were only stopping by the campus so he could get some forms from a secretary.

But did he have another reason for taking her here?

"It looks like a nice place," she said as they crossed the parking lot. "It's big."

He laughed. "It's not that big. You should see some of the other college campuses in the state. UK out in Lexington is huge."

"UK?"

"The University of Kentucky." Flushing, he said, "All my life I wanted to go there. I even used to want to play ball for them. But it wasn't meant to be."

"Why wasn't it meant to be?" she asked as he held the door open for her and they walked into the air-conditioned building. "I thought you liked this school."

"Oh, I do. But that didn't stop me from wishing I had gotten a scholarship to a big school like that." With a shrug he said, "None of it matters, anyway. I wasn't a good enough baseball player to get a scholarship and my parents couldn't afford to help me get there any other way."

Lydia sensed there was more he wasn't sharing, but she

had no idea how to encourage him to tell her more. And, of course, hearing about all his ties to the outside world made her feel insignificant and awkward.

She liked their life in Crittenden County. She liked how they were friends with most everyone, Amish or English. She felt more of an equal there. Here, she felt conspicuous in her dress and *kapp*.

And the crowds of people her age sitting in tables around them, listening to music on their headphones, chatting on cell phones, and working on their laptop computers felt overwhelming as well. Silently, she followed him down the hall and then up a flight of stairs.

When they came to an office door, Walker steeled himself before turning the knob and walking in. Lydia followed.

A lady who didn't look to be much older than them looked up from what she was working on at her desk. "Yes?"

"My name's Walker Anderson. I have some paperwork to pick up?"

She paused and smiled at Walker. "I remember you," she said lightly. "You came in, looking for information about some correspondence courses."

"Yeah."

"We set aside some information in a packet. Hold on and I'll go get it."

When she got up, Lydia looked at Walker suspiciously. He was standing tall right next to her, but he seemed distant. Removed. "What is she talking about, Walker?"

"Huh? Oh, I'll tell you in a minute."

Lydia held on to her patience as the woman gave Walker the packet. They talked about credit hours and prerequisites, and then Walker wrote down the woman's phone number and email address.

But the moment they were back in the hall, she turned to him. "Walker, what is going on?"

He guided her to an empty portion of the hall. "I've been thinking about taking some classes online next semester. On the computer."

"Okay . . ."

He took a deep breath. "And I thought you might want to do that, too."

She almost laughed. "Walker, I can't go to college. You know I never even went to high school."

"That's what's so great about what Alison found. You can get your GED online, Lydia. You can take classes with me back at home."

"I can't be taking classes, Walker. I'm working almost every day at the nursery."

"Yeah, but you don't want to do that forever, do you? I mean, now that we're together, we need to plan ahead, right?"

Lydia felt like smacking her palm on the side of her head. My, but it had certainly taken her long enough to figure out what Walker had been getting at. The whole time she'd been waiting and hoping for Walker to turn away from all he knew and become Amish, he'd been doing some planning of his own.

"We do need to plan," she agreed slowly. "But I'm afraid it's not going to be as easy as I'd hoped. Or you hoped either, Walker."

She could almost see the spark fade from his eyes. "You don't want to go to school, Lydia? Not at all?"

"I'm sorry, Walker. But I don't."

He held his silence as they walked down the stairs, down the hall, and back out of the building. Only when they were getting into his truck did he speak again.

"Lydia, I love you, I do. But I don't know how we're going

to manage to mesh our lives together. When we start talking about our wishes for the future, and start talking about plans for the rest of our lives . . . nothing seems to go together."

"I understand." She said nothing more because there was nothing left to say. Though their futures were at cross-purposes, they were in agreement on this: If one of them didn't change, they didn't have a future.

No, that wasn't true. They'd have a future.

It just wouldn't be together.

Chapter 6

"Perry discovered that if you stood in the middle of the trail, and crouched down just a little bit . . . he could see right into our windows. I never asked him how he found out. I suppose I didn't want to know."

JACOB SCHROCK

After supper, Jacob knew he couldn't sit for another minute in his father's company. Lately, his father had been hovering over him so protectively that Jacob was beginning to feel like a firefly in a jar.

He needed a break from the constant vigilance, and he needed it soon, or he was afraid he would say something he would regret. He'd been taught to always respect his parents and never argue with their directives. However, he was on the verge of breaking his silence.

Entering the living room, where his father was contentedly whittling in front of the fireplace, he announced, "I'm going out for a while, Daed."

With a start, his father got to his feet. "Going out? Where are you going? It's late, you know."

"It's eight o'clock, Daed. Not so late."

"But it's dark out—"

It had finally happened. His patience had snapped. "Father, of course it is dark. And furthermore—"

With a wary look his way, his mother jumped into the conversation. "Aaron, enough! My goodness, what's gotten into you lately? Jacob is twenty years old, not eight."

To Jacob's relief, his father looked more than a little shamefaced. "I know that."

"Then why are you watching his every move? I tell ya, Aaron, sometimes I truly worry about you." Waving her hand, she motioned to Jacob. "We'll see you later, son."

But his father stood up. "Hold on, Jacob. Are you taking the buggy? Because if you are, you should remember to get a lantern and be careful."

Reminding himself that his dad was only spooked by Perry's death, Jacob struggled to hold on to the very last bit of his patience. "I'm not taking the buggy. I'm only going for a walk. I'll be back in a while."

"Walking? Where to?"

"Daed, stop." He ground his teeth, working to control the bark in his voice.

"It's a father's job to look out for his child."

"I agree. Except I am not a child." Looking over his father's head, he met his mother's gaze and sent her a silent, plaintive plea for more help.

She shook her head in dismay. "Aaron, stop this. You are borrowing trouble, and we both know it."

"But—"

With a shooing motion, she waved Jacob out. "Go on, son. You worked hard today, and you did a fine job with the chores here, too. Go enjoy yourself for a few hours."

"*Danke*, Mamm."

The lines around her eyes softened. "Yes, of course. Now off you go."

He grabbed his coat and hat before his father could come up with another reason for him to stay under his watch.

Once outside, he walked down the gravel driveway, enjoying the way the rocks crunched under his feet. The lantern shining in the family room window guided him to the side of the house. He continued to walk until the darkness enveloped him.

Thick clouds had formed overhead, effectively creating a shield over the earth. It was so dark he could barely see his hands, never mind any trees and shrubs surrounding him.

He was glad for the small flashlight he'd put in his pocket the other night. One never knew who or what you could come across in the dead of the night.

The narrow pinpoint of light was all he needed. He continued to walk, enjoying the crisp night air and the pungent scent of new foliage. Most of all, he reveled in the feeling of freedom. He was so relieved to be away from his father's constant monitoring.

Walking aimlessly, he clambered over some rocks, and entered a field that had lay fallow for the past two years. Only then did he truly relax, and wonder what he was going to do with himself for the next few hours.

He hadn't thought of who he'd wanted to see or hang out with beyond the overwhelming desire to be free of his father's eye.

Then one thing led to another, and before he knew it, he was following the faint path toward Perry's house.

When they were still in school, Jacob had run down this path to pick up Perry so they could walk to school together.

Of course, Perry had never been ready, and Jacob had

never wanted to leave him. And Deborah? Deborah had been at Perry's mercy. Her mother would never let her go to school without the two of them. So they'd had many a morning where they'd arrived at school late . . . and he remembered those mornings like it was yesterday.

"Come on, Perry. Why aren't you ever ready on time?"

Perry laughed low. "There's no reason. It's just school."

Jacob felt his temper flare. Over and over Perry was making all three of them late. Not wanting to use himself as the reason, Perry used Deborah instead. "I'm surprised your sister doesn't go on ahead."

"Mamm and Daed won't let her."

"But doesn't she get sick of waiting for you? And sick of losing her recess because we're late?"

Perry paused and looked back at Deborah, who was once again following them both. "You mad at me?" he asked. The words weren't unkind but his tone was.

After a pause, Deborah shook her head.

"See?" Perry said with a laugh. "She's fine."

That was the exact moment Jacob had realized that Perry was a bully. He'd enjoyed exerting power over his parents and his sister. Even his friends. And why shouldn't he?

Yet again, Jacob hadn't said a thing. He had let Perry do whatever he wanted.

Like usual.

Little by little, instead of being bullied, Jacob began to be a lot more like Perry. He liked feeling powerful instead of victimized. Before long, both he and Perry had considered it a badge of honor being known as troublemakers. Growing up under his father's thumb, Jacob had often looked for ways to act up a bit. Perhaps Perry had felt the same way?

Only now did Jacob think about how unfair and selfish he and Perry had been to Deborah.

Why had he never thought about how hard it had been on her, to always be in her brother's shadow? And how he'd always just accepted that she would be there? To his embarrassment, he had never felt the slightest bit of guilt about ignoring her.

He sure had never apologized to her about how he'd acted. Even after all this time, he'd never said he was sorry.

His face flamed even though the night air was cool.

Then the trail widened and the brush cleared. And in front of him lay the Borntragers' home.

As he expected, it was mostly dark, though he did see a faint glow in an upstairs bedroom. Deborah's most likely.

He stopped and looked up at it. Staring at the glow shining through her window shade. What was she doing? Reading by the light of that kerosene lantern?

Sewing?

Just sitting and remembering? It seemed that was all he did these days. Still staring blankly at the window, he noticed the shade twitch. With a start, he realized if she looked out, she'd most likely see his shadow standing underneath her home—looking at her window like some kind of Peeping Tom. Now that would be embarrassing, indeed!

Jacob Schrock was wandering around in her yard. Deborah peered through the tiny crack between the shade and the window and wondered why he'd shown up.

A sudden, fierce anger emanated through her. First he had to go out of his way to make sure she was miserable at the store. Then he gave her an awkward, stilted, most likely very insincere apology. Now he was standing in her yard, below her window.

Could he never leave her alone?

Quickly, she turned off the lamp, grabbed her cloak and black bonnet, and put on both while she went downstairs. For a moment, she thought about telling her parents that she was going out, but decided against it.

Her mother had made an appearance for supper, but after eating only a few bites, had gone back to bed. Her father was closed up in his study, most likely reading a new book checked out from the library. Or staring at the blank walls, pretending he could go back in time.

Either way, neither of them would care one way or the other what she did.

Slipping on her boots, Deborah let her anger and frustration with their whole situation fall by the wayside and tromped outside.

Jacob Schrock had really gone too far today.

As she slipped down the porch steps, she wondered if he'd left, but then she saw his shadow. It looked like he was waiting for her. When she got closer, he stepped out into the clearing, letting the dim glow of a half-full moon illuminate him.

"Hey," he said.

Deborah's steps faltered. "Hello, Jacob. Care to tell me why you're lurking outside my house?"

He visibly winced, and she felt a twinge of remorse. But she had weeks of hurt to make up for. And she was terribly tired of turning the other cheek.

"I don't know why I'm here. I had to get out of my house—and next thing I knew, I was walking on this old path."

"The path you used to take to come get us for school."

Stuffing his hands into his pockets, he tilted his head to one side. "I was just remembering how Perry always made us late." After a pause, he added, "You always ended up getting punished, too. Did you ever tell your parents that it was never your fault?"

There in the yard, in the dark, where memories seemed to surface more clearly than they did in the daylight, she shook her head. That had all been a long time ago. However, the pain still felt fresh. "I think you know the answer to that," she said.

"Perry would've only gotten back at you if you'd told."

She opened her mouth to agree, but with a start, stopped herself. Would Perry have gotten back at her? Really?

Or was she just remembering the Perry who'd been so cruel his last few months alive? "Perhaps." She shrugged. "It doesn't matter now. Not really."

"I never apologized to you. I should have."

"For what?" She shook her head. "Jacob, it was not your fault that Perry was never ready and that my parents wouldn't let me go to school without him."

He stepped forward. "Then whose fault was it? If you don't want to blame Perry or me . . . who do you blame for all those recesses you missed?"

Back when they were younger, Deborah would've given money for him to accept at least part of the blame. But now?

Now it was pointless to dwell on the past. "It was no one's fault," she said quietly. "It was just how it was." She shrugged. "Besides, it was long ago. And I survived. We all did, *jah*?"

Slowly, he nodded. "I guess we did. So, tonight, I saw a light on in your room. What were you doing?"

For a moment, she thought about making up a story. Pretending that she'd been doing something valuable with her time. "Not much. Reading." Actually, she'd been peeking through the crack in the shade out the window. And thinking about Perry.

"Will your parents miss you if you go on a walk?"

"Nee." No, they wouldn't miss her at all. The only thing they seemed to want to keep them company was their depression. And Perry, of course.

"Want to walk? Not far," he said quickly. "Just somewhere close."

"How about we go to the old schoolhouse?"

"It will be just like old times. Almost."

Deborah said nothing. Because they knew nothing was like it used to be—and it was more than not having Perry with them. It also had to do with the fact that before, she'd been the boys' afterthought. She'd tagged along after them while Perry and Jacob had walked side-by-side.

Laughing about jokes she didn't understand.

With only his tiny flashlight leading the way, they kept their pace slow. It was dark and the path hadn't been used for years. Rocks and vines and broken branches littered what little they could see of it. Most of it was covered with thick brush.

"I don't know whether to be surprised this trail is so overgrown, or to be surprised it's in existence at all," Jacob mused.

"I'm leaning toward being surprised it's here. How many years has it been?" Deborah asked. "I certainly haven't gone to the schoolhouse in a long time. Not since our eighth-grade graduation."

Jacob chuckled. "Me, neither."

When it narrowed, Jacob reached out and grasped her elbow, holding her steady when she stumbled on a tree root.

The sudden brush of their bodies against each other felt like so much more than it was.

"Sorry," he blurted, when he seemed to realize that he was still holding her arm. He dropped his hand.

"*Nee*. I, uh, was glad you steadied me. It would be awful if I twisted my ankle out here."

"You're a little thing, though. I bet I could carry you home without a problem."

If he'd been anyone else, she would have teased him. Or claimed that while she was petite, she certainly wasn't all that small. Much too big to be picked up like a child.

At last, the glow of the white clapboard schoolhouse loomed in front of them. The white wood, combined with the reflectors that someone had nailed to a few trees in front of it, made it feel like they had stepped into the light.

Jacob turned off his flashlight.

As they got closer, Deborah noticed that an abandoned bike lay on its side next to the school's front door. "Look at that," she said.

"Wonder whose it is?" Jacob asked. "It's still in good condition."

"I've always wondered how a bike gets left here. I figure if a person needs to take it to get to school, he needs it to get home, too. Plus, if I had forgotten it, my *mamm* would have made me turn right back around and get it."

"Mine, too." They shared a smile, then their smiles turned to wariness as they heard the rumble of a car's engine approaching. "Guess we're not the only people out tonight, huh?" he asked.

Deborah felt strangely exposed, standing in the empty schoolyard. Making a sudden decision, she walked to the side of the building, then leaned against it. At the moment, she didn't care if Jacob was going to tease her for hiding.

But instead of teasing, he joined her. Pressing his back against the hard planks, too.

As the car approached, they slid closer toward the back, deeper in the shadows. Their bodies touched. Jacob's breathing quickened.

Deborah, on the other hand, practically held her breath. Suddenly, she felt like they had been courting trouble, walking out in the dark together.

But surely this was simply her imagination taking control?

Jacob reached for her hand. Squeezed it once. Obviously in an attempt to reassure her as they waited for the vehicle to pass them.

But then it slowed, turned slightly.

And just like a spotlight had shone down from heaven, the car's spotlights flashed their way.

Illuminating them as clearly as if they were standing inside a metal cage—

Waiting to be caught and inspected.

Chapter 7

*"Perry always said I didn't understand a lot of things because
I wasn't Amish. Now I wish I had asked what was so different
about his life. Or at least what was so wrong."*

WALKER ANDERSON

Jacob recognized the newcomer. It was Walker Anderson; he
would have recognized his dark green Explorer anywhere.
Someone was in the passenger seat, too. Maybe it was his
sister Abby?

When he saw both passengers looking directly at them,
Jacob suddenly became aware that he was still holding Deborah's hand. Hastily, he dropped it.

She must've felt self-conscious, too. The moment he released her, she stepped farther away. "Who is it, Jacob? Can
you see?" she whispered.

"It's Walker."

"Walker? Out here? What do you think he wants?"

"Ain't no telling," he answered flatly, feeling less than
thrilled about Walker joining them. He and Deborah were
finally talking about things that had lurked between them
for years. If they didn't clear the air, there was a good chance

nothing between them would ever get resolved. And now that she was working at the store, well, that would mean a lot of awkward conversations.

And he definitely didn't want that. Sometime over the last few days, he realized that there was another connection besides past bringing them together. There was a spark between them, and it had far less to do with past regrets than the way he liked feeling her hand in his.

But if they had to be interrupted, he was really glad it was only Walker. At least he could keep a secret.

"Don't worry, Deborah. I bet they only want to say hi."

As they walked toward the truck, she looked curiously over her shoulder at him. "What else would he want?" she asked before raising her voice. "Hello, Walker."

"Hey," Walker called from the open truck window before sliding down from the truck. Gesturing toward his sister who got out as well, he said, "Abby and I were driving by when we saw the two of you standing out here. So . . . what are y'all doing?"

"Just walking," Deborah said.

Walker looked from one to the other and smirked slightly. "Just walking in the dark, huh?"

"What are you up to?" Jacob said instead of answering. "I never thought I'd see you driving around Amish schoolhouses at night."

"We were visiting our grandparents," Abby said as she strode toward Deborah. With more than a bit of amusement in her voice, she added, "Then, of course, we had to go visit Lydia."

Jacob relaxed. That, he could deal with. Walker couldn't seem to stay away from his girlfriend for more than a few hours at a time. "And how is Lydia tonight?"

As Abby whispered something to Deborah, Walker replied. "Lydia is great. Plus her parents don't even look at me like I'm the devil-boyfriend anymore."

Jacob laughed. "Devil-boyfriend, huh? I knew they were suspicious of you, but that's taking things to a whole new level."

"They're kind folks, they just haven't been all that welcoming. I mean, it used to feel like they'd just about give their souls for Lydia not to fall in love with me. But some things just can't be helped."

Folding her arms over her chest, Abby said, "Walker and Lydia have become almost annoying to be around."

"We are not annoying," Walker countered.

"Oh, yes you are. When you two are in the same room, you stand right next to each other and hardly talk to anyone else." Looking at Jacob and Deborah, she tilted her head to one side. "Almost as close as the two of you were standing against the building."

Jacob was thankful for the dark so no one could see his face burn red. He had been standing awfully close to Deborah, and it wasn't only because he'd been afraid they were about to get caught.

"So now that I've told you my whole story, why don't you tell me what you two are really doing," Walker said. "I mean, no one goes walking in the dark to an Amish schoolhouse without a reason."

"There's no story here. Deborah and I had been talking about how I used to pick up her and Perry for school. We wanted to see if the trail was still there."

Walker folded his arms over his chest and nodded. "Ah. Yeah, I can see how you'd want to check out that trail in the dark. Makes perfect sense to me."

"We have to do something for amusement. Some of us work more than twenty hours a week, Walker," Jacob said. "Not everyone here gets to go to college and sit around talking about history or stars."

Walker narrowed his eyes, looking for a moment like he was going to tell Jacob that he knew nothing about college, which would have been true, but then he seemed to decide to let Jacob's comment go. "That's true. Not everyone does get to go to school."

Now Jacob felt ashamed. What was wrong with him? Why was he always letting his mouth get the best of him? His life would be a whole lot better if he'd ever learn to think before speaking. "Sorry. I didn't mean that how it sounded."

"I didn't think you sounded any special way." But despite what Walker said, Jacob thought he might've hit a sour chord because Walker readily turned to Deborah. "Deb, how are you doing?"

"Me? I'm fine."

Jacob noticed that she looked like she would rather be anywhere else but answering Walker's questions. "Deborah started working at the store."

"I know. I was there the other day. Remember?" Walker looked at Jacob strangely before focusing back on Deborah again. "I've been thinking about you and your parents, how hard it must be on you all, living without Perry. Abby drives me crazy, but I'd have a pretty hard time of it, if she wasn't in my life anymore."

Jacob couldn't believe that Walker was bringing up Perry's death. "Walker—"

But Deborah seemed relieved instead of annoyed. "It has been hard," she said softly. "It's my parents who are having a tough time. Actually, I don't know if they'll ever recover from losing their son."

Walker nodded, just like discussing death was something he did all the time. "I read somewhere that losing a child is the hardest experience a man or woman can have."

"I am sure that is right. We don't quite know what to talk about anymore."

"At least he is with God instead," Walker said. "That, at least, has to offer some comfort to your parents."

"I think so. Maybe one day it will . . ." Her voice drifted off, but not before Jacob noticed that there was a catch in her throat.

Seeing her becoming distressed, especially over Perry, made him talk without thinking. "Perry wasn't innocent, you know. It's not like he was a saint or something." The moment he said the words, he ached to take them back.

But Deborah looked at him straight in the eye. "All of us are sinners. There's no need to start throwing stones."

Her accusation made him feel defensive all over again. "There's a big difference between making mistakes every once in a while and doing the things Perry did, Deborah . . ." he said honestly. Probably too honestly.

She flinched, but held her ground. "That is true. But I also know that none of us knows what other people do in their own homes."

"What is that supposed to mean?"

"It means that I know for a fact that Perry was not the only person in the county to do things he didn't want other people to know about."

Walker lifted his hands. "Boy, I didn't mean to start a fight. I'm sorry I even brought him up."

"We've just been thinking about you," Abby added, acting

the peacemaker. "We've been concerned. A lot of people have. That's all."

Abby saved the moment by linking her arm through Deborah's. "You know, I've been thinking that it's a real shame that none of us have gotten together much since . . . well, since so much has happened. We should." Brightening, she added, "Anytime you want to talk, you ought to call one of us."

"I'll do that. I'll call you right up the next time I happen to be near our phone shanty."

There was more than a touch of sarcasm in Deborah's voice, which Jacob found surprising. Deborah was usually forthright, saying what she meant. He was the one who seemed to always have a snide comment these days.

But he didn't want to dwell on that. Instead, he hoped to keep the tone light and was grateful to Abby for leading them away from their dark memories.

"Abby, I heard that you've been thinking about being Plain. Have you already forgotten what it's like to be Amish? We don't have a lot of phones."

Abby bit her lip. "I know. I'm sorry, I was just trying to help—"

"You did," Deborah said quickly. "It is I who needs to apologize. I'm sorry. It really has been a hard couple of months. And since I'm an only child now, it's even harder. I do appreciate your caring thoughts."

"Maybe we could come up with some time to get together?" Walker suggested.

"Or we could get Deborah a cell phone," Jacob said quickly.

Deborah breathed in sharply. "Do you know how to get one?"

Well, here was his moment of truth. "I, uh, actually do have one. And I could get you one, too."

She blinked quickly. "My parents would be so upset. I could never get a cell phone."

"Why not?" Abby asked. "Lydia said her parents have let her get away with quite a few things right now. She went to the movies with us the other day."

"The Planks are different . . ."

Feeling his heart go out to her, imagining what life might be like in the Borntrager house, Jacob said, "What would it harm, Deb? You haven't joined the church yet. I mean, I bet half of our friends are doing something their parents wouldn't be thrilled about."

Obviously torn, she bit her lip.

"Don't tell them. Get a phone for yourself. If you had a cell, then you could call anyone you wanted."

Even in the dim light, Jacob could see that Deborah was intrigued by the idea.

He knew why: Freedom was a wonderful feeling. Just getting out from under his father's thumb for an hour had made him feel like he could breathe again.

"Jacob, I couldn't let you get me a cell phone."

"I'll pick you up one," Walker said. "There are some disposable cell phones at the Walmart in Paducah. Next time I'm there for school, I'll pick up one. If you really want one, that is."

To Jacob's pleasure, she looked his way for advice. He shrugged. "I don't see what it could hurt, Deb. It's just a phone. And if you are sitting alone in that house and I don't happen to be standing in your yard . . ."

She grinned. "Then I could call you all? Even if I only wanted to talk?"

Walker chuckled. "That's what they're for, Deborah. Call us, or text us, and we'll listen. Or shoot, we'll come out and meet you somewhere."

"I'd meet you in a heartbeat," Abby said. "I'm sure Lydia would come, too."

"I don't think Lydia will be getting a cell phone. At least not from me," Walker said, iron in his voice. "Her parents are letting me drive her around in my truck and go to the movies and such . . . but I'm afraid a cell phone would be crossing the line. I can't risk her parents becoming upset with me. But I could make sure she knows if you call. I bet Frannie and Beth would come, too."

"And I'll come up with a place for us to meet." Jacob waggled his eyebrows. "Someplace out of the way."

"I would like that," Deborah said. "I would like to know that I had a way to call you all. If I needed you, that is."

Jacob had to swallow back his burst of surprise. Since when was Deborah eager to start reaching out to them?

"Deborah, I'll bring you a cell phone next time I see you at work," Walker said.

"And you'll show me how to use it, too?""

"I'll do that. I'll program in everyone's numbers. Then all you'll have to do is call," Jacob said.

"I can't believe I'm saying this, but, okay."

"You're going to be glad you have it, Deborah," Abby proclaimed. "You never know when you're going to need it for an emergency. That's one part of being Plain I can't seem to wrap my head around."

Next to him, Deborah was stumbling over her response. "I know I would be glad to have it if something bad happened. Not that, you know, I want anything to—" Her next words were cut off by the sound of another vehicle approaching.

Since they were standing next to Walker's truck, there wasn't anywhere to hide. Jacob cursed their luck. Of course it wasn't against the *Ordnung* for them to be out at night, or even to be hanging out with *Englischers*. But their actions would be noticed and commented on, and he could do without that.

Luckily, the car turned into a driveway about a third of a mile ahead of them.

The close call scared him. "We should go," he said. "Sooner or later someone is going to see us all standing here. I'd rather not answer any more questions."

Walker crossed his arms over his chest. "I bet you're right. We should probably call it a night. So, Jacob, Deborah? What do y'all want to do?" he asked. "Do either of you want a ride home?"

Jacob looked at Deborah's face and saw her fear. It wouldn't do for either of them to be seen getting dropped off by a truck. "I think it would be better for me to walk her home," he said.

"All right," Walker answered as he opened his driver's side door. "Hey, be careful in the woods, though. There's no telling what will pounce out at you."

Walker was kidding of course, but beside him, Deborah shivered. Reaching out, he rested his palm on the small of her back. "We'll be careful, won't we, Deborah?"

Walker started up his truck, which sounded far too loud and telling in the quiet of the night. Jacob felt some relief when the truck pulled away and he and Deborah were alone again. "Ready to head back?"

"Not really, but I think we had better go."

He felt the same way. He wasn't ready to go home to the hundred questions his father would have for him.

He wasn't ready to say goodbye to Deborah, either. Somehow they'd become closer tonight—close, like a couple.

He'd felt that link between them, and he was sure Walker and Abby had sensed it, too. He ached to explore this new bend of their relationship. To coax her to tell him what she was really feeling.

But when they started back home, Jacob leading the way and Deborah right on his heels, neither of them spoke.

She seemed lost in thought, and he couldn't seem to quell the guilt he felt. Guilt for how he used to treat her, and guilt for the way he'd recently lashed out at her. But mostly, Jacob couldn't stem the feeling of despair that threatened to overtake him.

Because one thing was certain . . . if Deborah ever discovered what had really happened between him and Perry, she would never forgive him.

And he would never expect her to. Some things were unforgiveable.

Chapter 8

"Perry was never really a part of our group. Sometimes I felt bad about that. But then, of course, I remembered all the reasons he let me down."

FRANNIE EICHER

Long after she'd said goodbye to Jacob and had crept back inside her house. Long after she'd pulled off her tennis shoes, wiped off stray pieces of grass and leaves that had stuck to the side and had laid them under the bench by the back door. Long after she'd stealthily climbed the stairs and had washed her face and brushed her teeth, Deborah lay in her bed and thought about what had just happened.

In the span of a few hours, everything had changed.

She'd lived most of her life being afraid to show too much emotion and afraid to get too close to other people. Growing up with Perry, who'd been a champion of using her weaknesses to his advantage, made her that way.

For the last year, she'd begun to trust Jacob less, too. At first it was because he seemed to be such a follower of Perry's. She couldn't understand why the man she'd always idolized had decided to blindly accept Perry's faults. Deborah had ached to shake Jacob. Even though it seemed a betrayal to her brother, she wanted to make him see that Perry's ideas and actions were foolhardy and dangerous.

Later, her faith in Jacob faded when she'd learned what he had become. Sometime between following Perry and his disappearance, Jacob had become angry and intense. Whereas he used to talk to her patiently, he came to hardly even look her way. He'd snapped at her and it seemed as if they'd never been friends.

Now he seemed to have changed into yet another man in her eyes. The last few days in his company had been a revelation, to be sure. It was obvious that Jacob had been hiding under a raised guard as well. Maybe he was afraid of getting hurt?

Deborah heard her mother walk up the stairs, pause, then open the door to Perry's room. She seemed to do that more and more. In the middle of the night when she couldn't sleep, her mother would open the closed door to Perry's room and look at his things, crying softly.

After an hour or so, her father would guide her out, and the door would stay shut for another twenty-four hours.

As she heard the quiet echo of her mother's tears, Deborah attempted to close her eyes. Tossing and turning in her bed, she tried to imagine a different life. What would it be like to live in a home where there was joy and laughter? Where people were honest with their emotions, and honest with her?

Perhaps the only way to change her family was to change her own actions. The first step would be to help her mother, if she was brave enough.

Was she?

"You can do this," she whispered to the empty room. "You

can take your future in your hands and cast away your fears. If you are strong enough."

That was a vow worth making, she decided. Pulling on a robe and slippers, she opened up her door and walked into Perry's room.

With a start, her mother looked up from her perch on the end of Perry's bed. After a hasty swipe to her eyes, she blinked owlishly. "Deborah, what are you doing up? Did I wake you?"

"I was already awake." There was no need to admit that she hadn't gone to sleep yet. "I heard you in here. I thought maybe this time you wouldn't have to be alone."

"This time?" Her mother ran a hand along the thick quilt that covered Perry's bed. Almost like she was afraid to mess up the green-and-black log cabin design.

Leaning against the doorframe, Deborah said, "I hear you in here almost every night, Mamm."

She clenched her hands in her lap. "I feel closer to him when I come in here. It's silly, I know. It's not like Perry invited me in here to chat when he was alive."

No, that hadn't been his way. Perry would have met any person entering his room with a scowl. "Perry liked his privacy," she said with a smile.

To her surprise, her mother chuckled. "Indeed, he did. Why, I remember when he was four or five, he told me he no longer needed my help when he showered. He took a towel from my hands and closed the door right in my face."

"That sounds like Perry." Entering the room, Deborah took a seat next to her mom. Never would she have imagined that sitting in his room would help, but it did. There, on the comfy quilt, so much of the anger that always seemed to permeate his spirit dissipated. "I was always surprised Lydia put up with him," she said lightly.

"He was different with her, though. He was quieter, kinder."

Deborah nodded. That was true. Perry had been different around Lydia. Far more patient and far less self-absorbed. Everyone had commented on how good she was for him. "Frannie wasn't a good match."

Her mother smiled again. "Indeed, she was not."

But of course, by the time he courted Frannie, he'd already made the choice to take drugs.

"I saw Jacob Schrock tonight," Deborah blurted.

"What? When?"

"I snuck out," she said bravely. Deciding to let her guard down a little further. "I saw him walking by our house, so I went outside and talked to him."

"What in the world was he doing in our yard?"

"He was out walking. He said he was thinking about when he, Perry, and I used to walk to school together."

"And Perry always made you late," her mother mused.

"I didn't think you realized that."

"I realized more than you knew," she said cryptically. "So . . . what did you do tonight with Jacob?"

"We walked to the schoolhouse."

"In the dark."

"Yeah. He had a flashlight," Deborah explained. Although truthfully, that explained nothing. She knew that wasn't what her mother was wondering about.

Her mother must have thought the same thing. "And?"

"And? And nothing." She shrugged. "We just talked. I know I should have told you I was leaving, but I didn't want to risk you or Daed telling me no."

Her mother glanced at her out of the corner of her eye. "Jacob Schrock is a *gut* man. He always has been."

Deborah shrugged, "Lately, he's seemed mad at me. Angry."

"We're all dealing with our grief in our own way. Perhaps that was his?"

"Maybe," Deborah allowed. But that still didn't feel quite right. "I wish he wouldn't have taken his anger out on me. I could have used his friendship these last few months."

Perhaps it was Deborah's allusion to how alone she'd felt, or perhaps her mother had just had enough—whatever the reason, her eyes were pained when she stood up. "I know you're confused, Deborah. But I must admit that we've all probably done things we wished we hadn't."

With her words still hanging between them, she wandered out, leaving Deborah sitting on Perry's bed, wondering yet again when everything was going to start getting easier.

Jacob was still trying to read by flashlight when his mother knocked on his door.

"Jacob?" she whispered. "Jacob, are you awake?"

"I'm awake." Quickly, he tossed his book to one side and hurried to his door. "Mamm, is everything all right?"

"I don't know." She slipped by him, closing his door behind them. "You had visitors this evening. I thought I should let you know."

The news caught him completely off guard. "Someone came by after I left? Who?"

Warily glancing at his door, she said, "Detective Reynolds and Sheriff Kramer."

He wasn't sure if he was more worried about the unusual

nighttime visit, or that the sheriff and his detective friend had come to talk to him together. "I wonder what they wanted."

"They wouldn't say. Your father was mighty upset about their visit, though. No matter how hard he tried, they wouldn't talk to him."

Jacob could imagine that. His father liked to be in charge of things, whether they were at the store or in their home. He wouldn't have liked the two men arriving after dark unannounced, and then staying closemouthed about what they wanted to talk to Jacob about.

"What do they want me to do? Should I go by Sheriff Kramer's office tomorrow?"

His mother's eyes widened. "No!"

Jacob grew more concerned. What would be the harm in going to the sheriff's office? "Mamm, are you worried about something?"

"Not worried . . ." She ran a hand over her hair, which Jacob had just noticed was loose and down her back. "It's just that your father wouldn't want you to be seen there." She cleared her throat. "At the sheriff's office, I mean. People might talk, you know."

He knew they would. But that was beside the point. The last thing he wanted was to have to answer the sheriff's questions in front of his parents. That would only make a difficult situation ten times worse. "What do you want me to do?"

"Nothing. If those men want to speak to you, I'm sure they'll stop by again." Her smile wavered. "Or maybe they will have moved on and won't need to speak to you after all."

He doubted that. Sheriff Kramer didn't stop by people's homes for no reason. "Mamm, why didn't you tell me this right when I got home? We must have talked for ten minutes after I walked in the door."

"Your father didn't want to bother you." She bit her lip. "But I thought differently. I thought you should know that the policemen came by."

She looked so worried and unsure, he hugged her quickly. "I'm glad you told me, Mamm. Now I think I better get to sleep."

"You'll be able to sleep? You're not upset?"

"Of course not," he lied. "I've nothing to hide."

Pure relief filled her features. "I'm so glad to hear that, Jacob. *Gut naught.*"

"Good night, Mom." He kept his smile until she closed the door.

Then he crawled into bed and stared into the dark. Preparing himself for a long night ahead.

He was afraid that Detective Reynolds had finally discovered everything he'd tried so hard to keep hidden.

Chapter 9

"I've been holding on to our land, hoping to get a good price for it. But now that a man's gotten killed near our well? I doubt I could give those acres away."

HENRY MILLER

When Deborah saw Beth and Frannie's smiling faces as they entered the Schrocks' store the following morning, their smiles warmed her heart. After the drama of the night before and another long night of listening to her mother cry, it was so good to see happy people.

"How's work today?" Frannie asked.

"It's *gut*."

"It looks suspiciously quiet in here." Beth glanced around dramatically. "Are there no animals for sale?"

"Just a pair of kittens." She pointed over to the metal cage on the other side of the counter. In the cage, a pair of black and white kittens lay contentedly curled up around each other.

Deborah was wondering how they would react to being separated. Time and again, the kittens had proven to be rather skittish around the customers. Every time the pen's door opened and one of the kittens was carefully pulled out, leaving the other alone, both cats had made their displeasure known.

Just that morning, Mrs. Schrock had gotten scratched across her cheek.

"I'm right tired of these naughty things," Mrs. Schrock said. She was dusting a few of the shelves near the back wall. "I like animals, especially cats. But these two are quite the pair. I've never seen the like." With a frown, she said, "My husband made a poor choice when he decided to do a neighbor a favor and offer these kittens for sale. They are the most antisocial pets I've ever come across."

Most folks seemed to agree with Mrs. Schrock. It was a very good idea to leave them alone. Beth discovered that right away. Approaching the cage, she got the usual hiss and backed up warily. "Wow, Deborah. They're a lot meaner than they look."

From the back, Mrs. Schrock sighed. "They're a difficult pair, for sure. I doubt anyone will even take them for free." She looked to add more when a buzzer rang from the back. "Oh, *gut*! The delivery truck has arrived."

After the back door clicked shut, Deborah shook her head at the tiny pair of furballs. "They do seem to have little interest in being held or cuddled. I don't know what Mr. and Mrs. Schrock are going to do with them."

"Maybe they'll stay here and be your mousers?" Frannie suggested. "A good mouser is always needed."

"Perhaps, though I can't see them ever being that helpful." Turning to her friends, Deborah got down to business. "Now, how may I help you two?"

The girls exchanged looks. "Oh, we just came to look around," Frannie said airily.

Something was up with them. Deborah had never known

Frannie to speak so nonchalantly. Usually she verged on being too blunt.

Curious, Deborah walked around the counter. "Did you come in here to look for anything special?"

"Maybe," Frannie said. "I told Luke I'd make a little gift basket for one of his aunts who's coming here to visit. She's curious about his new life here, you know."

Deborah could only imagine. The fact that Luke had fallen in love with an Amish innkeeper in a small Kentucky town had to have caught his whole family off guard. "The baskets are over there," she said, pointing to a display of handmade baskets on metal shelves.

"Danke," Frannie said.

But Deborah noticed that Frannie wasn't all that interested in the baskets. And Beth didn't seem like she was looking around the store much, either.

Instead, it looked like they were more interested in chatting. And stealing looks her way.

Deborah grew impatient. "Something is going on. Come on, Beth, tell me what it is. Do you have news, too?"

Looking shamefaced, Beth bit her lip. "I do, but I don't think I should share it."

"You should definitely not share anything, Beth," Frannie admonished. "Gossiping helps no one."

Deborah could agree with that . . . to a point. Now, though, she was anxious to hear about anyone else's problems. It would be a relief to not only be fixated herself. "Come on. I know gossip isn't good, but I wouldn't say a word to anyone."

Beth bit her lip. "You promise you can keep a secret?"

"I promise. Now, come on. You girls are torturing me! Both of you look like you have the weight of the world on your shoulders. What do you know that I don't?"

"Abby told Frannie that Walker and Lydia might break up," Beth blurted in a rush.

That certainly was news! "What? It's obvious to everyone who sees them that they're meant to be together."

Ignoring her own warnings about gossiping, Frannie chimed in. "I guess Walker took Lydia by his college and was encouraging her to think about taking classes."

"Oh, my."

Frannie nodded, looking depressed. "I haven't known what to tell her. My situation with Luke has been much different. I've been more independent, and have enjoyed owning my own business. With Luke agreeing to move here, I felt like I could step away from the church with my father's blessing."

Deborah knew that Frannie always had doubts about her place in the community. But Lydia Plank was a far different story. She'd always seemed happy being Amish.

Yet, recalling the many times she'd smiled at other people and said she and her parents were "fine" when in fact the three of them were anything but, Deborah knew private lives could be much different than public ones. "What is she going to do?"

Beth looked at Frannie, then shrugged. "We don't know. I don't think Lydia knows, either. Well, that's what Abby Walker said. I've been praying, asking the Lord to give them guidance," Frannie said. "He has a plan for all of us, to be sure."

"He does," Deborah allowed, "but I would be sad if his plan was for Lydia to have her heart broken again."

"Love is a difficult thing," Frannie said. "It's not easy to find the right man, you know."

"Oh, I know that." Little by little, Deborah found her composure slipping. It wasn't their fault, but she suddenly felt like

the odd man out. Even though Beth wasn't romantically involved with anyone, Deborah had heard that she had developed a fancy for an *Englischer* for a short amount of time.

So, at least Beth was experiencing things.

And what had she done? She'd barely been able to find
a job.

Practically reading her mind, Frannie reached for her
hand. "Now all we have to do is find you someone special,
Deborah."

"We both know it's not as easy as all that."

"Well," she winked, "now that Lydia and I are off the
market, all the eligible men are free for you." With a teasing
smile, she added, "And for Beth, of course."

Sharing a skeptical look with Beth, Deborah played along.
"What eligible men?"

"Like . . . Micah."

Deborah shook her head. "He's not the man for me, Frannie."

"Or any woman, Frannie." Beth piped in.

Frannie shrugged. "Then how about Kevin?"

"Kevin Yoder?"

"Of course."

"Kevin is handsome, that is true," Beth said. "And he's
going to get his parents' farm. I suppose we can't forget that.
I'm not interested, but you can have him, Deborah."

Knowing that her girlfriends were merely teasing, Deborah
pretended to consider it. "Me and Kevin? I don't know." She
was about to add more when she noticed Jacob had walked
toward the counter and had heard them. Cheeks flushing,
she turned away quickly.

The other girls noticed. "Hello, Jacob," Frannie said. "How
are you?"

Jacob was returning their greetings when the door chimed and Walker strode in.

Thankful for someone new to focus on, Deborah walked toward him. "Hello, Walker. You aren't working today, are you?"

"No. I'm looking for Lydia." Sounding a little distracted, he added, "Have y'all seen her?"

"I haven't seen her all day," Frannie said.

Deborah realized that Walker didn't just look distracted, he looked pale and troubled. "Is anything wrong?"

He nodded, his head moving in a jerky motion. "My dad just called me. My grandfather collapsed at the farm. He's on his way to the hospital right now."

Jacob stepped forward. "Do you know what happened?"

"I think its his heart." He shrugged. "No one knows much."

"What can I do to help?" Jacob asked. "Do you want me to go with you to the hospital?"

"Thanks, but I was kind of hoping Lydia could be with me." Looking at the four of them standing in a semicircle around him, Walker said, "I hate to ask y'all this, but if any of you see Lydia, would you tell her what happened? I really need to get on to the hospital."

"You don't even have to ask. Of course, I'll track Lydia down and tell her your news," Frannie said.

"I'll pray for your grandfather's recovery," Deborah announced.

"Thanks, Deb. Thanks, everyone," Walker said before turning on his heel and rushing back outside.

"Poor guy," Jacob murmured.

As she watched Walker drive away, Deborah couldn't help but be envious of Lydia right at that moment. Walker's need for his girlfriend symbolized a perfect love, indeed.

Love wasn't just about feeling giddy and excited. No, it was also about comfort and security and being there for another person. If Walker was so anxious for Lydia at a time like this, Deborah was sure that things would work out for them.

Why, if she'd had someone like that, what would the past few months have been like? So often Deborah had wished for the comfort that comes from the presence of a person who would really understand her. She could only imagine that, if she'd had this kind of love, the stress and sadness consuming her could have been lessened.

Deborah was still thinking about Lydia and Walker when the door chimed.

Luke Reynolds walked in the door, and he wore an expression that made Deborah realize that he had no intention of shopping.

Frannie lit up. "Luke!"

"Hey, Frannie."

Like a moth to the light, Frannie practically danced across the floor to him. "I didn't know you were going shopping today. You should have told me, I would have waited to shop with you."

He smiled for a moment, brushed his thumb against her cheek, then shook his head. "I'm afraid I'm here for work."

"Work?"

And just like that, the room's atmosphere tightened.

Pursing his lips, Luke looked a little shamefaced. "I guess I really know how to ruin a party."

"It was no party," Frannie said quickly. "I know you have to do your detective work. It's an important job, to be sure."

As he looked at his girlfriend, Deborah noticed Luke's features soften. "Thanks, Frannie."

Oblivious to his amusement, she continued. "Beth and I

only came here to shop. And to see the mean kittens. And to visit with Deborah, of course."

Luke's lips twitched. "Of course."

"Walker was just here, but his grandfather has taken ill, so he left." Looking mildly chagrined, Frannie finished her summation. "Deborah and Jacob here are working."

"I was hoping they'd be here."

Deborah held her breath.

"Did you come to speak with me, Luke?" Jacob asked, his tone stilted and hollow sounding.

Realizing he'd moved off to the side, Deborah turned to him in surprise. Jacob looked as stiff and awkward as his voice sounded. She could have sworn he'd been standing closer.

But now he seemed to be holding himself apart.

Luke looked at Jacob, paused, then stepped toward her instead. "I actually need to ask you a couple more questions, Deborah. Can you talk now?"

His tone, though kind, was far different with her than with Frannie. Though he was politely phrasing the words, it was also very obvious that the detective wasn't asking permission at all.

"I can talk. Sure," she said.

"Let's go outside."

The day was sunny. Suddenly, she felt like she needed all the air and open space she could get. "Okay."

Detective Reynolds nodded at Jacob and Beth, lightly patted Frannie's shoulder, then led the way outside.

Deborah followed him out the door, down the front steps of the store, and along the sidewalk silently. The knot of trepidation in her middle felt tighter with every step she took. Her mind spun as she imagined what questions he was about to ask . . . and what answers she could tell him.

"How about we sit there?" He pointed to a bench near the back of the store. It had actually been one that she, Perry, and Jacob had often sat on after school.

Staring at the bench, memories returned. She remembered happier times, when her brother had shared a joke with Jacob . . . and how sometimes she had almost felt included.

He lightly rested his hand on her arm. "Or would you rather go someplace else? We could go sit in my truck. Or we could even go to your house."

The last place in she wanted to get questioned was in her home, under her mother's nose. And it was truly a beautiful day. If they talked here, they would be out in the open. That sounded better than being in his truck. She sat. "The bench is just fine."

He sat down beside her, then opened up the small notebook he carried, flipping through the pages until he got to an empty page. "Let's get started."

Deborah breathed deep and tried to prepare herself for the worst. Once again she was going to have to think about Perry and his faults.

And recognize that she should have tried harder to help him.

Chapter 10

"I think a lot of us have regrets about Perry. We should have stepped in and tried to pray with him, to help him see the error of his ways. It's a shame, that. But looking back at mistakes don't help much. It only leads to a stiff neck, you know."

AARON SCHROCK

Sitting next to Luke, Deborah looked frightened and awkward. As he made a real show of putting his notes together and getting organized, Luke berated himself. He realized now he shouldn't have approached her at work. He should have known that she'd put her guard up in front of her friends.

Even having Frannie there hadn't helped. Of course, Frannie was so proud of his occupation, Luke noticed she sometimes went out of her way to remind everyone that he wasn't just the man in her life, he was a police detective, too.

Which was exactly what Deborah hadn't needed to be reminded of. Now he was going to have to find a way to gain Deborah's trust, or at the very least, encourage her to relax so he could get the answers he needed.

"I hope I didn't make things too awkward for you, Deborah," he began. "If you're really uncomfortable, we could visit later, at your house."

"I promise, this conversation wouldn't be any easier at home. Besides, you are looking to find my brother's murderer, Detective. I want to help in any way I can. Feel free to ask me anything you want, at any time."

Her direct, honest way of speaking caught him off guard. She was the only person he'd questioned who didn't seem to have anything to hide about Perry.

"I appreciate that." Needing a moment to determine the best way to start, he pulled out a pencil, then set his cell phone on mute, then carefully placed it on the bench by his side.

"Deborah, tell me about the last time you saw your brother."

And just like that, her layers of composure fell away. Her smooth expression crumbled, and her wide, hazel eyes filled with tears. She wiped at her cheek impatiently. "The last time I saw Perry was on New Year's Eve."

Lydia had seen Perry that afternoon. Frannie far later.

"What time?"

"I don't rightly know, Detective. I never thought to look for the exact time."

"Was it dark? Close to midnight? Were you at home? Do the Amish even celebrate New Year's?"

"We do. Not with wine and all that. But we do stay up late and welcome in the New Year, same as everyone else." Smiling slightly, she said, "When Perry and I were little, my *mamm* used to make us donuts. We'd eat too many while they were hot, watching the hands on the clock slowly inch toward twelve."

"Sounds like fun."

"It was. When we were small, Perry was great fun. He was always game for anything." Shaking her head, her voice turned wistful. "He used to make my *daed* laugh and laugh. Goodness, I haven't thought about that in years."

Circling back to the point of their conversation, Luke said, "What about this New Year's Eve? Where was Perry?"

She closed her eyes. When she opened them, her expression was pained. "The last time I saw him was"—she paused, thinking—"some time about noon, I'd say. I'd been making lunch."

"And?"

"And, we talked about how next year was going to be better." Biting her lip, she added, "He kept saying he'd had a bad year, but he was hopeful that come January, things would improve. I told him I had faith that things would." Looking at him directly, she said, "That's all a person can do."

Luke sensed that Deborah was still hiding information from him. "So you never saw him that evening? You're sure?"

"Oh, I'm very sure. I looked for him the whole evening, you see. Even until we counted down to midnight. My parents were upset."

"They'd expected him home?"

"Yes." She looked apologetic. "Things aren't all that different with the Amish than the English, Detective Reynolds. Perry was twenty-two. Men his age don't usually choose to spend New Year's Eve with their parents and sister." She sighed. "But he had promised us that he would be there. He had started acting more like himself, you see."

Worried she was going to stumble over her brother's drug use, he attempted to get that off the plate. "It's common knowledge that he'd been taking drugs . . ."

She shook her head. "It wasn't that. It was that all of a

sudden he was acting like he cared again. Like a veil had been lifted from his face and he was seeing more clearly. We waited for him to come home." Her voice cracked. "But he never did."

"Mose told me that you didn't report him missing. No one in your family did. Where did y'all think he was?"

Something new flashed in her eyes. "I didn't know . . ."

"Come on, Deborah. You lived with Perry, you knew him better than just about anyone. Where did you think your brother was?"

"I thought he'd finally left," she said sharply, pain etched deep in her eyes. "I knew he'd tried to change, but it was also obvious that he'd burned too many bridges and that no one cared he was ready to make a new start. That upset him very much, you see. He had really thought we'd all forgive him easily."

"Forgiving is the Amish way." Though Luke was still learning much about the Amish culture, he did know that much.

"Yes . . . but repenting is expected. Perry never did." Looking even more disturbed, Deborah clenched her hands together.

Luke watched her knuckles turn white. Taking care to keep his voice even, he said, "Who was waiting for him to repent? You?"

"*Nee.* I . . . I had given up waiting." She swallowed.

He could tell she wasn't going to offer anything else. So he decided to go back to the night that so many had mentioned.

"So whose idea was it to go to the store the night before?"

"Mine, I suppose." She bit her lip. "But we hadn't gone to meet people. I had been sent to get some butter, and Perry decided to walk with me." A new hitch appeared in her tone. "I was so happy, he hadn't showed any interest in our friends in months."

"So, y'all saw everyone?"

She nodded. "When we approached, though, nothing went like it was supposed to. Or, like it used to." Looking beyond Luke, a wrinkle formed between her brows. "It was like our roles had switched." Looking directly at Luke again, she explained. "The girls asked me to join them. But no one wanted anything to do with Perry. Used to be, I was always the one tagging along."

Luke already knew that both Walker and Jacob had talked to him. "So did you stay with your friends or go back home with Perry?"

"I should've gone back with him, but I didn't."

"Why not?"

Tears formed in her eyes. "I was so tired of not belonging. Of having to live in his shadow. Then, finally, I was being asked back into the fold. I couldn't refuse."

"So what did Perry do? Did he go home right away?"

She stared at him in surprise. "I truly have no idea. I never asked him when we talked the next day. And then I never saw him again."

"Deborah, do you remember anything else? Anything someone might have said that could prove helpful now?"

"No."

"You don't remember any conversations? Or see anything unusual in his room?"

Her cheeks paled as she looked at him directly. "I didn't see a single thing of interest in Perry's room."

"Are you sure?" Even a rookie would have realized she was lying.

"I am positive, Detective. Like I have told you before, I don't know who killed my brother, but I would sure like to."

In the waiting room of the Crittenden County Hospital, a flurry of activity circled around them. Children cried, men and women filled out forms and looked at watches impatiently, cell phones buzzed, and two television screens played the news on muted screens.

But all Lydia cared about was the man sitting next to her. Squeezing his hand, she tried to sound as positive as she could. "I know it's hard, but try to relax. Your parents say your grandfather is in good hands, Walker. And we both know that God is watching out for him, too."

"I hear what you're saying . . . but I'm still scared, Lydia," Walker said.

"I know. But you heard the nurse's report. He will get better."

"I hope so." Squeezing her hand, he said, "I'm really glad you're here."

"Me too."

Looking over at Walker's parents, they met her gaze and smiled slightly. Abby was just outside the emergency room doors on her cell phone. Lydia was so glad that Abby had found her. She'd just gotten home from a walk when Abby had pulled up in her mother's sedan.

Once she'd heard the news, Lydia had barely taken time to tell her mother where she was going before hopping into Abby's car. Boy, was she glad Abby now had her driver's license!

After a time, Walker turned to her. "Lydia, sitting here, I realize that I've been letting too much get in the way of what's really important. It's taken my grandfather having a heart attack to realize I've been concentrating on all the wrong things."

Attempting to lighten his worries, she smiled. "And what should you have been worrying about?"

"You and me. Trying to find a way for the two of us to be together."

"We're working things out." It had been rocky, but Lydia had expected that. It was bound to be difficult, trying to mesh two very different lives into a successful couple.

"Things are going to be different from now on. I know what I should do. What *we* should do."

"And what is that?"

"I'm going to go help out at my grandparents' farm."

"You already do."

He shook his head. "Lydia, I'm talking about living there. Really helping. They're going to need me."

"What about your classes? You just signed up for the new semester."

"I know, but they're not important right now." Leaning close, he whispered into her neck. "Nothing is as important as family, Lydia. And being with you. I've been stupid, but not anymore. I'm going to become Amish, Lydia."

She was so surprised, she could only hold on to his hand and pray.

Chapter 11

"Along the creek is a wide bridge with hardly any sides. If you fell off the bridge in the spring, when the water is high and the current is strong, why it would be quite some time before anyone found you. You could be lost forever."

DEBORAH BORNTRAGER

Jacob couldn't help it. Every couple of minutes he found himself looking out the window, watching the conversation between Deborah and Luke Reynolds. The detective was sitting with his elbows balanced on his knees. Deborah sat beside him, straight and prim.

Looking pained.

They'd been out there for a while. Long after Frannie and Beth had gone, and after Mrs. Miller had come in for a dozen eggs, peeked at the hissing kittens, then scurried off.

Long after another delivery truck had come to the back door and he'd helped unload a dozen boxes.

Glancing out the window again, Jacob noticed Deborah was talking and talking. Luke was writing down notes.

What was she telling him? he wondered. And why was she so upset?

"Jacob, if you wipe the counter any harder, you're going to make a hole in the wood," his father said.

Abruptly, he straightened. "I don't think we're in danger of that, Daed. All I'm doing is polishing it."

"I polished it this morning." Carefully taking the rag from his hands, his father said, "Care to tell me why you're so concerned about what Deborah and the detective have to say to each other?"

"I'm not concerned."

"Sure you are. Admitting you have a problem is the first step, you know. And I think you are mighty concerned about what Deborah and that policeman are saying to each other."

"I'm not concerned. Only curious." And relieved that the detective wasn't speaking with him.

His father lumbered over to the window and peered out, his face so close to the pane that his nose was surely making a mark on the glass. "Well, for what it's worth, they seem to be done talking now, son."

Not even trying to hide his relief, Jacob straightened. "Really?"

"Uh-huh." Still with his nose next to the window, his father continued the report. "Let's see. Luke just went to his truck and our Deborah is right . . . here." He turned to Jacob and grinned.

"She's not 'our Deborah'," he snapped. "She's not anything to us."

"No. I'm just an employee, right?" Deborah asked from the doorway.

"I told you she was here, son," his father chided.

Turning her way, seeing the look of disappointment in her eyes, Jacob winced. For some reason, he always managed to sound rude and abrasive around her. "I didn't mean that how it sounded, Deb," he said quickly, his insides falling to mush when he saw that she'd been crying. "My father was teasing me about you and I was getting tired of it. It was nothing personal."

"I'm afraid that's a fact," his father added, sounding contrite. "I joke around far too much. It gets me heaps of trouble all the time," his father added, sounding inordinately contrite. "Why sometimes, I hardly know when to stop. Just like Jacob here hardly knows when to stop polishing wood."

As a look of puzzlement stole over her features, Jacob mentally rolled his eyes. He loved his father dearly.

But sometimes? . . . Sometimes, he seemed intent on driving him crazy.

Seeing that something had happened with the detective to shake her up, he pointed to the store's clock. "It's one, Father. Actually, it's almost ten after."

"And?"

"Deborah's shift ended ten minutes ago. You should let her get on her way."

"Oh, I don't have to leave yet," Deborah protested. "I haven't worked my whole shift yet. I spent the last thirty minutes talking to Detective Reynolds."

It had been forty-five minutes. But who was counting besides him?

"Being asked questions isn't easy," his father said. "Jacob is right. You should get on your way. Besides, the store's fairly quiet now."

"Oh. Well, all right, then. I'll go get my purse and cloak from the back."

"Hold on, child. Deborah, did you walk here today?"

"Yes, Mr. Schrock." Pointing toward the back door, she said, "I went the back way."

"You've been through quite a time of it. I don't like to think of you walking through the woods by your lonesome." As if he'd suddenly had a very bright idea, his father snapped his fingers. "Jacob, why don't you accompany Deborah?"

There was no easy way to refuse the request. "All right."

Deborah held up a hand. "I'm fine. Really . . ."

"Let him walk by your side now. Go get your cloak and enjoy the rest of your day." Making a shooing motion with his hands, his father said, "You two, get along now."

Jacob smiled wryly. "If we refuse, he'll only get worse. Come on."

"I suppose I canna argue with that." Without another word, she walked to the back, and returned with her cloak. After he watched her fasten it, he followed her out of the store.

They walked side-by-side down the steps and along the sidewalk.

When they approached the narrow trail leading toward the back of the store and to his house, he motioned her forward. Walking single file, they marched on until the grass rose and brushed their calves, the trees grew thicker, and they were completely out of sight of the back windows of his home.

Just as the path grew wider and he stepped to her side, Deborah turned to him. "You don't need to walk with me any farther, Jacob. I am perfectly fine."

He didn't want to leave. "Are you? You seem kind of shaken up. Did . . . did talking to the detective make you upset? Have you been crying?"

She swiped her cheeks. "Maybe. Being questioned scares

me. Detective Reynolds waits so long in between his questions that I'm never sure if I'm supposed to keep talking or that I've said too much."

"I've had that feeling, too. I think he does it on purpose." Clasping her elbow, he murmured, "But just because he has questions for you, it doesn't mean he should make you upset."

"It's not all his fault, Jacob. The whole situation makes me cry. Losing my brother makes me cry." Valiantly, she tried for a watery smile, but failed miserably. "I'm sorry. I don't mean to upset you with my waterworks."

"You're not upsetting me." Instead of going directly toward her house, he took a different fork in the trail. The one that led to the bridge that spanned one of the widest parts of Crooked Creek. "I'm just not used to girls crying."

His quip got what he wanted: a giggle. "I'm not much of a crier. But talking about Perry . . . and his last days on earth, it makes me terribly sad. Sometimes I still can't believe that I truly had thought Perry had gone off and left us, Jacob. Back in January, I missed him, but I didn't mourn him. I really did imagine that he was in St. Louis."

Jacob was torn between the need to comfort her and the desire to know what Luke had asked her. After weighing the two, his need for the information won out. If Luke was talking to her about Perry's last day, Jacob was sure he would be interviewed next. Why else had the detective and sheriff showed up at his house last night?

And he needed to be ready. "What did Luke ask you? What sort of things did he want to know about Perry?"

She swung her head his way as they walked deeper into the dense foliage. In the distance, they could hear the faint sounds of water rushing. "Why?"

"No reason. I just was curious." Glancing at her, he noticed most of the light from the late afternoon sun was getting blocked as it shone through the leafy trees. Shadows formed around her face.

"I mainly talked about New Year's Eve."

"Not when you two came to the store?"

"I talked about that some. But he wanted to know what Perry's last day had been like." Her boots crunched on the broken branches, old leaves, and pinecones underfoot. She ducked once, dodging a leafy tree branch.

"Really?" Worry gnawed at his insides as he attempted to sound aloof. "He doesn't think you're a suspect, does he?"

"I certainly hope not! Perry was my brother."

"Yeah. Sorry. Of course he'd never think that. Did he ask about me?"

She looked at him curiously, then blinked. Her voice growing deeper, she said, "Not so much. Are you worried that he would?"

"It's no secret that I was mad at him."

"I know you were."

They were next to the creek now. With the recent rains, it was fuller than usual. The current ran fast, and the water level was so high that it covered all the rocks that were usually visible. "Look how deep the water is," he said, trying to calm them both down.

"It is. If someone didn't know rocks were under the surface, they might be tempted to jump in. It would be so easy to get hurt."

The water did look deep and luminous. Deceiving.

"I bet one day something like that will happen," she mused. "It seems we're all susceptible to accidents. To things we never counted on."

He knew that was true from his own experiences. "We have to be vigilant."

"Yes . . . or grateful." Softly, she added, "We mustn't forget that every day could be our last."

He was a little taken aback by her train of thoughts. "That's mighty morbid, Deb."

"But true. Most of the time I don't even appreciate my days. Sometimes I don't even appreciate the people I see, or even the people I know and love."

"I'm sure you do—"

"Not always. On December thirty-first? I was too busy thinking about my own selfish wants. And focused on wishing Perry would finally do something he promised to do. I was too busy holding on to hurts to really enjoy his company." Looking up at him, she whispered, "I'll always regret that."

"You shouldn't. You don't owe Perry anything, Deb." Before he knew it, he was gripping both her shoulders, holding her tightly. Not letting her go. "Deborah, what happened to Perry wasn't your fault. If you can't make yourself believe anything else, believe that."

Ignoring his words, oblivious to his grip, she shook her head. "That's almost impossible to do. He was my brother."

"You were his younger sister. Of all people, I know how he treated you. At best, you were his sweet pet, the girl he tried to protect and shield. At worst? At worst, he only saw you as one more person who could betray him. Perry wasn't a saint, Deborah."

She shrugged. "So what if he wasn't?"

Remembering . . . remembering more than he wanted to, more than he ever wanted her to know, he grasped at what to say. Trying to figure out how to get her to trust him. To listen to him forever. To know that, he, too, wished he had done things differently. "You're right. It doesn't really matter," he finally replied.

Stepping closer, still holding her shoulders, dipping his head so that they were standing eye to eye, so close that their lips were mere inches apart, he murmured, "You have to learn to forget about the things you can't change and move forward."

"Where is forward?"

Her voice was raspy. He heard a note of tension in her voice, the same one that had been drumming inside of him.

There was something new between them . . . Something dark and strong and slightly dangerous.

Whatever it was, he was tired of denying it. "It's here," he said before he closed the gap between their lips and finally kissed her.

As their lips brushed again, learning each other, she stiffened in his arms. Immediately, he let go of her shoulders, freeing her. Allowing her to break away, to berate him for taking the liberty.

But instead of doing either, Deb tilted her head and slipped her hands around his neck. Her warm hands glided along his bare skin, making his flesh burn.

And then she kissed him again. Right there, deep in the darkened thicket next to the too-full river that covered up a multitude of sins. She tasted sweet. The moment was perfect, like everything he'd ever imagined.

But then he remembered what he had done. With a jerk, he lifted his head and pulled away. "We shouldn't have done that. I mean, *I* shouldn't have done that. I . . . I'm sorry."

Deborah looked anything but apologetic. "I'm not. I've wanted to kiss you for most of my life."

Then to his shock, she turned and walked back to the path, toward her home.

He lengthened his stride to keep up, but inside himself, Jacob knew he had far longer to go than just a few steps. His world had just turned on its side. And in this new place, Deborah seemed to have all the answers, while he had only one.

After what he'd done, he would never deserve her, and one day soon, she would think that, too.

Chapter 12

"Perry used to tell me that just because he was the son of a farmer, it didn't mean he had to become one."

WALKER ANDERSON

"Luke? Is there anything I can do to help?" Frannie asked as she brought him a plate of fried chicken, scalloped potatoes, and stewed vegetables.

Looking at the plate filled to the brim, he raised his eyebrows. "Frannie, you bring me the tastiest meals I've ever had in my life. You don't need to do another thing."

She waved off his compliment. "It's just food, Luke."

It was more than that, he realized as he took his first bite of potatoes. Frannie continually made an effort to make his day better, whether it was by fixing him a delicious meal or sitting next to him and just listening.

Now he couldn't believe that he'd been so stubborn when he'd first met her. Had he really thought her efforts to look after his needs were simply to pry into his business?

"It's more than food. I'm grateful for everything you do."

She smiled, her obvious happiness echoing the way he felt about her. Then, as if sensing his stress, she narrowed her eyes. "Luke, what has made you so upset? Is it the investigation? Or is it something else?"

"It's just the investigation." He picked up his fork, then put it back down. "You know I can't talk about it."

"I don't need to know the details, though I promise if you told me something in confidence, I would never betray it."

She meant that, too, Luke realized. Somehow, she'd transferred her loyalties to him, and was now willing to go against her father's wishes and out of her comfort zone. Her belief in him and their relationship was humbling.

"I know you'd keep every secret that I asked you to, Frannie. I can't tell you how much I appreciate that. But I'm not going to put that burden on your shoulders. Besides, it wouldn't be right, professionally. I need to keep this case close to my chest."

She took the chair next to him, perching on the edge like she didn't want to get too comfortable. "May I tell you something? Something you might not know about Perry, or about the rest of us?"

"You can tell me anything you want."

"Luke, I've traveled to Holmes County in Ohio. I went once up to Lancaster County in Pennsylvania, too. To an outsider, the Amish might all look the same." She leaned back while he took another bite. "Oh, an *Englischer* might notice that our *kapps* are different, or our buggies vary a bit from community to community, but he might not realize that our norms can be far different from each other."

"What do you mean?" He wasn't sure he was seeing her point.

"Up in Lancaster? The Amish there are a wealthy lot. The land is expensive, and some Amish have even invested in stores and hotels built for the tourists. That money gives people security, I think. And with that security, they might be inclined to take more risks."

Luke didn't disagree. Money, or lack of it, had played a role in almost every group of people he'd investigated. He'd seen a wide variety of crimes committed for a few hundred dollars. Or far less. "The Amish here in Crittenden County aren't wealthy, are they?"

She shook her head. "No. I don't know anyone here, Amish or English, who would consider themselves rich. Because of that, we keep to ourselves. Maybe it's because we can't afford to move away? We couldn't afford to get out if we were desperate." Laying her palms flat on the table, she said, "What I'm trying to say is that our community here in Crittenden County is a close-knit group, maybe closer than most. We keep our problems close to our hearts, and we try to make do in spite of our difficulties. Because there ain't nowhere else to go. We know each other real well, both the good and the bad things."

"And?"

She took another breath. "What I'm trying to say is that a great many people might know more than they're letting on, Luke. They might decide that they'd rather live with what they know than take a chance on what might happen if they betray each other."

He was catching on now. "Because they have nowhere else to go."

"Exactly. And they may never trust you enough to tell you the whole truth."

While he understood what she was saying, he didn't agree with the reasoning. "Sooner or later, the people who are responsible are going to have to come forward. They have to, Frannie. Laws are greater than one person or one community or one state. I swore to uphold the law and I will. And I know Mose and I are very close to getting to the bottom of this case."

Her expression softened. "Oh, I know you're going to solve things, Luke. You are a wonderful-*gut* detective, of that I have no doubt. I just don't want you to be too upset when a whole lot of people aren't happy when you solve the case and make an arrest."

"What about you?"

"Me?"

"Are you going to turn your back on me if I arrest someone you're close to, Frannie?"

She shook her head slowly. "I will never turn away from you. I love you."

He picked up his fork again. "Then that's all that matters to me. Because I love you too, Frannie."

When Frannie's smile grew, he smiled right back.

And thought again that no matter what the consequences, coming to Crittenden County had been the right decision.

After debating whether to speak her mind for the last mile, Lydia turned to Walker. "I'm glad you asked me to come with you to visit your grandmother, but I'm worried she might not want me here."

"Of course she wants you to visit. She knows how much you mean to me."

"But with your grandfather still in the hospital, she might not want an extra visitor. She seemed real upset at the hospital."

"We were all upset, but you made a world of difference for me, Lydia. Besides, I heard Grandma Francis say you were welcome to visit her anytime."

"I have a feeling she was talking about a time in the future . . . not me coming over the next day!"

Walker turned to her in surprise. "I can't believe you are worrying about this." Taking her hand he said, "Lydia, I told them that I intend to ask you to marry me."

"You did what?"

"It's true," he said with a smile. "I know we're going to have to work everything out, but it can be done. I feel sure of it."

Lydia felt her cheeks heat. Walker was so outwardly affectionate, it sometimes took her off guard. He hadn't been shy at all about telling his grandmother about his intentions. And he hadn't been shy about holding her hand in the hospital, either. His easy, affectionate way with her was so different from the usual circumspect way of the Amish.

It had taken some getting used to, the way he liked to give her a hug when he saw her. Last night, he'd even kissed her cheek in front of his parents.

Luckily, they hadn't looked shocked. No, they'd only laughed.

Yes, it was hard to get used to, but it was nice, too. Lydia was discovering that she couldn't help but enjoy the way he was so open and honest with his emotions. Instead of feeling awkward, it felt wonderful to have the man she loved be so loving to her.

But all that aside, visiting his grandmother while she was worried about her husband resting in the hospital? That seemed to be pushing things a bit. "If you want me beside you, then that's where I want to be," she said as he parked the truck and turned off his headlights. "It's just that sometimes a family likes to only be around family during difficult times."

Still holding her hand, he squeezed gently. "You are family, Lydia. Plus, I think having you visit is going to help Grandma. I know your presence will help me."

She kept his words close to heart as they walked toward his grandparents' front door—and when he seemed to stumble when he grasped the door handle. "You okay?" she said gently.

"Yeah. It's just that I've been over here dozens of times and it's never looked so quiet here." Pain was etched in his eyes when he turned to her. "What if my grandfather never comes home?"

Lydia knew better than to offer false promises. All she knew to do was to rely on her beliefs, that the Lord was in charge. "If he doesn't survive, then the Lord has plans for him up in heaven. And plans for us here on earth."

"You truly believe that, don't you?"

"I can't help but believe it. I feel it with all my heart."

She noticed that the hard lines etched around his mouth eased a bit as he turned the handle and led the way inside. Glad of heart, she felt a renewed sense of peace.

It was moments like this when she knew that she'd made the right decision to accept her relationship with Walker. Yes, it was difficult to fall in love with someone who was so different than herself. But he gave her things she needed, like openness and freedom.

On the other hand, she seemed to give him a security he longed for. It was becoming apparent that they needed each other to thrive.

"Grandma? It's Walker. Lydia and I are here to visit," he called out.

Slowly, his grandmother appeared at the end of the darkened hall. "I was just lying down. I'll be right there." Her voice sounded thready and weak.

"I think she was sleeping, Walker," Lydia whispered.

Raising his voice a bit, he added, "*Mommi*, I'm sorry. We'll come back another time."

"No, no. I need to be getting up. Why don't you wait for me in the kitchen?"

"All right," he said.

Seeing how upset and worried he was, Lydia slipped her hand into his and led him into the cozy kitchen. "Sit down, Walker. I'll heat up a kettle and make us tea."

He paused behind one of the old oak chairs surrounding the table. "It's not a normal oven, Lydia. It runs on gas. And you have to light it with a match."

She couldn't help but chuckle. "It's not 'normal' for you, but it is for me, Walker. Have a seat and stop worrying."

Looking chagrined, he did as she asked.

Happy that he was letting her take the lead, Lydia opened cabinets, discovered tea and a kettle, then slowly began the process of making a pot of tea.

She'd just set the tea leaves to steep when Walker's Grandma Francis joined them. "Lydia, you are a dear. A cup of hot *tay* sounds wonderful-*gut!*"

"I'm glad about that." Holding up the plate of orange marmalade scones, she added, "I made you some scones, too."

With a smile, Walker's grandmother lifted the napkin and took one out. "These look delicious."

Walker pulled out a chair for her. "Sit down, Grandma. Did you not sleep much last night?"

"Not too much. It felt strange, being here all alone."

"How is Grandpa James? Have you heard?"

She shrugged. "I walked down to the phone shanty early

this morning for an update. He's not doing too well, Walker. The *doktah* at the hospital told us that he had a narrow escape from a heart attack." Tears forming in her eyes, she said, "He is going to have to have surgery. They need to open a blockage in one of his arteries."

"When is that going to happen?"

"In the next week or so." She bit her lip. "Your father has been such a blessing. He said he visited with the doctor this morning, and has been helping your stubborn grandfather understand that the doctor wasn't just making a suggestion. It's an order."

"Did Grandpa James actually consider not getting the surgery?"

"You know your grandfather," she said as Lydia placed a steaming cup of tea in front of her. "He doesn't want to think about his weaknesses."

"I'll talk to him."

His grandmother smiled. "Be prepared, Walker. Just because you are full of advice, it doesn't mean he wants to listen to it. All he really cares about at the moment is spring planting. I'll talk to him more when your father takes me back to the hospital in a few hours."

"Lydia and I can take you as soon as you're ready."

"You're a dear, Walker."

Lydia sat down across from Walker and saw a look of puzzlement play across his features.

"Tell me about spring planting."

"Oh, yes. Grandpa James was hoping to get some wheat, corn, and alfalfa planted. It's all he seems able to talk about."

"Now that he's in the hospital, how will it get done?"

When Lydia saw Walker's worry carry over to his grandmother, she stepped in. "Don't dwell on that, Walker. It's our way to help each other. I'm sure other Amish families in the church district are already making plans to come here and help plow."

The older lady smiled. "Of course you are right, dear. They'll help us. We are blessed for many hands at a time like this."

"I don't know how I feel about all your friends and neighbors helping with the plowing, Grandma. It should be your family."

"You mustn't look at things like that. Your father is helping us with the doctor and the driving. And you are here, paying me a visit. That is a true blessing right now."

"But I could do something . . ."

"Walker, please don't fret. If I need you to help me with errands, I'll ask."

"Look, I've been trying to find a way to say this without feeling like I'm stepping on your toes, but maybe there's no way to do that." Taking a breath, he said, "I decided to stop going to classes, Grandma. I want to help you here on the farm."

Grandma Francis looked taken aback, and more than a little surprised. "I appreciate your offer to help on the farm, but I'm afraid you don't know much about planting a crop. It might be more work than you were prepared to do." She looked Lydia's way and Lydia felt like she could practically read her mind.

"Most of the Amish men who would be helping have farmed from practically the time they walk. It would be hard to learn how to do everything quickly," Lydia said diplomatically.

Walker knew he needed to appreciate his gifts and talents, not try to step into things he had no control over and would only make worse. But he felt strongly about doing something meaningful. "But I could learn, right? I mean, I might not be the best at anything, but I'm reasonably smart. And I'm strong and healthy."

His grandmother nodded. "Yes, of course, Walker. That is true . . ."

"Grandma, I came over here to tell you that I want to live with you for the next few months. I want to help with the farm, and I want to stay here with you so you won't be alone."

His grandmother looked so worried about hurting his feelings, Lydia took pity on her and said what needed to be said. "Helping other farmers with their crops is our way, Walker. The men have plows and sturdy horses. I'm afraid you wouldn't be able to use a tractor or anything like that."

"I know that. I didn't mention using a tractor." Placing both of his palms flat on the table, he said, "Grandma, when do you expect the other men to come help?"

"In the next week or so."

"Then when they get here, I'll ask them to let me join them. I can't imagine that they'd refuse my help."

"Walker, there is no need—"

"I am considering becoming Amish, Grandma. I want to live here with you and help."

His grandmother's eyes widened as her cheeks flushed. "I know your faith is mighty strong. And I know your willingness is true and honest . . ." Her voice drifted off, obviously struggling to put her doubts into words.

But Walker picked up on her words. "If my faith is strong, and I am willing to try my best to adjust . . . isn't that enough? Haven't you always said that God is looking out for us, that he never gives us burdens too big for us to handle?"

"I have said that. And I do believe that."

Looking at Walker, Lydia felt tears prick her eyes. Before his grandmother could reply, she felt herself nodding. "You are right, Walker. Your faith is enough. Faith in the Lord is always enough."

The room fell silent as both she and Walker turned to his grandmother. She, too, seemed incredibly touched by his faith—and his passion to do everything he could to help his grandparents.

With a trembling hand, she reached for his. "Thank you for reminding me about what is important. A true heart and a willingness to serve is all anyone really needs."

Walker squeezed his grandmother's hand, then leaned back in his chair. "It's settled. I'm going to live here with you and farm." He paused. "Just, ah, don't expect too much."

"You're going to tell me that, after your pretty speech?"

His cheeks flushed. "You always have told me that I talk too much. I am now merely trying to keep your expectations low."

Grandma Francis chuckled. "Don't you worry about that, Walker. You will soon find that the Amish men you work with won't expect much from you at all."

Covering her mouth with her hands, Lydia hid a smile. She feared Walker's grandmother was exactly right.

Chapter 13

"If we had known what was eventually going to happen with Perry, we would have kept a closer eye on his comings and goings."

BETH ANNE BORNTRAGER

"Deborah, do you plan to see Jacob again tonight?" her mother asked from the doorway.

Deborah's hands froze as she wrung out the dress she'd been hand washing in the laundry tub. When had her mother approached? Had she been so deep in thought that she wasn't even aware of movement around her?

Or maybe she was so used to her mother keeping to herself that she hardly even listened to her anymore? "I have no idea. Are you upset? I was safe with Jacob."

"I debated whether to tell your father about your meeting. But in the end, I let him know. It's best that he knows what you're doing, Deborah."

Deborah didn't see the reason for that, but she refrained from arguing. "And what did he say?"

"Nothing much. Though we both agree that it is mighty

dangerous to be out at night. A lot of terrible things could happen. It's not safe."

"I was with Jacob," Deborah reminded her needlessly. "I wasn't alone."

"That's the only reason your father didn't speak to you about your outing." She cleared her throat. "Jacob is a good man. To my knowledge he's never strayed."

Shaking out the dress, Deborah slowly hung it up on the clothesline strung through the middle of the room. "I'm sorry you got worried. But like I told you, we weren't doing anything much. Just walking."

"So what did you two do, besides walk?"

Her mother's questions sounded almost normal. Almost like she was her old self. It was disconcerting, and made her wary, too. She didn't know how much her mother could handle.

"Nothing, really. We started out talking about those days walking to school together. Next thing we knew, we were out at the old trail." Taking a chance, she added, "It was fun, walking through the fields in the dark like that."

Her mother's gaze turned sweet and affectionate. Almost girlish. "You've always liked Jacob, haven't you?"

Deborah wasn't sure how to answer that. Yes, she had always liked him. Until he'd been so mean to her that she'd wished she'd never see him again. "Jacob and I, we have a difficult relationship."

Her mother chuckled. "*Jah*, I suppose it could be described that way."

"I didn't get home too late." Plunging her hands in the water, she pulled out another wet garment and wrung out the water. After, she shook her father's shirt, then set it on the side of her basket. All the while, she felt her mother's gaze rest on her. It was a bit unsettling—was she watching to make sure Deborah didn't make a mistake?

"Deborah, I wanted to tell you that I am sorry that I haven't been a better parent lately."

Deborah sighed. She hadn't been any sort of parent, or mother. But Deborah didn't blame her. Any woman would have a hard time doing much if she'd lost a child. Besides, her mother's neglect wasn't all that unusual. In a lot of ways it felt like just another episode in a lifetime of being her parents' afterthought.

Perry had always come first. Whether that was good or bad ceased to matter. They'd become used to Perry's needs and wants always taking precedent.

"There is nothing you need to apologize for, Mother. I've been fine." And she had been fine, she realized with some surprise. She'd found a job and had renewed relationships with her girlfriends.

She'd also taken care of as much as she could around the house. For months now, with the exception of her two weeks in Charm, she'd taken care of the laundry and the cooking. She'd dusted and cleaned and tried to be everything to everyone. In short, she'd grown up.

"Perhaps we could start spending more time together?"

Pleased, she smiled at her mother. "I would like that."

"I would like that, too." Looking satisfied with their conversation, she handed Deborah a towel. "I also think it's time for me to start living my life instead of passing each day in bed. Why don't you to let me finish the washing?"

"Mamm, there's no need. Besides, I'm almost done with it."

"And that, child, is all the more reason to let me finish this chore. It's a small enough task that I should be able to handle it, even though I might be a little rusty."

Impulsively, she gave her mother a hug, not even caring that she was likely getting her mother a little wet from her damp sleeves. It was simply so nice to have her back. "Mamm, being rusty is just fine with me. I'll take you any way I can have you."

Lifting her chin a bit, her mom teared up, "You've always had me, Deborah. I'm sorry I haven't made sure you knew that. I . . . I shouldn't have neglected you like I did."

There was no need for apologies. They'd all been dealing with their grief in their own ways. Her father had been working, her mother holed up in the comfort of a dark room. She'd found solace by reaching out to other people.

Who was to say that one way was better than the others? "Let's not apologize anymore. Let's just move forward."

Her mother's face eased into a smooth relief. "I'd like that."

After giving her mother a hug, Deborah left the washroom, then decided to walk to the store early.

She was halfway there when she spied Walker's truck parked in front of a coffee shop. He was standing with Jacob, and when they saw her, they motioned her over.

"I haven't looked at the schedule. Are you working today?" Jacob asked.

"*Jah*. You?"

Looking pained, he nodded. "Always. But listen, it's good we saw you. Look what I have for you." He held out a paper shopping bag.

She peeked inside it and almost gasped. There was a cell phone. "Is this mine?"

"Yep. I just picked up Jacob and we've been charging it in my truck and entering in everyone's phone numbers," Walker said.

After briefly showing her how to access the phone numbers, he said, "Now you're good to go, Deb."

The phone symbolized so much to her: independence, trust from friends . . . and a bit of awareness that she was now challenging the rules that she'd always adhered to. "How much do I owe you?" Mentally, she counted up the money she recalled in her wallet. Perhaps forty dollars?

"Jacob bought it, not me," Walker said before waving goodbye.

"You bought it?" she sputtered. "Jacob—"

"It was no big deal. And before you start throwing money my way, stop."

"I want to pay what you're owed."

"You don't 'owe' me a thing, Deb," he said quietly. "You've done a lot for me, and you've been able to forgive me when I've acted like a total jerk. I had some extra money, and it made me happy to spend it on you. Take it."

"But—" She hardly knew what to think about this.

"Consider it a gift."

A gift? "But that isn't what we talked about."

"Then consider it a surprise. Now, put it in your purse and say thank you."

Feeling like she was in daze, she did as he asked. *"Danke."*

"You're welcome." He smiled. "Come on, let's walk to the store."

She fell to his side, keeping pace with him. The sidewalks were narrow, and more than once, he paused so she could precede him during an especially narrow patch.

A buggy passed them, and when Jacob fingered the brim of his hat at the driver, Deborah knew their walking together would be remarked upon. But instead of feeling wary, she felt like standing up a little taller, or smiling a little bit brighter.

This was a moment out of her dreams. A moment that until recently she never thought would be realized.

Only when they passed the sheriff's trailer, where they saw the silhouettes of Sheriff Kramer and Detective Reynolds inside, did reality return.

Their footsteps slowed.

Until Perry's murder was solved, nothing about their lives would get back to normal. Questions would remain about his disappearance and his death. And who knew more than they were letting on.

"Well, would you look at that? Jacob and Deborah Borntrager are walking together," Mose said, lazily watching the couple walk together outside the front window.

Having gotten tired of staring at his notes, Luke stopped tossing up the squishy stress ball he'd found in the back of Mose's supply closet up in the air. "You're worse than a neighborhood gossip."

"By now, I'm sure you've realized that Deborah's had a crush on Jacob Schrock for quite some time."

"And?"

"And, it does my heart good to see them walking together, like a couple. Why, back when they were small, we all thought it was only a matter of time before they began courting."

"We?"

"Everyone in the church district," Mose grumbled. "And at Mary King's."

"Let me get this straight." Tossing the ball up in the air again, Luke chuckled. "You were discussing relationships with the rest of the old biddies over coffee?"

"And pie." Mose's chastised expression lasted only about thirty seconds. Then he chuckled, too. "Don't knock it, Luke. Since you've decided to settle here with Frannie, I'd guess you'll soon be taking an interest in other peoples' love lives."

"If I turn into a gossip, heaven help us all."

"Indeed." Mose winked, then turned back to the window. "Hmm. Jacob is grasping Deborah's elbow. That romance has bloomed, for sure."

"We still need to question Jacob, you know."

"I know. I read your notes from Deborah's interview. I think she was withholding something."

"I thought so, too." Standing up, Luke crossed the room and stared out at the departing couple beside his friend. "But I'm not sure if they're only lying to us . . . or to each other as well."

When they were out of sight, Mose picked up his car keys. "I think there's only one way to discuss this further, Luke."

"Let me guess . . . at Mary King's?"

"Of course. I heard she's been baking up some lemon chess pies. I aim to have a slice before it's all gone."

Chapter 14

"The older a man gets, the farther he had to walk to school as a child."

AARON SCHROCK

After only the briefest knocks, Jacob's dad opened his bedroom door. "Jacob, I'm afraid you are going to have even less free time now," he said in a rush.

Jacob scrambled to a sitting position on his bed. "And why is that?"

"I just spoke with Walker. He's quitting."

"What? I just saw him. He didn't say a word about it." When he saw his father's gaze had centered on his *Sports Illustrated* magazine . . . and his cell phone, he hastily pushed both under his pillow. It wouldn't change what his father had seen, but maybe it would prevent a lecture.

"I guess it's a sudden thing," his dad replied as he walked across the room and sat on the old recliner in the corner. "He's got a good reason, though. He's going to live on his grandparents' farm and help out there for a time."

"He mentioned that his grandfather was sick. Is he worse?"

"I don't think so." He frowned. "Your mother heard that

he's going to have to have a procedure done on his heart, but he's out of the danger zone, praise God."

"I wonder what Walker's family thinks about him going out to help on an Amish farm."

"Oh, I'm sure they're proud of him . . . and maybe worried a bit, too." He raised his brows. "Something tells me that the Planks might not be losing a daughter as much as gaining a son."

Thinking about Walker, with his city ways and the truck he loved so much, Jacob felt his lips curve into a smile. "I think you may be right," he mused. "Daed, do you think Walker knows anything about plowing?"

"Jacob, I'd be surprised if he knew which end of the horse to hook the plow up to! I'd have a difficult time plowing, and I did it when I was a boy. It ain't an easy thing to get used to." With a chuckle, he added, "Walker Anderson has a great many skills. Farming ain't one of them."

"That is one thing I think we can agree on."

They chuckled, making Jacob happy that for once he and his father were on common ground. The warm atmosphere seemed to affect his father as well. Before Jacob's eyes, his father's shoulders and back relaxed and he sank farther into the old brown recliner.

"I've always liked this chair. Don't know why your mother put it in here."

"She didn't," Jacob corrected. "Mamm was going to give it to charity because it was so worn out and ugly. I decided to rescue it and bring it into my room."

His *daed* patted the armrest. "It may be big and weathered-looking, but it's still in good shape. Why, it's far more comfortable than my new chair."

"Oh, I bet you'll get used to the new one soon, Daed," Jacob replied dryly. "After all, it's only been two years."

"Time does heal all wounds." He paused, his eyes on the pillow. "So, you got yourself a cell phone, do ya?"

There was no point in lying. "I do."

"You know I can't bless that."

"I don't expect you to approve, Daed. But I haven't joined the church yet."

"I wish you would. So . . . who do you call on this phone of yours?"

"If I told you, then I'd be giving away other names. I can't do that."

His brows rose. "Other Amish kids have cell phones?"

"I'm hardly a kid, Daed. I'm twenty years old. And yes, other people my age have them." He waved a hand. "You know, even some members of our church have them."

"They use those phones strictly for work. The bishop ain't too happy about it, neither."

Jacob didn't want to talk about the rules of their *Ordnung*. The only thing to come out of that would be an argument about what was right and what was wrong.

The conversation would be a little pointless, anyway. He'd already done so much that was wrong. Scooting to the side of the bed, he sat on the edge and faced his father. "I'll work at the store whenever you need me to. You know I will."

"I was hoping you'd tell me that. You are a *gut* boy, Jacob." He squirmed. "*Jah*, a fine man. But maybe I won't need you as much as I fear I will. After all, Deborah seems to be getting the hang of things. She likes working, too."

Thinking about how natural it was starting to feel to be working by her side, Jacob nodded. "She does like being at the store."

"The detective sure talked to her for a while. Do you think

Luke suspects she had something to do with Perry's death?" His father sounded perturbed.

"I certainly hope not." The strain in his *daed*'s voice didn't come near to matching how he felt. He would never forgive himself if Deborah was blamed unjustly for Perry's death.

"He's questioned a lot of people, Daed. But that doesn't mean that everyone he's been talking to is guilty." Sounding more confident than he felt, he added, "I bet he's merely trying to get more information."

His father looked startled, though he tried to cover it up quickly. "I bet you're right. I, ah, feel certain that Deborah had nothing to do with her brother's death."

"I know she wasn't involved."

"She's turned into a pretty woman, don'tcha think? She was always such a tiny thing, like a doll."

Jacob liked how delicate Deborah had felt in his arms by the creek. He'd wanted to hold her close and protect her from everything bad in the world. He nodded in agreement.

"I always thought her eyes were pretty."

Deborah had hazel eyes, the exact shade as Perry's. Until lately, her eyes had only served to remind him of how much he'd disliked the guy.

But lately he'd been thinking about her eyes, about all her features. And realizing that she was more than simply pretty. She was beautiful.

However, these new feelings were not anything he was anxious to share with his father. "We all grew up," he said. "I suppose we all look better than we did at fourteen."

His dad's smile widened. "Indeed. And hopefully you're smarter, too."

As he thought of his recent actions, Jacob felt his smile

fade. He was struggling to think of something to say to explain his mood swing when his mother's voice floated up the stairs.

"Aaron? Jacob? Are you two in Jacob's room?"

"We are." His father hopped to his feet. "Gloria, what is it you need?"

Instead of hearing her answering yell, they heard the pounding of rushed footsteps on the wooden stairs.

Jacob stood up and opened his door just as his mother approached. "Mamm? Is everything okay?"

Her face was flushed, full of anxiety. "I'm not sure. Detective Reynolds and Sheriff Kramer are here."

His father gripped the edge of his bed. "Both of them?"

Her gaze still on Jacob, his mother nodded. "They came to talk to Jacob."

"Only Jacob?"

She nodded. "Shall I send them up?"

"There's no need, Gloria," Mose said from the doorway. "If you don't mind, we'll be speaking to Jacob in here. This is as good a place as any, I think."

"All right," his father said. "The room is crowded, but we can make room—"

"I'm sorry, Mr. Schrock," Detective Reynolds said. "But we'll be speaking to Jacob alone."

His father's expression fell. "Alone? Are you sure you—"

Jacob interrupted. "It's all right, Daed. I'll be fine."

"Does he need a lawyer, Mose?"

Mose turned to Jacob. "We're merely going to ask you questions. But you're welcome to get a lawyer if you want."

"It's your right," Detective Reynolds added.

The last thing in the world Jacob wanted was a lawyer. "I don't want a lawyer, Daed. I'm fine."

"Goodness, Jacob," his mother wrung her hands. "Maybe your father is right?"

Before his parents could prolong things further, Jacob hardened his voice. "Daed, take Mamm out of here. Please."

Grudgingly, his *daed* ushered his mother out of the room. When only the three of them were left, Mose closed the door, and leaned against it.

His heart racing, Jacob clasped his hands behind his back with a sense of doom.

"Jacob, it is like this, I'm afraid," Mose said. "Detective Reynolds and I believe you were the very last person to ever see Perry Borntrager alive." He paused, took a breath, then plunged in. "Furthermore, we believe you were with Perry on the Millers' farm on the evening of December thirty-first."

The words were so damning, Jacob felt himself sway. His whole life seemed to flash before his eyes. All his good decisions. And the bad ones, too. His struggles with his parents. The good times with his friends.

The walks to school with Deborah and Perry. The kisses he and Deborah had just shared.

The pain he felt whenever he thought of the moment his whole life had changed. When he and Perry had been together for the very last time.

He contemplated lying. Considered trying to cover his tracks. Thought about blaming what he did on somebody else.

But he had already evaded the truth for long enough.

And there was no way he was ever going to let Deborah, or anyone else, get blamed for what he'd done.

"Why did you *really* go to Lexington as soon as Abby Anderson found Perry's body, Jacob?" Luke said from his position by his desk.

The relief he felt about admitting the truth was almost overwhelming. "My father sent me. So I wouldn't have to be questioned."

"And why didn't he want you questioned?"

Jacob shrugged. "Probably because he knew I disliked Perry." He paused, debated about revealing too much, then decided to go ahead and tell all. "I think he suspected I killed Perry."

There, he'd said it. He half expected the ceiling to come tumbling down, now that he'd admitted his worse fears. But all he felt was relief from finally voicing his secrets, and a deep sense of finality.

It seemed now his future was out of his hands. It was now in God's hands, and these men's, too.

Mose walked to Luke's side. Now the three of them were facing each other, the sheriff and detective standing side by side, Jacob smack in front of them. He shifted uncomfortably, wanting to look them both in the eye, but afraid, too.

He'd known Sheriff Kramer all his life. How could he bear to see the disappointment in his eyes?

"Did you hate Perry, Jacob?" Mose asked.

Time passing had served to let him remember those days with stark honesty. "I thought I did."

The detective scowled. "Either you hated him or you didn't."

"It wasn't that easy," Jacob said. "I knew Perry my whole life. We used to all walk to school together, me, Perry, and Deborah. I loved him like a brother."

Mose narrowed his eyes. "But?"

"But then we drifted apart. Perry started wanting different things. He wanted to jump the fence, he wanted more money than I could dream of. He wanted to get high . . ."

Knowing he wasn't making a whole lot of sense, Jacob swallowed. "After a time, I gave up hoping he'd change."

When the two other men did nothing, just stared, Jacob took a deep breath and continued. "I've realized lately that I didn't hate Perry. I had hated the things he did, and the things he had been making me feel."

"Did you meet him at the Millers' farm on the evening of December thirty-first?" Mose asked.

Jacob swallowed. Felt the rest of his life fade. He was going to go to jail. To prison. He was sure of it.

But perhaps going to jail with a clear conscience was better than lying to everyone he loved? Surely God would be glad about that?

"I did. But I didn't go out there to kill him."

Stark sympathy filled Mose's expression. "Tell us what happened, Jacob."

He closed his eyes, prayed for strength, then began. "Perry and I argued when he and Deborah came by the store on the thirtieth. He was acting so different. Like he was lost or something." He frowned, remembering how his temper had flared. "To be honest, he asked if he could hang out with us. I told him he couldn't." Raising his chin, he looked at Mose. "It made me so mad, the way Perry had expected that we'd just take him back. After everything he'd done."

"How did you end things that night?" Luke asked.

"I told him to go away. I told him that it was too late," Jacob admitted with a wince. "I told him that a man couldn't take back his sins, he could only live them." Hearing his words now, Jacob felt his cheeks redden. He'd been so sanctimonious!

So mistaken, acting like he'd never done anything wrong.

"So how did you end up seeing him the next evening?"

"I was working late at the store. Actually, I was out on the front sidewalk sweeping when I saw Frannie Eicher running from the edge of the Millers' farm. She was crying, said she'd just gotten in a fight with Perry. I tried to talk to her, but she pushed right by me. She was really upset. Actually, she looked terrified."

Swallowing hard, he dared to look at Luke. He knew Luke and Frannie were practically engaged. Was Luke going to be upset with Jacob for not doing more for Frannie?

But instead of frowning, Luke's face was a careful mask. "So what did you do?"

"I went to go talk to him."

"But it weren't your business, Jacob," Mose said, his voice sounding frustrated. More like a father's than a sheriff's.

Sitting on the edge of the bed, Jacob nodded. "You're right. I shouldn't have gotten involved, but I kind of already was. We'd all been friends for so long, and all of us had gotten hurt by Perry, one way or another. We felt helpless. Well, I did, at least," he amended. "For weeks, I'd tried to stand up to him, but instead of getting involved, I looked the other way. When I saw Frannie crying, something inside me just snapped. It felt like the last straw."

"What did you do?"

Remembering how he'd pushed by his father, only saying he was going to find out what happened, he said, "I went to go find Perry. I went to finally tell Perry what I thought of him, and about everything that he'd been putting us through."

Luke leaned forward slightly. "Are you sure you didn't go to the Millers' farm to kill Perry?"

Jacob felt his mouth go slack.

"This is important, Jacob," Mose warned.

"I didn't! Oh my gosh, no." Jacob shook his head for emphasis. "It was nothing like that. I looked for him so I could tell him to stop bothering Frannie. And Lydia. All of us." Even though the truth hurt to tell, he continued. "I was such a jerk. I was sure someone had to tell him the truth, so I thought it should be me."

"And did you find him?" Luke prompted.

"I did. I found him standing by the well, staring off into the woods." Remembering Perry's posture, the way his expression was so sad, Jacob lowered his voice. "Perry looked as bad as I'd ever seen him. And . . . and it was obvious that he wasn't himself."

Mose's voice hardened. "Stop glossing over things, Jacob. What do you mean when you said Perry wasn't himself?"

It hurt to say the worst. It felt like the worst sort of betrayal. But Jacob forced himself to give the details Mose seemed to need. "Okay, it was obvious he was on drugs. His eyes were glazed, his attention was scattered, and he was really keyed up. Nervous. When he saw me he got angry."

"What did you do?"

Suddenly, it was very easy to recount what had happened. It still felt so real to him. As if it had only happened a few days ago, not months. "I did what I set out to do. I told Perry that he should leave the girls alone. I told him that we were all tired of the way he was ruining himself, and trying to ruin our lives along with him. I told him that he was being selfish again, only thinking about himself."

Mose nodded. "And how did Perry react to that?"

"About how you'd think," he said, unable to ignore the smile in his voice. It wasn't funny, of course, but the question hit him in a funny way. To anyone who had been around Perry his last few weeks, they would have known how he would have reacted to Jacob's accusations. "Perry freaked out and said I should mind my own business." Remembering the hurtful things they'd said to each other—things that could never be taken back—Jacob struggled for control. "We argued."

"And then?" Mose asked.

"After that, after I told him that he'd never be good enough for Lydia, that he wasn't fit to even be in the same room with Frannie . . . he hit me."

Luke exchanged a glance with Mose. "Where did he hit you?"

Remembering, Jacob pressed his fingers to his chin. "On my jaw." The force of Perry's fist had made him see stars, and had spurred his anger. Swallowing, he confessed the rest of it. "So I pushed him back. Hard."

"And then what happened?"

"And then we started fighting." Everything became a blur, the way his fist had felt against Perry's body, the pain that had shot through his shoulder when Perry had pulled him hard. The sweat that had run down his back and brow. "We ended up half wrestling on the ground . . . and then Perry fell backward and hit his head."

Luke held up a hand. "Wait a minute. Perry hit his head on one of the rocks?"

"Yeah." Remembering it as clearly as if it was happening right in front of him, Jacob said, "He fell back, and then . . . his head hit one of the rocks that lined the old well."

"And?"

"And he started bleeding." Jacob looked at Detective Reynolds curiously. He would have thought it was obvious.

"I mean, was he dead?" Mose asked impatiently. "Is that how Perry died, Jacob?"

Jacob jumped to his feet. "*Nee!* Perry was bleeding, and we were both banged up and bruised. But he wasn't dead."

"Was he passed out? Was he conscious?"

"He was awake." Remembering exactly how Perry was sitting, Jacob said, "Actually, Perry was more than that. He was yelling at me."

Luke looked incredulous. "I find that hard to believe."

"Well, that's how it was. Perry sat there against the rocks and yelled at me something fierce."

Mose lifted up his glasses. "What did he say, Jacob?"

"He called me a coward, called me worse than that. He called me names, said how I'd only become a weakling, still waiting for my father to tell me what to do."

"What about you? How badly were you hurt?"

Jacob held up a hand. "My hands were bruised and cut. My jaw was swollen. And my shirt was torn. I had a couple of cuts on my arms. But nothing too bad."

"Then?" Mose asked.

Jacob swallowed and confessed the last of it. "And then I ran back home."

The other men exchanged glances again. "Wait a minute. You left him on the ground?"

"Of course. I didn't know what else to do. I mean, it weren't like I could have made him leave or he would have let me help him walk home. Sheriff Kramer, you know how big Perry was—he outweighed me by at least thirty pounds."

"You didn't shove him in the well?"

"No! I don't know how he got in there."

"You sound so sure of yourself."

"That's because I am sure of myself. I don't know what happened to Perry after I left, but I can promise you this. The last time I saw Perry Borntrager, he was lying in the Millers' field bleeding and cursing at me."

Taking a deep breath, Jacob added, "I know what I did was

wrong. I know I should have gotten him help. I should have called for an ambulance or something. And I know you're probably going to arrest me. But I swear to you, I left him lying there on the ground. He was alive and yelling at me. I never put him in a well. If you believe anything I've said, please believe that."

Chapter 15

"Do you ever wish you could go back and relive a certain day of your life? You know, do things differently? I asked Perry about that once, asked him what day he'd do over. He said he had too many days to choose from. Me? I only know of one."

JACOB SCHROCK

Luke turned to Mose. His friend looked stunned, whether by the story or by the confession, he didn't know. As for himself, he was pretty shaken up. Rarely had he ever gotten as emotionally connected as he had with everyone involved with this investigation.

And while he felt a true sense of accomplishment for finally rooting out the person who'd ended Perry's life, he felt very sad for Jacob. The boy was obviously lying, and after he went to trial, it was a very good possibility that Jacob would spend the rest of his life behind bars.

It was a terrible place for any man of course. But for an Amish man, who was used to a peaceful life, used to the structures and rules set by his community? It was very near a death sentence.

But of course, they had no evidence that said Jacob had

actually killed him. All they had was some evidence that they fought. It was enough to question Jacob, but not enough to charge him with murder, or even manslaughter. They needed to look again at the evidence, even Perry's toxicology reports. He needed to pin down just how much meth Perry had been on.

And how much it took to kill a man.

Only by keeping his emotions firmly in check was he able to continue. "Jacob, we're going to take you into the sheriff's office for more questioning."

Jacob's expression crumbled. "You're not going to arrest me?"

"*Nee*," Mose said grimly. "I'm not arresting you, but you are a person of interest, and your story does bring up enough questions that I want to talk to you some more. Given that, I think it would be best to do this someplace other than your bedroom."

Once again Luke was ashamed of the way he'd come to Crittenden County, fully expecting to advise Mose and get out of there fast. He'd been hopelessly naïve.

It was painful to investigate someone he knew. Luke was desperate for some emotional distance. Every time he looked at Jacob, he remembered Frannie's recent warning about how they were a close-knit bunch, and how there was never anywhere to run if things got bad.

Though by sending him to Lexington, Jacob's father had certainly tried.

"Do I have to go? I mean, do I have a choice about whether or not I go with you?" Jacob asked.

The skin around Mose's mouth was tight. "You do. But I would advise you to come along with me."

Jacob's face turned white. "I didn't kill Perry, Sheriff Kramer. I swear I'm telling you the truth."

Mose only crossed the room and opened the door.

Luke sensed the pure dejection in the young man's attitude, and the heartbreak in Mose's heart. They'd both secretly hoped that Jacob was somehow going to lead them to a faceless stranger. Looking at Mose, he asked, "Do you want to read him his rights?"

"Not just yet. I'll do that when we get to the office," Mose said, vaguely referring to an interrogation room. Turning to Jacob, he motioned him with a hand. "Let's go."

"Wait a minute. Mose, can I call someone on my cell phone before I leave?"

Still looking at Jacob, Luke asked, "Who are you going to call?"

"Deborah."

"You sure you want to do that?" Mose asked.

"Yeah. I don't want her to find out about this from someone else." Flushing, he said, "May I talk to her? You can even dial the number if you want. I won't be long, and you can stand here and listen."

In Cincinnati, Luke would've laughed at such a request. But here, where he knew so many of the people involved, he could see Jacob's point of view. But he also figured there was no harm in it. And who knows? Maybe they'd even learn something new.

Picking up the cell phone, he scanned the numbers, found Deborah's listing, and handed it to Jacob. "Go ahead."

"Thanks." Slowly he punched the send button then placed the phone to his ear. After a ring or two, she answered.

"Deborah? This is Jacob." He paused. Almost smiled. "*Jah*, your phone does seem to work good. Ah, listen. I'm in . . . I'm in trouble. Detective Reynolds and Sheriff Kramer are with me. They're going to take me to the sheriff's office. They're questioning me about Perry's murder."

Luke exchanged a glance with Mose as they listened. That boy had a lot of nerve, he would give him that.

"No, no! I didn't kill your brother, Deborah. We fought and I knocked him down. . . . When I left him, he was lying on the ground, bleeding." He closed his eyes as Deborah said something into his ear. Then he sighed. "I . . . I just wanted you to hear that from me."

"*Nee*. I don't know who put him in the well. I have no idea. I promise! Listen, Deborah. I know you won't believe me, but I'm sorry. I know I should have told you all this weeks ago." Glancing at Luke, Jacob said, "I should have told a lot of people about the fight a long time ago. I . . . I just wanted you to know. No matter what happens, I wanted you to know that I'm sorry. I never meant to hurt Perry, and I really never meant to hurt you."

After another moment, Jacob clicked off the phone and handed it to Mose. "Thanks."

"I have to say, I wouldn't have expected you to be calling Deborah right at this moment."

"She's come to mean a lot to me. She's been having such a hard time, feeling so alone, I know that I should have told her what I did."

"And now you did."

"Yeah. Finally."

"Well, I can understand that." Gripping Jacob's arm, Mose opened the door. "Are you ready to face your parents?"

"Yeah."

The three of them exited Jacob's room, Luke leading the way, Jacob second, then Mose bringing up the rear. As they walked down the stairs, Mr. and Mrs. Schrock appeared in the foyer.

"What are you doing with Jacob?" Mr. Schrock asked.

Luke took it upon himself to tell the news so Mose wouldn't have to.

"We're taking him down to the station for questioning, Mr. Schrock."

Mr. Schrock's whole expression fell. His wife looked on the verge of fainting.

"Questioning for what?"

"It's about Perry's death of course, Aaron," Mose said. "All of us know that."

"*Nee!* But you can't take him. He didn't kill Perry!"

Alarms went off in Luke's head. He could understand a father's belief in his son, but he seemed so certain it sounded suspicious. Glancing Mose's way, Luke noticed a tightening of his shoulders. He was picking up on the same thing.

Obviously they were going to be talking about this soon. Tamping down his curiosity, Luke did his best to keep things low-key. "Now's not the time to discuss this, sir."

"But it must be if you're going to take my son away."

"We're just going to talk to him some more," Mose said.

"When will you let him come home?" Gloria asked.

"Not for a few hours at least. I'll send someone over to let you know what's going on."

Mr. Schrock glared. "I'm going to call a lawyer."

Mose stood stoically next to Jacob, who looked like he was trying to stay on his feet. "Aaron, if that's what you want to do, I think you should," Mose said.

His expression still looking stunned, Mr. Schrock rushed forward, reaching for his son. "Oh, Jacob. I'm so sorry." Jacob shied away from his touch.

Mose stepped forward and tried to regain control of the situation. "Aaron, there ain't nothing to be said now," he said as he put both of his palms on Jacob's father's shoulders.

"But I need to speak with him quickly. Tell him not to worry—"

Sensing the same warning bells, Luke turned to Mose.

And like the professional he was, Mose easily diffused the situation. "Now . . . that ain't going to happen," Mose said firmly. "We're going to visit with Jacob."

"But Jacob is my boy. You shouldn't be talking to him without me."

Luke was on the verge of reminding Aaron Schrock that Jacob was an adult when Jacob spoke. "Don't make this any worse than it is, Daed. Please don't."

"But, this is such a terrible thing. I hate that it's happening to ya."

"I know, and I'm sorry." His voice cracking, Jacob turned to his mother. "I'm mighty sorry, Mamm."

"Can I hug him, Mose?" she asked.

"Of course, Gloria. Don't forget, we're just bringing him in for questioning. Nothing else."

She nodded. "I understand."

Luke took hold of Jacob's elbow and took him to Mose's cruiser. The short drive to the sheriff's department was done in silence.

Once they were there, Luke and Mose walked Jacob into the interrogation room in the back. The receptionist watched them walk by and handed a few papers to Mose.

Through it all, Jacob had been stoic. He'd spoken only when spoken to, and seemed to search for the right words then.

In his gut, Luke felt that Jacob was telling the truth. The story Jacob told rang true. The young man wasn't acting like a killer, and he honestly seemed bewildered about how Perry's body had gotten into the well.

He looked relieved when Mose gave Jacob a soda, then left him in peace for a few moments.

As for himself, Luke felt queasy. Luke took a seat next to Mose's desk and tried to make sense of what had just happened. Something didn't feel right, and he wasn't sure why.

He'd been certain Jacob had met Perry that night. And Jacob had admitted as much. So what didn't fit?

He was still stewing on that when Mose came back and sat down behind his desk with a grunt.

Then Mose looked at him and frowned. "Something was fishy about Aaron. He said more than one thing that got my gander up."

"I felt the same way." It was a relief to admit his worries.

Sitting on the edge of his chair, Mose fussed with a couple of his metal paperclips, pulling them apart and twisting the metal. "So help me, Luke . . . I don't think the boy killed Perry."

Luke liked Jacob, but he forced himself to concentrate on the story he'd told them. "They fought. Perry fell and hit his head."

"*Jah*. That much is true. I can believe that."

"If you believe that . . . what doesn't sound right to you?"

"Jacob doing anything else." Scratching his head, Mose rose and started pacing. "I think that fight happened, Luke. It makes sense. Perry was volatile, and Jacob had more than his share of hurts. He's got a temper, too."

"Okay. Let's say Jacob did go out to the Millers' and that he fought with Perry. So what if he didn't kill him immediately? Perry probably bled out and died."

"Then we could charge Jacob for criminal negligence, or involuntary manslaughter." Mose pointed a finger Luke's direction. "But even if he was bleedin' out and dying on the ground, he wasn't crawling into wells, Luke."

"And if Jacob had pulled Perry into the well, he would have gotten Perry's blood all over him. Someone would have seen that."

"Which means he would have either had to go back home with blood on him, or he took off his shirt and hid it."

"I don't think he did that. Someone would have noticed Jacob walking without a shirt on. And we would have heard about it by now," Mose stated.

Luke threw his pencil on the table. "Okay. Let's say you're right. Let's say Jacob and Perry fought, Jacob hit Perry, and Perry fell and lay bleeding. Jacob gets scared, so he leaves. Who shows up and finishes the job?"

"That's the million-dollar question, ain't it?" Mose asked. "Who hated Perry enough to stuff him in a well?"

"Or maybe the question is this," Luke said slowly. "Who cared about Jacob enough to hide Perry? Or hates Jacob enough to let him take the blame."

Grimacing, Mose closed his eyes. "It's moments like this, Luke, when I wished I would have listened to my father and farmed."

"At times like this, I wish you would've, too," Luke said with a grin. "Then I wouldn't have gotten roped into this case."

Chapter 16

"Years ago when I would follow Jacob and Perry to school, I used to imagine that it was Jacob walking by my side, and that it was Perry who was following. Of course, Perry would have never followed either of us. That wasn't his way."

DEBORAH BORNTRAGER

Overcome, Deborah threw the cell phone down and stared at it like it was on fire. Jacob had been fighting with Perry the evening he died? They'd been arguing and fighting and Perry was left bleeding while Jacob ran away?

Her head pounded as all of the consequences ran together in her mind. Jacob was to blame for Perry's death. Maybe completely to blame. In addition, he'd been hiding the truth from her for months. No matter what he'd said, he hadn't trusted her. Or maybe, rather, it was that he hadn't wanted her to know his guilt.

And all this time, she'd been harboring her own secret about the man she'd loved for most of her life.

Feeling like each of her feet weighed a hundred pounds, she slowly walked over to her desk drawer, pulled out an old devotional, and carefully pulled out the note she'd hidden inside.

The one she'd snuck out of Perry's room.

The note that Jacob had written to Perry, promising him that he would one day make Perry sorry for all the pain he'd caused them.

She'd been sure it was just another example of Jacob letting his emotions get the best of him. Afraid that someone would get the wrong idea about his words, she'd kept the note hidden.

But now it seemed that there was a very good chance that she'd been the one who'd completely misunderstood Jacob. Feeling sick to her stomach, she knew she was going to have to show the note to Mose.

Even if it meant admitting her folly and caused Jacob to hate her for the rest of her life.

Even it if helped Mose and Detective Reynolds arrest Jacob. She had to do this for Perry.

But this was going to hurt. Giving in to her grief, she laid down on her bed and let the tears fall for what she was going to have to do.

All this time, she'd been sure no other man could ever measure up to Jacob. She'd refused to see his faults. Instead, she'd made excuses for his rudeness or his selfish ways. Instead of realizing that he was never going to be the man for her, she gave him second and third chances. How could she be so stupid?

She hiccupped after a few moments, reliving Jacob's phone call. And then she realized what he hadn't said. He hadn't mentioned his reasons for looking for Perry. He hadn't even said whether the fight had been an accident or on purpose. All he'd said was that he and Perry had fought, but that he hadn't killed him.

With the policemen standing right there, he'd taken the

time to call her. Almost as if she mattered to him as much as he mattered to her.

Did he still?

Maybe, just maybe, she hadn't been as foolish as she'd thought? Deborah realized that God was testing her right there and then. She could either have faith in Him, or she could use this moment as yet another reason to close herself off from the world and wallow in grief.

Thinking about that, she reflected about how many days and nights she'd done just that. She had chosen to stay by herself, letting her doubts comfort her instead of other people.

Looking at her closed door, she knew this was an important moment for her. She knew Mose would stop by the house soon and speak to her parents. And they would once again be thrown into a combination of righteous grief . . . and anger at the rest of the world.

But one thing she was certain they would not do was reach out to her. It would be up to her to hold the family together, to comfort them.

She would. She intended to do her duty.

But over the last week, Deborah had realized that she was so much more than the dutiful daughter. She was a grown woman with needs and fears all of her own. It was time she reached out to people who could help her.

Looking at the cell phone still clasped in her hand like an invitation, she made a sudden decision. She scanned down the five phone numbers and clicked on the name.

Frannie answered immediately. "Deborah, you are using the phone! I am mighty glad of that."

"I didn't call simply to talk. I need help."

"What is wrong? Are you hurt?"

"I'm not hurt, at least not on the outside. Frannie, to be honest, I'm afraid I'm pretty shaken up. Jacob just called and told me that he fought with Perry on New Year's Eve."

"But . . . that was the day I saw Perry."

"I know. I'm not sure what happened. Maybe he saw Perry after you did? He said they fought and he left Perry alone in the field, bleeding. Now Detective Reynolds and Sheriff Kramer have taken him to their office for questioning. I don't know what to do."

"Oh my word." Her voice was weak as she continued. "I don't even know what to think, Deborah. All I know is that I feel certain that Luke wouldn't do anything without believing it to be the right thing."

That was what she was afraid of. "I know. I can hardly wrap my mind around everything that he said. I feel like Jacob has been hiding a whole other life from me. Like he's taken everything that I believed about him and twisted it up into something I'm not even sure I recognize anymore."

Taking a breath, she blurted the awful truth. "Frannie, all this time while Mose and Luke have been here, questioning all of us, making us all doubt each other . . . all this time, he's been the one," she added, forcing herself to continue even though saying the words was breaking her heart.

"We don't know that for sure. I must say I'm surprised by the news. I had been sure it was a stranger. Like it could have been one of those men who the undercover agent had been following."

"I wish it had been a stranger."

"Maybe it still was. We don't know, right?"

She breathed deep. "You're right." Oh, she hoped Frannie was right! It was so much easier to blame and hate a mysterious stranger instead of the man she'd secretly loved for most of her life! "But I need to go to the sheriff's office and deliver something. Would . . . would you go with me?"

"Of course. But, Deborah, I can't change Luke's mind."

"I wouldn't want you to do that. The only way all of us can go forward is if we understand what really happened in the past. I just don't want to go to the sheriff's office alone."

"You won't have to. I know one thing for sure—you cannot be alone right now!"

"I was hoping you'd say that. I don't think I'm going to be able to stand another minute with only my thoughts for company."

"You don't need to do that. You've got your friends, Deborah, and we're not going to make you handle this on your own. Now, where are you?"

"I'm home. I'm sitting in my room." Sneaking a call on the cell phone Jacob had gotten her. Unable to help herself, she winced. Was it even right what she was doing?

"Do you want me to come to your house, and then we can walk to see Luke together?" Frannie asked. Deborah could tell by her tone that her mind was clicking away, debating various options of how to help her out.

"I don't want to stay here another moment." No, she wanted to run and run. To get as far away from her life as she could. Maybe if she did that she wouldn't hurt so badly?

"Then, how about you walk over here to the Yellow Bird Inn?"

"Are you sure you don't mind walking with me to see Luke? Oh, is Luke going to mind you getting involved?"

"First of all, I am already involved. And secondly, last I heard, I haven't given Luke any reason to think he could decide who I wanted at my bed-and-breakfast," Frannie replied with such a dose of salt and vinegar in her voice that

Deborah had to grin. "You need to come over right now, Deborah. Then, after we talk to Mose and Luke, I'll call Beth and Lydia. They can come over here and sit with us. All night if we need them to."

"You don't think they'd mind?"

"Not at all. News like this calls for girlfriends and chocolate."

"I'll be over soon," she said, tears of relief pricking her eyes. She was so glad she'd called Frannie. What would she have done if she'd just sat in her room, with only her dark thoughts for company?

Clicking off the phone, she stared at it. The right thing to do would be to turn it off and hide it, too.

But just as she was about to slip it between her mattress and box springs, she paused. And remembered the frantic tone in Jacob's voice. He'd sounded so scared, and so alone.

And out of everyone in the world, he'd called her. What if he tried again and she didn't answer?

As she thought about that, she berated herself for even thinking about such a thing. She shouldn't care about his feelings . . . should she?

Deborah found herself immobilized by fear and indecision. Weighing what was right and what wasn't.

"Deborah?" her father called out. "What are you doing in your room? I thought I heard you talking to someone."

"I was only praying out loud, Daed," she lied, immediately flushing. Oh, but that was the worst sort of lie. Not only was she lying to her father, but she was using the Lord in her deception. She had no doubt that He was shaking his head in disappointment.

But though she felt guilty, Deborah wasn't about to take back her words. She needed some time to herself and with people she could be completely honest with.

At the moment, those people were not her parents. Carefully, she slipped Jacob's note back into the devotional, then put a nightgown and a change of clothes into the tote bag, too.

Her father was standing outside her door, looking concerned and confused. "Daughter, what is going on?"

"I'm going to go to Frannie Eicher's for the rest of today and to spend the night as well."

His brows rose. "At Frannie's? Why?"

She knew she should tell him about Jacob's phone call. She knew she should stay home and be there for her parents. But though her sense of duty was strong, her need to think of her own sanity remained just as important.

Keeping her voice light, she said, "Frannie has invited several women over for the evening. It's a chance for us all to talk about her courtship with Luke. It's a 'girl thing,' Daed."

He frowned. "But Frannie is courting a man who is not of our faith. I hardly think you should be celebrating that."

Out of all the things they had going on, she found it hard to believe her *daed* was concerned about Frannie's love life. "Frannie and Luke have fallen in love. Frannie's never been happier, and Luke is willing to leave his city life and his position in the city police department for a life in Crittenden County. I think that's something to celebrate."

"But he is not Amish. And that man carries a weapon."

"I know. But I don't think you can always choose who you fall in love with, Daed."

Folding his arms across his chest, he looked at her with more than a little skepticism. "Is that right? Well, if you don't do the choosing, who does?"

"God, Daed. I think God helps us find the right mate in life. And for reasons we don't know, He's chosen Luke for

Frannie. I'm going to spend the night at Frannie's house, then go straight from there to work at the Schrocks' store."

His frown deepened. "I wish you had never taken that job. Whenever I think of the store, I'm reminded how working there ruined Perry's life."

Deborah gulped. Her father's words seemed to have double meanings. It now was evident that Jacob Schrock had ruined Perry's life. And perhaps all the hatred and violence had begun at the store.

Put that way, her father's words made a lot of sense.

So why wasn't she also thinking the same things? Why was she still holding a cell phone, all for the slight chance that Jacob would call her again?

And why wasn't she anxious to quit her job? She should want to put as much distance between herself and the Schrocks as possible!

"I'm going to leave now, Daed. I don't want to walk to Frannie's in the dark."

His face fell. Steeling herself, she turned and walked out the door.

Chapter 17

"When Mr. Schrock said he could never keep a secret from his wife, Perry had laughed. 'Everyone has secrets they don't want anyone to know,' he said. Maybe he was right?"

WALKER ANDERSON

"Uh-oh," Mose muttered just seconds before Frannie and Deborah Borntrager entered the office. "I do believe things just got more complicated."

Luke was afraid his old friend was right. He loved seeing Frannie, of course. But this was not the right time. "Frannie, honey, I can't chat now."

Her blue-gray eyes flashed in annoyance. "Oh, Luke. Of course I know that."

"*Of course?*" He raised his brows. "If you didn't come here to talk, why are you here?"

Some of the fire in her expression faded. "Deborah asked me to come with her."

Silently, Deborah nodded.

Mose sighed. "Deborah, I'm not going to let you talk to Jacob."

"It's not that," Deborah protested. "I didn't come to talk to Jacob. I . . . I have something to show you both."

Curious, Luke turned to Deborah. "What do you have?"

"A note."

She looked on the verge of tears. Luke grabbed a box of tissues and handed her one. "Why don't you sit down, Deborah?"

"Danke," she said, taking the chair next to Mose's desk.

When Frannie looked about to pull up another chair, Luke shook his head. "Frannie, it's a nice day out. Would you mind sitting on the bench outside?"

"Oh. All right, Luke." Turning to Deborah, she said, "Just tell them what you told me and it'll be all right. I promise. I'll be out here waiting."

Once the door was closed behind Frannie, Mose pulled up another chair, so they were all sitting in a semicircle around Mose's metal desk. Once he was settled, he looked at Deborah curiously. "What is this note you have to show us?"

Her hands shook, but she opened up her purse and pulled out a worn-looking devotional.

Luke shared a glance with Mose. Deborah had decided they needed to pray more? "It's a prayer book," he muttered. When she flinched, he knew he should apologize, but his patience was near its end.

"Luke, I've got this," Mose murmured as he picked up the book. "This looks mighty nice, Deborah. I am sure I'll put it to good use this evening."

She blinked owlishly. Then frowned as she pulled the book back out of his hands. "Sheriff Kramer, I didn't walk over here to bring you a devotional. I slipped a note inside it." Taking a deep breath, she opened the book to the center and pulled out a neatly folded white sheet of paper. "A few weeks ago, I found this inside Perry's bedside table. I thought you might use it against Jacob, so I took it and hid it."

Luke opened the note and read carefully. "'Perry, you're going to regret the things you've been doing. I'll make sure of it,'" he said out loud. After he passed it to Mose, he rested his palms on his knees. "Any idea when Jacob sent this?"

Deborah shook her head. "No. When Perry went missing, I looked through his drawers, thinking maybe I'd find a clue about where he went."

"And this didn't look like a clue to you?" Mose asked.

"Maybe it did, maybe it didn't." With a grimace, she squeezed her hands tight. After it looked like she got her nerves back under control, she spoke again. "Detective, I was afraid for anyone else to see it. I thought Jacob was simply mad about how Perry had been acting at the store. I never thought he'd act on it. But after his call, I knew I wasn't going to be able to rest until I showed this to you."

Standing up, Luke handed her back the devotional. He felt beyond frustrated with her. Withholding this from them had been foolish and had cost him and Mose valuable time. But, he knew venting his annoyance wasn't going to make anything better. "Thanks for coming by, Deborah."

She bit her lip. "Does . . . does this make things worse for Jacob?"

"Let me walk you out," Mose said, completely ignoring her question. "Are you and Frannie going to be together for a few hours?"

"Yes. We are going to her home. Some other girls are going to meet us."

"Then if we need you, we'll know where to find you. Thank you, Deborah," he said, then shut the door tight behind her.

When they were alone again, Mose folded his arms over

his chest and shook his head. "I'm telling you what . . . if we don't discover what really happened soon, I'm going to strangle the whole lot of 'em."

"I know the feeling. So far, not a person we have talked to has told us the complete truth from the very beginning." Luke pointed to the door. "You ready to go see how Jacob reacts to seeing this note?"

Mose waved a hand. "I'm more than ready."

Walker insisted on taking Lydia to Frannie's bed-and-breakfast. "I like picking you up and taking you where you need to go," he said. "Plus, with all the work I've been doing, we've hardly been spending any time together."

Lydia felt the same way. "I've missed you." Patting the cushion on the couch next to her, she added, "I am glad you had time to come over a little early. I haven't seen you in two days."

Stifling a yawn, he asked, "Are you sure you don't want to beg off? We could spend the evening together."

"I wish I could, but Frannie said getting together was important. She said Deborah is feeling pretty blue tonight."

His eyebrows rose, but to her relief, he didn't object. "I'm just teasing you. My mom likes to go to her book club meetings once a month. But my dad and I get the feeling that she doesn't talk about books as much as laugh with her girlfriends. Maybe one day when we're married, you'll be wanting to do the same thing."

Lydia felt her pulse jump a little bit. No matter how hard she tried to take all the changes in her life in stride, she still got as giddy as a schoolgirl whenever she thought about being Walker's wife.

"Perhaps," she teased. "Would it bother you if we did have a girls' night every once in a while?"

"Probably not." With a sneaky grin, he added, "But of course, then you would have to let me have a hunting weekend with the boys every once in a while."

"I suppose I could let you do that." When she noticed he yawned again, then winced as he tried to stretch, she took a better look at him. He wasn't just sleepy—he was exhausted!

When he winced again when he shifted, she said, "Walker, you look like you're hurt."

"I'm not hurt. I'm just more sore than I've ever been in my whole life." He lifted an arm with another wince and rolled his neck. "Plowing behind a horse is a whole lot harder than I thought it would be. Five-hour pitching practices have nothing on that plow."

"Are you doing too much?" She hated to worry over him, but the plain and simple truth of it was that Walker was not used to all of the hard labor that came with the life of an Amish man working in the fields. "Do you need some more help?"

"Believe it or not, my father came out and helped me this morning."

She'd only seen his dad dressed in suits. Not even trying to hide her surprise, she gaped. "Your father?"

"Yeah." He stretched his arm again. "Funny thing happened when I told my dad that I was going to live out at Grandpa James's farm and try to help. It turns out that he knows a whole lot more about being Amish than I do."

"I suppose he would. He was raised Plain."

"Even twenty years of driving a car hasn't prevented him from guiding a plow a whole lot better than me." With a sheepish smile, he added, "Between my father showing me the right way to muck stalls and watching the other Amish men hold their tongues while I continually make mistakes, it's been a lesson in humility."

"Poor Walker." When he rolled his neck with another grimace, she twisted to sit behind him. "Relax and let me rub your shoulders for a bit."

He obediently shifted so his back was turned her way. "You don't mind?"

"Of course not, Walker," she said, rubbing his shoulders— and frowning when she felt all the knots in his muscles. "My goodness, no wonder you're sore! I think all of your muscles have frozen in knots."

"It feels like it. I felt a little better after a hot shower, but now it feels like I'll never be pain-free again."

Massaging his neck, Lydia smiled as his shoulders and neck relaxed, little by little. When he sighed in relief, she chuckled softly. She could get used to this, she realized. There was something about helping him at the end of the day that made her feel worthy.

She could imagine the two of them spending many an evening together. Of course, they wouldn't be sitting like this, they'd be on their front porch. Or sitting together, enjoying the peace and quiet of their home after they each had spent most of their days outside.

"Can you rub just a little to the left, Lydia? I've got the worst crick right . . . there."

Feeling another knot, she massaged harder. "I hope your mother is rubbing your father's shoulders right now."

"He probably doesn't even need it."

"He needs it! His head might remember how to plow, but I assure you, his muscles haven't missed the activity. Coaxing a horse to pull a plow through acres of land isn't easy to do."

She took a breath, remembering all the evenings her father came home, looking muddier than the horses. "Then there's the mud. The rain makes the plow move easier, but it brings on its own set of problems, too. Why, one evening, my *mamm* made my *daed* wash up outside, he was so dirty!"

Her hands slowed as she realized Walker hadn't said a word. "Walker?" she murmured.

When he still said nothing, she leaned around to see his face.

Then, of course, she had to smile. Walker Anderson had fallen asleep.

Getting to her feet, she went to go get him a quilt.

Her mother stopped her at the door. Frowning at Walker's body slumped in the chair, she asked, "Is Walker okay?"

"He fell asleep," Lydia said. "After plowing all day, I think he's more tired than the horse!"

Her mother chuckled. "I'm sure he is. Plowing is mighty hard work. I bet he is sore as well."

"Mamm, I was on my way to get a quilt to cover him up. I thought I'd let him sleep for a while. Is that okay with you?"

"That is fine. A nap will do him good."

"It will, though I have plans to go to Frannie's tonight. Walker was going to take me there."

"How about I make him a bowl of stew? You can bring him a bowl in about fifteen minutes. After that, he should be fortified enough to drive you to Frannie's."

Lydia was touched. Her mother was really bending over backward to develop a relationship with Walker. "Thanks for being so nice to him, Mamm."

"He loves you, Lydia. Every time he's near you, he looks like the sun rises and sets on you. I can't fault that. All a mother really wants is for her daughter to love a man who loves her back."

Lydia knew Walker loved her. It gave her such a sense of security, knowing that she'd found the right person to spend the rest of her life with. "He's still seriously thinking about adopting our ways, Mamm," she whispered. She wanted that so badly, she was afraid to even mention it out loud.

Practically reading Lydia's mind, her mother said, "If Walker chooses to became Plain, that would be an answer to a prayer, Lydia."

When her mother went to the kitchen, Lydia ran to get a quilt and softly laid it over Walker's chest and lap. Then she sat beside him and watched him sleep.

And gave thanks to the Lord for all of her blessings.

"Frannie, only you would make a cake at a time like this," Beth Byler said when the four of them watched Frannie bring in a chocolate cake, plates, napkins, and forks all on a tray.

"As I told you, a time like this deserves chocolate. That can't be denied."

"You're right," Beth said with a comforting smile toward Deborah. "Do you think you'll be able to eat?"

"I don't know. Frannie, the cake looks good, but right now I feel like everything is going to send me rushing to the bathroom. My stomach seems to be tied up in knots."

"Well, who can blame ya?" Sitting at the far side of the coffee table, Frannie said, "Are you glad you went and talked to the detectives?"

She thought about it. "I'm glad, I suppose. Even if it hurts Jacob's feelings, I didn't want to harbor any more secrets."

"I think that's a *gut* plan."

"I hope so. I am glad he called me, too."

"That says a lot. He didn't have to call just to tell you his side of the story."

"It was good to hear the truth from him. Well, at least most of the truth." After weighing the options, she went ahead and told the other girls the whole story. "He said they fought, and that he hit Perry and Perry hurt his head."

"And that is how Perry died?"

"I don't know." Shrugging, she added, "Jacob promised that Perry was alive when he left him. And he swore up and down that he didn't put him in the well. Perry sure wouldn't have gotten in the well himself."

"Does it make a difference if he did that or not?"

"I'm sure it will to the police."

"I mean to you. Does it make a difference to you? Will you ever be able to forgive Jacob?"

Forgive? "I don't know," she replied, weighing each word with care. "There's a part of me that doesn't want to forgive him for anything. I want to put all my energy into hating him, and blaming him for Perry's death."

Beth crossed her arms over her chest. "No one would blame you if forgiveness came hard, Deborah."

"Though forgiving is who we are," Lydia reminded them quietly. "If he told you the truth and repented, you need to forgive him."

"I know. I've been thinking about that." Actually, she'd been weighing the pros and cons of forgiving him already.

But not because she was Amish, and that it was the right thing to do. But she was considering forgiving him because she'd fallen in love with him.

And she knew in her heart that he'd told her the truth . . . that Perry had gotten injured in an accident. And that someone else had put Perry into the well and left him to die.

But was that wrong? Was that disloyal to her brother and her parents? If Jacob had gotten help, would her brother still be alive?

"What is going to happen now?" Frannie asked.

"I don't know. After I talked with Mose and Luke, I walked out to you. Maybe Jacob's still in the sheriff's office."

Beth pointed to Frannie's cell phone. "Can you find out what's going on, Frannie? I bet since Luke loves you, he'd tell you everything."

She shook her head. "I'm afraid not. Luke wouldn't tell me if I asked, and I don't want to ask him. I don't want to put him in that position. I need to trust him to do his job . . . and he needs to be able to trust me to give him space."

"I think Jacob's parents will get a lawyer. And if they do, he might get out on bail," Lydia said.

When the other girls looked at her surprise, she shrugged. "Before Walker moved to his grandparents, we spent quite a few evenings watching *Law and Order* at his house. His parents love the show."

Deborah couldn't help it, she giggled. So did Beth.

Frannie's face split into a wide grin. "You've been watching crime shows with his parents?"

"Only once or twice," she said as a faint blush colored her cheeks. "That show was good. Plus it's helping tonight, yes? I'm the only one who has a clue about what to expect."

Feeling much better now that everything was out in the open, Deborah said, "Would you please slice me a thick piece of cake, Frannie? I think chocolate cake is going to help me this evening."

"Of course, Deborah." With a wink, she said, "Then I know just what we should talk about."

"And what is that?"

"What else Lydia and Walker have been doing when they've been together."

"Definitely not!" Lydia exclaimed, her cheeks bright red.

"I'm talking about plowing his grandfather's field. You two have been leading a very busy life, I think."

In answer, Lydia held out her hand. "Give me a piece of cake, too, Beth. If we're going to talk about so much, I'm going to need to be fortified."

Picking up the knife again, Frannie grinned. "I knew this cake was an excellent idea."

Chapter 18

"I used to blame Perry whenever I got in trouble. It wasn't fair, of course. He only led me, I followed. Now that he's gone, I've got no one to blame but myself."

JACOB SCHROCK

Sitting alone in the interrogation room, Jacob realized that he'd never sincerely given thanks for his parents or for their store. He should've, he knew that. Schrock's Variety Store was a part of who he was.

It was his legacy.

His earliest memory was sitting on a counter, his father holding him steady while a pair of customers chatted with them both.

When he was older, he used to work beside his mother, folding bags for people who checked out, or straightening a shelf. Often, he'd been given a job like holding a kitten or sitting with some customers who had come inside for ice cream in the summer.

Through the years, there had always been something eventful going on. When he was younger, Jacob, like his father, had fed off the chaos. Only when he was older did he realize that there were better, smoother ways to run the market. Little by little, he implemented his ideas. Now his father relied on him to manage the deliveries and inventory. Actually, he organized most everything, except for his father's penchant for selling animals.

Through it all, Jacob had always known that his father was proud of him. For hours, his father had shown him off at the store, or had taken him on buying trips. Always his father had treated him with patience. Patience with his endless questions and mistakes.

And he'd definitely made his share of mistakes lately. He'd resented his job and had begun to take his parents' unwavering love for granted. He'd let his anger with Perry stew instead of forgiving him and letting it go.

And of course, he'd fought with Perry, injured him . . . and then lied to everyone.

Just an hour ago, he'd been shocked when Mose set his old letter to Perry on the table. He'd forgotten he'd even written it, and had been mortified when he read the words again.

They sounded angry and malicious. Petty. No wonder Mose had looked at him like he was a horrible person.

After talking with Mose, Jacob realized he certainly wasn't the only person to be keeping secrets. He was very surprised to discover that Deborah had seen that note and had only brought it to Luke and Mose reluctantly.

But nothing had floored him as much as the news that she'd had the note for weeks. And that she'd actually hidden it from the police in order to protect him.

Even when he'd been so rude to her, she had wanted to believe the best in him. It was becoming more and more obvious that he had a lot to learn about friendship and loyalty.

That was why he wasn't upset with her for ultimately

bringing the note to the authorities. She wanted to believe in Jacob, but she had loved her brother. It made sense that, now that he'd revealed that he'd been keeping secrets from her, she would share her secrets, too.

Thank goodness Mose didn't act like the letter was proof that Jacob had killed Perry. All Mose had said was that it proved that Jacob had been angry.

And that was true.

But the thing he was sorriest about was his lack of prayer. He'd never sat with God and asked him for guidance. Instead of praying about his concerns, he'd locked them up inside himself, trying in vain to ignore the hurts.

He was paying for that now. Sitting in the back room of the sheriff's office, he'd never felt more alone. But he was beginning to realize, surely if anyone could have the patience for him, it would be God?

Leaning forward, he braced his elbows on the small table. He closed his eyes and forced himself to relax, and then, little by little, he had a talk with the Lord.

Only then could he sleep.

Three hours after they'd taken Jacob Schrock into custody, his parents showed up with a lawyer. After talking briefly with the man, Mose released Jacob into his lawyer's care.

They couldn't hold him anyway; there were still too many inconsistencies in Jacob's story for them to actually charge him with anything. Though he felt he had gotten Jacob's whole story, Luke felt that they still were missing something important. Luke knew there was one more part to the story of Perry's death. He just wasn't positive about who he suspected had shown up after Jacob had left.

As he and Mose stood at the front window and watched the lawyer drive the Schrocks away, Luke stuffed his hands into his back pockets.

"What do you think?" he asked Mose.

"I think I feel like a fool," Mose said baldly.

"Why's that?"

"I feel like we've interviewed everyone who could have anything to do with Perry's death, that we've scoured the area, and that I've written over a hundred pages of detailed notes. But even after doing all that?"—Mose folded his arms over his chest—"This case still ain't closed."

Luke forced himself to bring up his fear. "I don't think Jacob stuffed Perry's body down that well, Mose. I don't think he was the last person to see Perry that evening."

"I agree with you." His scowl darkened. "And that, of course, makes me even more frustrated with myself."

"What does the D.A. say?"

"About what you'd imagine. We don't have any actual evidence to prove that Jacob killed Perry. Only a whole lot of stories, which won't make a difference on the stand. He also pointed out the levels of methamphetamine the labs discovered in his body. It could've been a lethal amount. Luke, Perry could have overdosed." Mose picked up a paper clip. "I feel like an idiot, Luke. I'm a smart man, and a good sheriff. But for the life of me, I can't seem to get either the evidence or the confession I need to close this case."

Mose's venting wasn't a surprise; Luke felt the same way. But his frustration didn't make their task any easier. "Any ideas about who we should talk to next?"

"I was thinking I'd go talk to the Millers, but they've said time and again that they saw nothing."

"I think we've missed something, Mose, and I think it has

something to do with Perry's relationship with his friends. I'm going to go through my notes again."

"I'll do it, too. And I'm going to reread our notes about Jacob. I must have missed something. Pull up a chair, Luke. I'll go brew some coffee. I have a feeling we're going to be up late."

For a brief moment, Luke let himself think of Frannie. He knew she was most likely wondering how he was doing . . . and how her friend Jacob was doing.

Because Luke didn't want to tell her anything about the case, he pushed back the urge to give her a call. No, it would be better to keep quiet and stay with Mose.

They were so close, he could feel it. The wrong thing to do now would be to give up. He needed to hold steady and power through. Only then would he and Mose succeed in putting this case to rest. He just needed to remember that.

Something wasn't right, Jacob knew that with every fiber in his being. Every time he looked at his father, the man looked wary. Almost guilty.

For the life of him, Jacob couldn't understand it. What did his dad feel guilty about? And why wasn't he yelling at him nonstop, or at the very least offering bits of wisdom and advice?

Instead, he only kept reassuring Jacob that he believed in him. That he knew Jacob hadn't meant to hurt Perry. That he certainly knew Jacob hadn't thrown Perry into an abandoned well.

That they would get through this difficult time together.

After his lawyer, Mr. Meyer, had arrived at the police station, the four of them drove back to their house. His father had gone so far as to close the store early so that they could discuss Jacob's case at length together.

Outside, the skies darkened. Jacob's *mamm* turned on a lantern and made a fresh pot of coffee on the stove, then fussed in the kitchen, popping out to join them for a few minutes at a time before returning to her haven.

Jacob and his *daed* joined the lawyer in the living room. If Mr. Meyer was uncomfortable, sitting in his dark suit in the warm house, he didn't act like it. Instead, the middle-aged man answered every question of his father's easily, even when the questions were repeated several times. Exhausted and nervous, Jacob elected to stay silent most of the time. He knew that he'd told the detectives everything he knew. He had no secrets left.

But his father, on the other hand, seemed far more uneasy. It almost seemed like there was something on the tip of his father's tongue, some secret he was trying hard not to divulge.

And Jacob couldn't help but fixate on it.

As the lawyer continued to explain terms like involuntary manslaughter and criminal negligence, Jacob leaned back in his chair and wondered what his father was hiding.

A look to his right revealed his mother hovering near the entrance to the kitchen. She, too, seemed perturbed and nervous.

Of course she had to be worried about what was going to happen to him . . . but was that all that was bothering her? Jacob just wasn't sure.

"Did you have any questions, Jacob?"

With a start, Jacob turned to the lawyer. "I'm sorry, no."

His father cleared his throat. "Jacob, was your mind wandering? You should be paying attention! This is important, son. I'm sure you have much to ask Mr. Meyer."

"I realize it's important, father. However, at the moment I do not have any questions."

"Do you have access to a phone?" Mr. Meyer asked.

"We have a phone shanty down the road," his mother said.

"And I have a cell phone," Jacob admitted.

Mr. Meyer looked relieved about that. "Please give me your cell phone number, Jacob. I think it would be best if we could stay in contact over the next forty-eight hours. I wouldn't be surprised if you heard from Sheriff Kramer sooner than later."

Thankful he had memorized the number, Jacob wrote down his cell phone number, and took one of the lawyer's cards, too. He sat back down to watch his parents escort Mr. Meyer to the door.

Thinking back, Jacob recalled when he was a small child, thinking that the worst thing that could happen to him would be not to be able to play basketball with his friends on Saturdays.

Then the worst thing he could imagine was working too much, never having a day off.

Then, of course, the worst thing he could imagine had had to do with Perry. Oh, he'd been so worried that Perry was going to always disturb his perfect life!

Now Jacob realized he'd been hopelessly naïve. There was a very good chance that soon he would be forced to leave everything he'd known and loved . . . all for a lapse in judgment.

And because the real guilty party wasn't going to come forward.

Jacob didn't blame him. After all, the need for self-preservation was a powerful thing.

Chapter 19

"Perry and I used to argue about who did the most chores. Now that I seem to do them all, I wonder why it used to matter so much."

DEBORAH BORNTRAGER

When Deborah walked down the stairs to greet the other women in the inn's kitchen, Frannie bustled over. "Do you feel any better this morning?"

They'd talked late into the night . . . and for the first time in weeks, Deborah had gone to sleep the moment her head hit the pillow. Obviously, being around her friends had been good for her soul.

But now, in the light of early morning, Deborah realized that nothing had really changed. "I slept well, and I'm glad of that. But I have to admit that I'm still awfully worried about Jacob. What if he spent the night in jail?"

Frannie set down the bowl of pancake batter she'd been beating. "He didn't. Luke told me that when I called him this morning."

"I'm so relieved."

"You should go see him," Lydia piped up. "It's not a good idea to sit and stew."

After getting herself a cup of coffee, Deborah sat down, "Maybe I will go see him. I've got to go to work anyway. Do you think his parents will let me talk to him during my lunch?"

"Oh, you are so practical," Beth chided. "Work hardly matters at a time like this. It's people we care about who matter."

"I would agree, except that I feel like I should be at the store as much as I can—with Walker quitting, and Mr. and Mrs. Schrock now busy with Jacob's problems. Someone needs to be there."

"Deborah, you are too thoughtful," Lydia said as she joined them. "Do you want some help at the store? I could ask my parents to let me help you today. My brother can take care of things at the nursery."

"Thank you, but I don't think that's a good idea." Deborah would have loved to lean on her friends, but she knew it would be wrong to start asking her friends to help her work.

Lydia shrugged. "If you change your mind, let me know."

"And if you want our company again, you should call us," Frannie said as she carried out a plate of pancakes sprinkled with fresh blueberries to the kitchen table. "Getting together last night was fun. Now, all of you, grab some forks and eat the pancakes while they're hot."

Against her will, Deborah smiled. Last night had been fun, especially eating Frannie's chocolate cake. "I was stuffed last night, but I bet I'll be able to eat a couple of these."

"And you'll call if you need me?" Lydia asked.

"I promise, I will."

An hour later, she entered Schrock's Variety. The silence that greeted her was almost suffocating. "Hello?" she called out.

The back door opened, and Mrs. Schrock stepped out, looking exhausted. "Deborah, you did, indeed, come to work! I wasn't sure if you would."

"I still have a job, don't I?"

"Of course you do . . . but with everything that's been happening with Jacob, I wasn't sure if you would want to continue being around us."

"Of course I want to still work here." She ached to say so much more. Ached to tell Mrs. Schrock that she believed in Jacob, that she knew he wasn't capable of murdering Perry. But this wasn't the time or the place.

Instead, she focused on her job. "What would you like me to do today?"

Wearily, the lady looked at the two kittens curled up together in their cage. "I think the kittens need their cage cleaned. And then, of course, I'll need you to help with any customers that come in."

"I can do that."

"Oh, bless you, Deborah." All at once, she enfolded Deborah in her arms and squeezed her tight. "You are our angel. What would we do without you?" Before Deborah could respond, Mrs. Schrock hurriedly left the main room.

Staring at the kittens, Deborah thought about getting right to work on their cage, but a sharp hiss from one kept her away. Feeling somewhat at a loss, she got out a dust rag and wiped down the counter, walked around to the front of the store and straightened some of the brochures and maps of the area that had fallen down.

Then stared at her purse that she'd left sitting by the cash registrar. Her cell phone was in it. Did she dare call Jacob, just to see how he was?

It was probably a very bad idea.

Walking over, she spent a few minutes organizing a few bricks of cheddar cheese in the dairy case, keeping an ear ready for customers. But none came.

A few minutes later, Mrs. Schrock called out. "I'm going back to the house, Deborah."

"I'll be fine," she replied.

Still the store remained empty, and still she couldn't help but wonder how Jacob was doing.

Giving into temptation, she strode to the counter, plucked the phone from her purse, and quickly dialed.

Jacob answered on the first ring. "Deborah, what is wrong? Are you all right?"

"I am. I . . . I was worried about you."

"So you're still talking to me?"

"I have questions, but I do believe you, Jacob." Softening her tone, she said, "I know you didn't kill my brother. Are you all right? How awful was it, being at the sheriff's office?"

"Please don't worry. I am fine. My lawyer says there's nothing to do now but wait. I . . . I haven't been arrested. Yet."

She felt dizzy. Walking to the back of the store, she sat in one of the rockers for sale, no longer caring what people would think if they saw her talking on the phone. "Jacob, what are we going to do?"

"We?" He laughed dryly. "Deborah, there's no 'we.' I'm in big trouble. You are not."

"Tell me what happened, Jacob."

"I'd rather I told you in person. Could . . . could you bear to see me?"

This was a completely different Jacob than she'd ever

known. Always he'd been the assured one, she'd been the hesitant follower. Now, though, it seemed like it was her turn to be the strong half of their relationship.

"I would like to see you. I'd like to hear what happened face-to-face." She paused. "Do you want me to come over later?"

"I don't think that's a good idea. The lawyer asked me to lay low right now. And . . . and I think that's best." After a moment, he said, "How about I go to your house tonight? Or do you think your parents will be upset if I show up?"

She didn't even know if her parents had heard the news about Jacob yet. But if they had, she knew they wouldn't be in any condition to talk to him.

"I don't think that would work, either."

"I figured as much." He cleared his throat. "How about I come up to the store, then? That's a fairly neutral place."

"I think that sounds like the best choice."

"I'll leave in a few minutes. I'll see you then."

After she hung up, she hurried back to her purse and slipped the phone back inside. As she did so, she steadied herself against the counter.

The only way to deal with it was to keep busy. And that meant that she could no longer ignore the chore Mrs. Schrock asked her to do.

With a sigh, she eyed the cage of kittens in the corner. It was time to tackle the cats. "Kittens, try to be nice, now. Remember, I am only trying to help."

In reply, one of them stood up and bared its teeth.

Jacob hadn't known what to expect when he slipped into the back of the store and saw Deborah for the first time. Would she be in tears? Angry at him? Or, was she going to be ready to talk?

Whatever her mood, he was prepared to accept it.

Well, except for hearing her squeals. "Deb, what's wrong?"

"Get over here quick," Deborah called out. "These kittens are tearing up the store something awful."

For the first time in twenty-four hours, he laughed. "Deborah, you've got a scratch on your cheek and an empty cage. Where are the cats?"

"On the loose." With a moan, she halfheartedly pointed to the cage. "Your *mamm* asked if I could clean the cage. But they didn't take kindly to it, I'm afraid."

"Any idea where they could be?"

"I heard them meowing a few moments ago over by the baskets." With a wince, she added, "I fear they're systematically tearing up all the merchandise."

"I fear you're right. Come on, follow me and get ready to grab a kitten." When she followed him around the corner, Jacob glanced her way and smiled. "I can't say that I'm glad you lost the cats, but I have to admit that it's nice to be doing something so normal."

"If you're saying tracking naughty kittens is 'normal,' that pretty much sums up the way of things," she teased. "This store has had more animals for sale than seems possible."

"It's a habit of my father's, I fear. He's always had a soft spot for animals." He frowned. "For anything in need, actually."

"I've noticed that."

"Yes. I, uh, imagine you have." He glanced her way again, and felt his mouth go dry. There was so much between them, so many words said, and so many words left unsaid. Years' worth, really.

How did a couple ever overcome such differences?

For that matter, how could a woman ever forget the circumstances of her brother's death?

Looking uncomfortable all over again, she spied a kitten, swooped down, and picked it up. After a few irritated meows and one halfhearted swipe, it settled in against her.

Deborah beamed. "Success!"

As he'd suspected, the other kitten appeared when its littermate was picked up. It sat on the ground, meowing franticly, as if it were worried it was about to be left behind.

Jacob quickly picked up the other kitten, but had to hold it away from his chest as it squirmed and scratched. "Yours is far happier than mine, I fear."

Once both kittens were safely contained, he braced his hands on the counter and began. "Deborah, I should tell you that I never intended to harm your brother." He shook his head. "For a while there, it felt as if the Devil had gotten ahold of me. I was so angry at Perry, so angry that I could hardly think about anything else." Glancing at her sideways, he said, "Have you ever felt that way?"

"No. I've been upset with people, and upset by a person's actions, but never like you are describing."

"I hope you never feel anger like I did." He pursed his lips before continuing. "Because I'm an only child, and because we don't have extended family here, I've always felt it was the three of us against the world. When I saw how Perry was continually hurting my family, disregarding all my *daed* has tried to build with this store, I couldn't see beyond that."

"I know you were upset . . ."

"I knew the feelings were wrong. I knew my thoughts weren't Christian. I knew I needed to turn the other cheek. So I kept everything inside . . . I pretended I was okay."

"But you weren't?"

"No. I wasn't. I wasn't even close to being okay. Just before Christmas, I wrote him that note you found."

"He kept it. It must have meant something to him."

"I don't know if it did or not. All I know was that my anger had consumed me." He turned her way, afraid she could see how vulnerable he felt. "Everything came to a head on the night you and Perry came by the store on December thirtieth."

"After Christmas, Perry was really withdrawn," she said. "I think he finally realized that he had made some very bad acquaintances, with some really dangerous men. He never said anything to me, but I do know that he had a lot of regrets, and that he was afraid."

After a moment's pause, Deborah continued. "That day was the first day we'd talked in ages. It felt like I had just gotten my brother back from a very long trip."

"I didn't know any of that when you two showed up," he admitted. "All I felt was that Perry had come by my family's store again, with the intent of doing something illegal. Or, at the very least, to make trouble."

"So you yelled at him."

He winced. "I did. You know what happened next . . ."

Deborah nodded, feeling a chill run down her spine. It was all so clear in her mind, it could have happened yesterday. "Frannie and Beth invited me to join you. And you made sure Perry stayed away." She remembered feeling so torn. She'd ached to be included. After all, none of Perry's actions had been her doing.

Jacob nodded. "Yep. I made sure he stayed away. And then, the next day I saw Frannie crying. She told me that she and Perry had been arguing." He swallowed. "Her sleeve had ripped . . ."

"But that was the next day. Why did us coming by upset you so much?"

"Now, it seems hard for me to explain. But that day, I felt like he was never going to listen to any of us. He wasn't going to change. He was never going to leave us alone. And Frannie . . ." Jacob reached out to her, looked like he wanted to touch her, but dropped his hand. "Deb, I've never had any romantic feelings for Frannie . . . but I do think she's just about the nicest person I know. I hated that he'd made her upset."

Frannie did have that way about her. "Did she confide in you? Is that why you went to go see Perry?"

Raising his chin, Jacob looked beyond her. "She was crying, and admitted that she'd been with Perry at the Millers' old well." His eyes bleak, he said, "All this time, I felt like no one had really stood up to him. So I decided to go find Perry and do my best to convince him to stay away from all of us."

Deborah was trying to see Jacob's side of the story. But she couldn't refrain from speaking her mind. "Jacob, that wasn't your place. Not one of us had asked you to be our savior."

"I know. But that evening I didn't care." He blinked. "I'm sorry, Deborah. I wish I could tell you that I was a better person, but I'm not. I made mistakes. Terrible ones." He turned away then, walking to the other side of the counter.

Deborah glanced at the store's entrance, half hoping for a visitor, for a reprieve from hearing the awful details of what had transpired.

But no one appeared. They were alone. "So you went to the Millers' farm angry."

"*Jah*. And when I got there, I yelled at him." His cheeks flushed. "I said some terrible things, Deborah, things I'll always regret. He yelled at me, too. Then, next thing I knew, we were pushing each other. Fighting."

"Fighting?"

"Me and Perry had known each other all our lives, Deborah. Though neither your parents nor mine condoned violence, it doesn't mean we always listened. There were many times we wrestled when we were small. Anyway, one thing led to another, and I pushed Perry hard. He landed on the ground, his head hitting the stones of the well. He started bleeding."

Her heart was racing. Everything inside her was fighting against Jacob's words, against the story. She hated hearing about her brother's last moments alive and that they were filled with so much pain.

In that moment, she knew she could have gone her whole life without hearing about Perry's last moments on this earth.

But to shield herself from the pain wouldn't make anything better or easier. Not now, and not in the long run.

It was important that she hear the rest of the story. She knew she needed to hear it in order to heal. Even if hearing it hurt. "And then?"

"And then he started yelling, and I, God forgive me, got scared. It was like something had all the sudden snapped inside of me, and I had finally opened my eyes to the person I had become. I was horrified, Deborah."

"What did you do next?" she whispered.

"I ran. I left him there, bleeding." Reaching out, he gripped her hand hard. "Deborah, I'm telling you everything because you need to know. Admitting what I did, how I behaved, what I was thinking—to you, of all people? Telling you is far more difficult than telling the police. But Deborah, please believe this: I didn't think he'd been mortally wounded.

Never in a million years did I think he was hurt that badly. I thought after I left he'd get himself up and go home."

She wasn't going to let him off that easily. "But he didn't."

Jacob was still gripping her hand. His fingers were digging into her skin, keeping her next to him. His gaze was tortured and raw. There was no charm or covering up of the truth.

And that's when she knew that everything he'd told her was the truth.

"If you left him lying there . . . how did he end up in the well?"

"I'll tell you the same thing I told Sheriff Kramer. I don't know."

"But weren't you concerned? I mean, didn't you worry when you never saw him again? When me and my parents told everyone how he'd gone missing?"

"If he'd died after I left him there, wouldn't someone have found his body? It never occurred to me that he'd passed away. Deb, I thought he'd finally left town."

"Truly?"

"Absolutely. I was so full of myself, Deborah, that I had thought I'd scared him enough that he had listened to me and left. That he went to St. Louis or wherever and starting living with the English. I thought he'd jumped the fence and never looked back."

"I had thought he'd moved away, too," she admitted. She'd been so hurt, so upset that he could leave her without a goodbye . . .

"But Jacob, what do you think happened to Perry after you left?"

"I don't know." Finally his death grip on her hand eased. "I promise you, I have no idea what happened. It was as big of news to me as to anyone when I heard his body had been found."

Remembering the day Sheriff Kramer had delivered the news, Deborah shuddered. "My parents could hardly believe it. I was shocked, too." She'd also felt so incredibly guilty. Here she'd been so sure that Perry hadn't been a good enough brother to her . . . when she hadn't even questioned where he'd gone.

She'd never even attempted to look for him.

"The day I heard, I thought that maybe I actually had killed him. It wasn't until I heard that he'd been found in the well that I knew it couldn't have been our fight. But I was still upset. So upset that my parents sent me to Lexington for a horse auction."

"I went to Charm. My parents didn't want me around during the investigation. They thought it would be too hard for me to take, I guess."

"But we had to deal with it anyway, didn't we? The Lord wasn't going to let us run away."

"Yes, we did." Her heart warred with the heartbreaking facts of his story, and her feelings for him. Deborah didn't know what to do, or what to say.

But though she knew it might take a long time to understand what had led Jacob to resort to violence, she realized one truth—Jacob Schrock had not set out to kill Perry.

That was not who he was.

"Deborah, listen. I don't know if you'll ever be able to forgive me. Maybe even hoping you will is too much for me to ask. But please know that I am sorry. I am sorry I hurt your brother. I'm sorry I didn't tell everyone about his injury. I'm sorry I kept the fight a secret. And I'm sorry I was mean to you when I returned. It might not mean much, but I promise . . . I will regret my actions until the day I die."

Could she forgive him?

Then, she realized . . . how could she not?

Forgiveness was a cornerstone to their community. Acceptance of others, even if they weren't perfect, was something she'd been taught since she was a young girl. If she refused to forgive Jacob, it would be as if she was turning her back on everything that was good and special about her community.

If she refused, she'd be no better than her parents. And their refusal to forgive was damaging them both.

"I'll do my best to forgive you," she said. She felt almost as if the Lord was right by her side, coaxing her on, offering the words to say when she hardly knew what to think. "Though, I'm not sure if I'm even the person you should seek forgiveness from . . . I promise, I'll do my best."

Tears dampened his eyes. He blinked twice. Then, as if he was unable to help himself any longer, he reached for her and hugged her. His arms around her felt like everything she'd ever needed. A hug from her brother. Support from her friend. A touch, letting her know that she wasn't alone.

And, God help her . . . being in Jacob's arms felt right. She lifted her chin to look at him.

He was staring at her with love. With a tenderness that left no doubt of how he felt about her.

"Deb," he murmured. Lowering his mouth, he kissed her carefully, as if she was so fragile, she could break in his arms. She could feel her resistance melting. Felt desire spring forward again.

After all, this was the man she'd always loved.

Then the store's front door opened, breaking them apart.

"Deborah?" Her father stood at the open door, a look of shock and betrayal on his face. "How can you be standing here, hugging Jacob?" her father called out. "He killed your brother."

Once again, Deborah felt her insides twist up into knots. As everything seemed to spiral out of control.

Chapter 20

"We all make mistakes, to be sure. However, some mistakes cannot ever be fixed. They merely bring forth pain. Forever and ever. It's a terrible shame, that."

AARON SCHROCK

Jacob quickly stepped away from her side, but the damage had already been done. He'd forgotten where they were, had forgotten how vulnerable she was, and had kissed Deborah right in the middle of the store.

And her parents had seen it all. By the looks of her father's thunderous expression, Jacob knew he would never be forgiven. At that moment, Jacob wasn't sure if he even should be.

Beside him, Deborah looked shaken and a little embarrassed. But she looked far more composed than he felt. "Daed, what are you doing here?"

Before her father answered, her mother appeared behind him. "Sheriff Kramer came by the house last night, Deborah." With a wary glance in his direction, she added, "He told us about Jacob. Since you were with Frannie last night, we knew you wouldn't have heard. We came here to tell you the news."

Deborah blushed. Her parents had no idea that she had a cell phone.

"Jacob, my question is why you are out of jail," Mr. Borntrager said, his voice full of menace. "They should have never let you around decent people."

Jacob felt like his throat was so filled with a lump, he doubted he was going to be able to swallow much longer. But he didn't dare to defend himself. What could he say to Perry's parents that could possibly ease their pain?

"Daed, you mustn't say such things," Deborah said. "Jacob is innocent."

"No, daughter. He is far from that."

"If you talked to the sheriff, then you know what happened with Perry and Jacob was an accident. We mustn't blame him."

"I know no such thing." Turning to Jacob, Mr. Borntrager glared. "You killed my son, and have been lying about it all this time."

"That is not what happened!" Deborah said fiercely.

Jacob was stunned. Never would he have imagined that she would be defending him, and especially not to her parents. The only way he could imagine dealing with this situation was to let them have their say. Therefore, he bit his lip and stood still. Completely prepared to take whatever vitriolic words were flung his way.

"Deborah, come with us now," her mother said quietly. "You need to quit this job and never come back. We'll shop somewhere else."

But instead of letting her mother coax her outside, Deborah stood her ground. "That's not fair, Mamm."

"It's not fair that Jacob killed your brother," Mr. Borntrager said. "Worse, you are demeaning his loss by hugging his murderer. You've shamed us. Never have we been so ashamed of a child."

"Never before?" she whispered. "Never before have you been so ashamed?" Deborah's eyes filled with tears.

Jacob couldn't blame her. For them to be forgetting how much Perry had shamed them all? It was almost unforgiveable.

Unable to keep silent any longer, Jacob stepped forward. "Don't blame Deborah. The hug you saw, it wasn't her doing, it was mine. I hugged her."

"That's not true," Deborah whispered.

"I asked to her stay here and talk to me. And I kissed her without asking her permission," Jacob said quickly. Almost standing in front of her so that he could shield her from the terrible looks her father was shooting their way.

But if Jacob had imagined his words would make things easier, he was mistaken.

Looking even angrier, Mr. Borntrager folded his arms tightly across his chest and raised his voice. "Well, of course Deborah being here is your fault. All of it is your fault. You've ruined our family, you murdered my son. You've lied to us for months, concealing your part in my son's death. And now you're attacking my daughter."

Jacob knew that Mr. Borntrager wasn't speaking the truth. It was at best exaggerated and at worst flat-out lies. But what did it really matter? His future was doomed because no one but Deborah seemed to care that he had no intent to kill Perry and had no idea who had hidden his body.

So he kept quiet, choosing to let her parents yell at him. At least then they would ease up on their daughter.

But Deborah pushed her way past him, standing in front

of her parents, looking as brave as he'd ever seen anyone look. "Father, you must stop saying such things."

"I've held my tongue all this time. No longer."

"But you're wrong. Daed, my hugging Jacob wasn't like you are describing. We were merely—"

"I don't want to hear another word."

"But I think we should talk about this!" Her expression crushed, she turned to her mother. "Mamm, don't you think we need to face the truth now? Don't you think you need to hear Jacob's side of the story?"

"My Perry is gone, Deborah. That is all I need to know."

"Nee!"

Reaching out, her father grabbed Deborah's arm. "Daughter, I've never laid a hand on you, but if you don't stop, you will leave me with no choice. We will leave now. And you will not say another word to Jacob Schrock ever again. Furthermore, we will never step foot in this store again. It's done nothing but bring shame and pain into our lives."

Tears now fell down her face. "It wasn't the store that hurt us, Father," she said quietly.

Looking at the three of them, Jacob knew there was nothing he could do. Her father was right. He'd done terrible things, and they should feel nothing but scorn for him.

"You should leave, Deborah," he murmured. "It's okay."

She shook her head. "But this isn't okay. You aren't like that. We aren't like that . . ."

"Deborah!" her father thundered. "You will obey me now."

"Go, Deb. It's okay. Everything's going to be all right," he said.

Tears now running down her face, apology bright in her eyes, Deborah said, "I'm so sorry, Jacob."

"I understand. I promise, I understand." He did understand, and he almost welcomed the pain of her family's rejection. It was no more than he deserved.

Without another word, Mr. Borntrager ushered his wife and daughter out of the store. Jacob stood stoically as he watched them walk down the front steps and down the sidewalk. Deborah's father was grim-faced as he led the way, his steps proud, his gait fast. Mrs. Borntrager followed, her face tilted toward the ground, her back hunched as if she was in pain.

And slowly following was Deborah. Her chin was up, her posture was straight. As if to all the world she had nothing to be ashamed of, and nothing to answer for.

It was only when he saw her swipe her face with the side of her hand that he realized she was still crying.

When they were out of sight, he glanced around the store, amazed at the silence. His family's store was rarely silent. Usually his father's voice echoed down the aisles, or his mother's gentle coaxing floated from the back storage room.

More often than not, the store was bustling with customers. Tourists, too.

And of course, the animals made their own noise. They chattered or buzzed or barked or chirped. But this morning, there was nothing. Only him and two kittens who always seemed to prefer their own company to his.

Standing in front of their cage, he watched them snuggle. They were wrapped around each other, curved so tightly that at first glance they looked like one. In slumber, their calico fur blended together, and their soft purring was as gently infectious as almost anything he'd ever heard.

Showing him that some things were meant to be a pair. Just like he and Deborah.

"Well, cats, I guess it's just you and me. For a time, at

least." Until the trial and a jury convicted him of his crimes.

Once in prison, he'd be living in a cage of his own, always at the mercy of people who were free.

Thinking about his future that way, Jacob knew he fostered many regrets. He wished he'd been a better son. Often, a better friend.

But more than any of that, he wished he'd treated Deborah better. He wished he'd seen her as more than Perry's little sister when they were younger. He wished he'd seen her as more than just a girl of his acquaintance during that short period of singings and courtship.

But most of all, he wished he'd never taken out his anger on her. He'd been wrong to see her as only a reminder of his faults. And then, when he'd finally realized how wrong he'd been, he wished he'd taken the time to let her know how much she meant to him.

Now, all he could do was prepare for his new future. The best thing for them both was for him to keep his distance, and to make sure she kept it, too. It wouldn't do for her to risk her parents' wrath. Or to risk facing others' disapproval.

Yes, certainly the best thing for him to do would be to keep to himself.

Because he'd finally realized that it didn't really matter what the future had in store for him. No matter what happened, there wasn't a thing he could do about it.

After all, no matter how much a man might wish to change the past, there was one thing they could all count on: You could never go back. What was done was done.

Chapter 21

"Good character—like good soup—is usually homemade."

AARON SHCROCK

"Would you like another piece of peanut butter pie, Walker?" Lydia asked after the rest of her siblings had left the table. "I'd be happy to get it for you."

He patted his stomach. "Lydia, you know I can't eat another bite. And if I do, I'm going to get so huge you won't like me anymore."

"You know that would never happen."

"It might. You don't know how I've been eating at my grandparents."

Lydia's mother stopped by their chairs on the way to the kitchen. "Have you been eating lots of *gut* Amish food, Walker?"

She smiled broadly, letting Lydia know that she was mighty amused by Walker's quandary.

"My grandmother is a wonderful-*gut* cook," he said with a grin. "Too good, I'm afraid."

"Walker's been working hard at their farm, Mamm," Lydia said, feeling so proud of Walker. She'd always thought that he was a man to proud of. She loved the way he was so confident and easy-going. But watching him in the fields, seeing him with his grandparents, hearing praise from other people about how hard he worked, and how determined he was to learn things the "Amish way," she'd never been more proud.

Her mother squeezed his shoulder. "I must say I'm amazed at how well you've been doing, adjusting to our ways, Walker. Living Plain is not easy."

Looking at Lydia, he smiled slightly. "I'll admit to being as confused about what to do as anybody. I was even hoping that Lydia would give living English a try. I was enjoying going to college and I thought she would, too."

As Lydia expected, her mother became reflective. "But now?"

"But now I'm starting to feel like God has been guiding me toward my grandparents. I would never have wished for my grandfather to have heart trouble, but I can't ignore how glad I am that I've started working at my grandparents' farm."

"He is guiding us both, Walker," Lydia said with a gentle smile. "Together, we will find a way."

"I hope so."

She was vaguely aware of her mother leaving, giving them a few minutes of privacy.

"We just need to keep our faith and not try to rush things. I do think living Amish is in my future, but I think it's going to take some time. I want to be sure."

Lydia knew it would most likely take several years for Walker to feel comfortable enough to meet with the bishop and take his vows. Until then, she needed to be satisfied with their love, and knowing that they were headed toward future happiness.

Unlike other couples they knew.

She wasn't anxious to bring up bad news, but Lydia couldn't help finally mentioning what had been on both of their minds for the last twenty-four hours. "I'm so worried about Jacob. What if he goes to prison? What will happen to him? What will happen to him and Deborah?"

"I'm worried, too." He pursed his lips. "Jacob wouldn't talk to me. I went by his house last night. I'm really starting to fear for him, Lydia."

"I know." Darting a look at the open doorway, she lowered her voice. "I would have never guessed that he would have been capable of killing Perry."

"I don't think he did. All anyone knows for sure is that he and Perry were fighting."

"Walker, Mr. and Mrs. Borntrager have said he admitted it."

"Is that what Deborah told you? Is that what Jacob told you?"

"Of course not." Deborah was defending Jacob with all her heart. But Lydia just wasn't so sure that he was completely innocent. "My parents said that I mustn't go to Schrock's Variety until Jacob is back behind bars."

"I'm still going to go there."

"But Walker—"

"I don't think he did it, Lydia. I worked side by side with that guy for months. We've been friends longer than that. He needs our support."

"I've been friends with him since we were children," she murmured.

"The last thing he needs is to think that we've all abandoned him. Lydia, we need to be there for him." Turning to her, he said, "I think we should go see him tonight."

"But I'll get in trouble if I disobey . . ."

"Lydia, if you don't want to come because you don't want

to, I'll understand. But if you are refusing because you don't want to disobey your parents, I think you should rethink that. You're a grown woman, Lydia."

"I know, but—"

"Lydia, I intend to ask you to marry me soon. I want to know that you're mine, even if we have to wait months and months until I can enter the Amish faith. Are you prepared for that? Or will you be waiting to see what your parents say? It's time to grow up, don't you think?"

She was so surprised that he even thought she was acting like a child, she leaned forward and kissed him. It was quick, barely more than a light brush of lips.

But it finally shut him up. "Walker, I am a grown woman. Don't worry about that anymore."

"Um, all right." He looked a little dazed and confused.

Standing up, she picked up their dessert dishes. "And if you would like to take me out for a drive this evening, I think I would even say yes," she added, being very careful to not mention out loud that she was willing to follow his lead.

But Walker's smile told her everything she needed to know. "I'd love to take you out for a drive, Lydia. It's a beautiful night for a drive."

Because her back was to him, she smiled broadly. "I'll let my parents know. I'll be back in a minute, Walker." There. He might have some opinions about how to manage her . . . but she had opinions, too.

Lydia had a feeling they now had a chance for happiness. One day. When their lives weren't so torn over the loss of Perry. When they weren't all so exhausted from the investigation.

When they weren't all so very aware that even when things were bad . . . they could still get much worse.

Chapter 22

"My Perry, he used to bring over as many boys after school as he could. In no time at all, the house would be overrun with noisy boys—all as hungry as could be. But that was okay, I didn't mind one bit. I always knew those days wouldn't last."

BETH ANNE BORNTRAGER

Their home felt emptier than ever. As they walked into the front entryway, Deborah couldn't help but contrast the quiet feeling of despair that pervaded the air with the noisy brightness of earlier days.

The bench near the back door was empty and spotlessly clean. Back when she and Perry had been teenagers, it had been constantly covered with books and gloves, old boots and sheets of paper. The coatrack held two coats, the kitchen table was empty. Years ago, the coatrack had always been filled to overflowing. Friends would come over, then rush off without retrieving their cloaks or jackets or sweaters. It had been a constant source of irritation for their mother.

And the kitchen? Well, that hardly was worth thinking about. Her mother had often cooked soup or cookies or bread.

It had been impossible to enter the house without being hit with the aroma of something fresh and warm to eat.

Walking into the quiet kitchen, Deborah turned on the gas, lit the stove with a match, then filled a kettle and set it to heat up. "I'll make some tea," she said.

"I don't care for any."

Deborah turned and noticed that her mother was standing next to the post at the bottom of the stairs. "Where are you going, Mamm?"

"Back to bed."

Dismayed, she asked, "But don't you want to sit with me for a little bit?" Realizing her parents had probably not had lunch, she said, "I could make us something to eat."

"I'm not hungry, Deborah."

"But what about Daed? When did he eat last?"

Her mother's eyes turned vacant. "I don't know," she murmured before heading up the stairs.

Her departure hurt. Deborah was so tired of trying to make things work between the three of them . . . and now she had nothing else to think about. She had no job, no other place to be . . . and now no Jacob in her life.

The kettle whistled, spurring her to action. Jumping to her feet, Deborah made herself a cup of tea, then opened the refrigerator and pulled out some vegetables.

She was slicing some carrots and celery for soup when the back door opened. "Daed, I'm making soup."

"You don't need to do that."

She looked at him in surprise. "Daed, you need to eat." She needed to eat, too. And she needed to keep busy.

"Deborah, I'm afraid I don't have much of an appetite. This morning's events have been terribly difficult on me."

Slowly, she set her knife on the counter. "Daed, are you talking about seeing Jacob and me hugging?"

"And kissing. You shamed us, Deborah. I don't know when I'll ever be able to forgive you for throwing yourself at that boy."

"Jacob is as old as I am. He's not a boy. We're grown adults. And I wasn't throwing myself at him." Feeling desperate, she pulled out a chair. "Daed, sit down and I'll tell you about what happened. And I'll share with you his side of the story. Then I think you'll feel a lot better about Jacob."

Ignoring the chair, his eyes turned cooler. "There is no 'his side.' There is only the truth and his lies."

"I disagree. If you'd just sit and talk to me, I think you'll change your mind."

"I'm not going to change it. Our Perry is dead, and Jacob Schrock is responsible. That's all I need to know, and all you should be worrying about as well."

"You're not being fair."

"Being fair has nothing to do with any of this. You'll have a lot of time to think about your poor judgment now that you're staying home."

He turned away then, leaving Deborah to stare at the pile of neatly chopped celery and carrots in front of her.

This was what her life was going to be like. Yes, her parents were still grieving for Perry, but they'd developed new habits over the last few months. They were content to keep the house quiet and dark. In a perpetual state of mourning.

And it looked like they were eager for her to stay that way, too. She could make tea and soup, do the laundry and the sewing, keep to herself and be quiet . . . but it was never going to be enough. She was never going to take the place of Perry.

Never would they start concentrating on her needs or her feelings.

Leaving the cut vegetables on the counter, she turned off the stove, added more hot water to her tea, then carried her mug up to her room. After closing the door firmly behind her, she took her teacup to the window seat and she curled up on the worn, frayed cushion.

Outside spring had arrived. Leaves were sprouting on the trees, flowers had begun to bloom. And the path that led to the Schrocks wasn't quite as worn down as it usually was.

With a sense of doom that surely matched the rest of the house, she realized that the weeds around the path would surely grow tall and unruly again.

Because there was very little chance she'd be visiting Jacob ever again. Yes, she was once again being a dutiful daughter . . . but she wasn't very happy about it.

Once again, she didn't know how much longer she was going to be able to last.

"I can't understand why today's sales are down so much," Jacob's father said at the kitchen table that evening. Looking up from the receipts on the table, he turned to Jacob. "Why do you think it was such a bad day?"

"Probably because everyone thinks I killed Perry?" Jacob said dryly. Of course it wasn't a laughing matter, but he was so uneasy, he knew if he didn't try to joke, other, darker emotions were going to get the best of him.

"No one thinks that."

"Daed, the whole town now knows I was taken in for questioning."

"But not charged. That's an important distinction, for sure."

His father was right. But he was tired of talking about it, and at the moment, he could care less about the day's totals. "Daed, I don't understand why you're looking at the store's receipts, anyway."

"I look at them every evening."

"But what would it hurt if you skipped one night?"

"Jacob, I'm disappointed in you. I've grown this store all my life, so you'd have something to depend on when you built a family of your own."

"Daed, I appreciate all that you've done for me. You've been a mighty good father."

"There's no need for thanks. You are my son."

"What would you have done if I hadn't wanted to take over the store one day? What if I had wanted to do something else?"

"Such as?"

"Oh, I don't know. Maybe I would have wanted to be a farmer or something."

Taking off his glasses, he stared at Jacob in confusion. "Why would you have wanted to do that?"

"Because it's my life. Not yours."

He laughed dryly. "When you have a family, you'll understand. My dreams are yours. I've lived my whole life preparing for the day when you would follow in my footsteps."

"But if I hadn't wanted to follow?"

"I would have stepped in and set you back on the right path." Slipping on his glasses again, he added, "I have done it before. No way was I ever going to allow anything to get in the way of your bright future."

A twinge of alarm coursed down Jacob's spine. "Daed . . . what do you mean by that?"

"Nothing."

"No . . . it was something." Looking at his father carefully, Jacob said, "What did you do? How did you 'step in'? Were you speaking about Perry?"

Staring at the receipts, his father smoothed the top one over and over again. "Perry passed away, son. He is no one you will ever need to worry about. He won't harm you or the store." Raising his head, he looked Jacob in the eye. "Plus, we've got your Mr. Meyer. He's costing a pretty penny, but he's sure to be worth every cent, don'tcha think? He'll get you off."

Bitter foreboding hit Jacob hard. At last, everything made sense.

And no sense at all.

"Daed, did you have something to do with Perry's death?"

His father turned chalky white. "Jacob!"

Feeling like he was stepping into another person's dream, Jacob shook his head in shock, "Daed, when I was talking to Frannie on the front porch, and she told me about her argument with Perry on the Millers' farm, you overheard. Didn't you?"

"Don't ask me to answer you."

"You did, didn't you?" he pressed. "What did you do, Daed?" But with a sinking feeling, Jacob knew. He knew it as clearly as if he'd been watching his father's actions on the kitchen wall. "You went out to the Millers' farm and found Perry, didn't you?" Feeling sick to his stomach, he asked the next question. "Daed, did you follow me?"

Almost imperceptibly, he nodded. "That boy . . . that Perry, he was nothing but trouble. He was going to hurt you, he was going to hurt your reputation. So . . . I did follow you."

"Oh, Daed . . ."

He raised a hand. "Oh, I wasn't going to do anything, Jacob. I was just going to stand out of the way. Just in case you needed me, you know."

"You shouldn't have done that."

"You're my son, Jacob." Frowning fiercely, as if it had happened only yesterday and not months before . . . his father continued. "After you two fought, and you ran off, I stood and watched Perry bleed. At first, I only stayed because I was sure he was going to stand up and run after you, and I didn't want that. But then, he didn't get up. He just kept bleeding. And eventually, he closed his eyes."

Jacob wanted to cover his ears, or run from the room. Anything to delay what seemed to be the inevitable. "What did you do, Daed?" he said, his voice hoarse.

"I marched up to that boy and finally told him what I thought of him," his father said. "Even though his eyes were closed and he wasn't moving, I explained how he was shaming his family, and how he was an embarrassment to us all. I told him how he'd been hurting you."

"Oh, Daed."

"I did it, Jacob," his father said, his eyes gleaming with pride. "I finally stopped holding my tongue and turning the other cheek. I stopped quoting well-meaning sayings. Stopped trying to turn everything that had happened into a positive. I yelled at Perry, Jacob." His voice cracked. "I yelled at that boy while he sat there on the ground bleedin' something awful."

"And then?" Jacob could hardly bear to say it.

"And then? Nothing happened. Perry just sat there, motionless. He'd likely passed out. Or died. He could've very well been dead by then." His father's eyes filled with tears. He pursed his lips, frowning at the memory. "I couldn't leave him there, Jacob. If I left him there, someone was going to find him. Then, all of the sudden, I realized he was leaning up against the well! It was like the Lord had placed it there, just for me."

"Daed . . ."

"It wasn't hard to put him down there. All I had to do was lift up his shoulders some, twist his body . . . and then let it fall."

Jacob felt stunned and scared and completely at a loss. "Father, you killed Perry."

If his father heard him, he didn't let on. Instead, he continued with his account. "After I got him down, I noticed there was some blood on the rocks. You know, the rocks he'd been leaning on? So I tossed those down the well shaft, too. Then I went back home a different way and prayed for a good rain."

"Rain?" Jacob swallowed.

"To cover up the tracks, you know? I didn't want anyone to see the tracks and decide to start following them. Someone might have taken a peek down that well."

He swung his gaze toward Jacob. "But no one did. No one even guessed he was down there. I had done it! I had protected you."

"Me?"

"Well, yes. To be sure. I didn't want anything to happen to you, Jacob. And for months, nothing did. Why, everyone thought Perry had left."

With a sudden burst of memory, Jacob swallowed. "Daed, you're the one who told me that Perry had left town."

He shrugged. "It was an easy enough rumor to start. No one wanted the boy to be here in Crittenden County, anyway. Not even his parents. See, they didn't love Perry like parents should, Jacob. If they had, they would have tried harder with him. They would have given him more attention."

Gingerly, Jacob took a chair and wondered what to do. If he said nothing, he could very well be blamed for Perry's death. But if he told the truth, he could be sending his father to prison.

"Daed, I don't understand your thinking. I don't understand how you could have hid his body. You hurt so many people. You took another person's life."

His father turned so that they were face-to-face. Looking at him with a solemn expression, he said, "That is what you don't understand, Jacob." Quietly he added, "See . . . all I had to do was think of you. I would have done anything in the world to save you pain, son."

Jacob believed his father completely.

But unfortunately, it didn't make him feel any better. Only a whole lot worse.

Chapter 23

"In the middle of the night, when I can't sleep, I make up things. I try to imagine what would have happened if I had never discovered Perry Borntrager's body. There's a part of me that feels like my whole life would be different if I'd never been there that rainy day."

ABBY ANDERSON

"Daed, we have to tell Sheriff Kramer," Jacob said.

"You can't, son. If you tell him what I did, he could arrest me. And right now, the lawyer feels certain nothing will happen to you. They can't prove you did anything wrong."

"What you did . . ."

"I did it for you, Jacob. I did it because I love you."

"Daed, I love you, too. But we have to tell Sheriff Kramer the truth. You can't keep this hidden."

His father stood up. His legs were shaking and his eyes were wide. It was obvious to Jacob that his father had never imagined that he wouldn't be thanked for what he did. "Jacob, are you going against me?"

"If telling the truth is going against you, then yes I am."

"Jacob, I forbid you to tell them. I will never forgive you if you betray this family."

"But the police think I did it. I could go to prison."

"Perry took lots of drugs, too, Jacob. Everyone knows that. I imagine no one will ever figure out how he really died. And because of that? You won't be charged."

Jacob looked at the kitchen door. For a moment, he was tempted to run out of the room, and keep running until the memories of all that happened had faded.

Then he remembered that he had his cell phone stuffed into his jacket pocket. "Telling lies won't help anyone, Daed. I'm going to call Sheriff Kramer."

His father's hand whipped out and gripped his arm hard. *"Nee."*

"I have to."

"You don't know what you're saying."

"Aaron, stop," Jacob's mother ordered from the doorway. Looking like a shadow of her former self, she was holding the doorframe like it was the greatest support. "I've been standing out here while you and Jacob have been talking. I heard every word."

His father leaned back against his chair. "Then you understand what I am saying, don't you, Gloria?"

"Not at all." Turning to Jacob, she said, "Do you know how to get a hold of Sheriff Kramer?"

"I have his card."

"Then you'd best go ahead and call."

Struggling to his feet, his father's expression turned dark. "Gloria, you can't let Jacob call! We can keep this hidden if none of us says a word."

"Oh, Aaron, you don't know what you're saying. I truly

don't think you do." Shaking her head sorrowfully, she added, "We have no choice but to tell the police."

"That's where you're wrong. There's always a choice."

"Perhaps for you, Aaron. For me? There is no choice. There's only one thing to do."

"Gloria, I beg of you . . . don't let him do this."

A glazed look of despair washed over her face. "Jacob, go call."

About to turn, he looked at his parents warily. "Mamm, will you be all right?"

"I'll be just fine. Go now. Waiting won't make things easier."

He left then, left the two of them staring at each other across a kitchen table where there'd always been three of them.

Picking up his jacket, he pulled his cell phone and Mose's business card from the pocket, and finally began to dial.

"Crittenden County Sheriff," a chipper voice answered. Jacob recognized the woman who had been sitting in the reception desk when he'd been brought in for questioning.

Clearing his throat, he said, "This is Jacob Schrock. I need to speak with Sheriff Kramer, if I may."

"I'll put you right through," she said.

His pulse raced.

"Jacob?" Mose said from the other side of the line. "What can I do for you?"

"Sheriff Kramer, I'm afraid I have something to tell you." Taking a deep breath, he pushed through the pain and began.

Luke looked up when Mose motioned for him to pick up the extension. Carefully, Luke picked it up and then closed his eyes briefly when he recognized the voice and understood what Jacob was saying.

Aaron Schrock had watched Perry Borntrager die, then had deliberately hidden his body.

As Mose carefully asked more questions, Luke wrote notes. Finally, it all made sense. He knew right then and there that they finally had the full, complete story. Just as he could sense when something was not right, he also had learned to recognize the signs of hearing the truth.

After promising to be at their house in a few minutes, Mose hung up. "So it was Aaron Schrock. All along." His voice was flat.

Luke ached for Mose, and for everyone involved. This was going to rock this community. "I think the fact it was Aaron kind of makes sense," he said as they grabbed their jackets and walked to Mose's cruiser.

"Unfortunately, it does," Mose agreed. "It makes sense, but it breaks my heart. I always liked Aaron."

Luke had, too. "I guess this proves a man will do almost anything to protect his son."

"*Almost* anything," Mose corrected. "That word makes all the difference, I think. Most men would offer their own lives for their children. But they'd draw the line at committing murder." Slapping his hand on his steering wheel, Mose bellowed, "What a fool." When he turned to Luke, his gaze was pain-filled. "Why didn't Aaron come to me right away? I could have tried to help him. Now we'll be lucky if he's not charged with murder in the first degree."

"Who knows why he didn't come to you. "

After backing out, Mose drove carefully across town and to the store. Jacob stood waiting for them in the parking lot, standing alone and looking dejected. As if the whole weight of the world was resting on his shoulders.

When Luke got close, he patted the young man's shoulders. "Who's with your father, Jacob?"

"My *mamm*. She told me to stay out here to wait for you."

"You doing okay?" Mose asked.

Jacob shook his head. "Not really. I never would have thought my *daed* could do this. I keep thinking I'm going to wake up from a nightmare."

Luke glanced Mose's way. The young man needed a helping hand. He really looked to be on the verge of collapsing.

Mose nodded at Luke before wrapping an arm around Jacob's shoulders. "Jacob, why don't you sit down here and let Luke and me go in without you."

"Are you sure?"

"Positive. I promise, there's nothing more you need to hear. We'll take care of things now."

"I should warn you, my father is pretty upset."

"It's okay, son. Your dad did the right thing by confessing to you," Luke soothed. "And you did the right thing by calling Sheriff Kramer. But just because you did something right doesn't mean it was easy. Stay out here, Jacob. No son wants to see his father like this."

Luke was thankful that Jacob sat down. Then, with Mose by his side, they walked the narrow path along the side of the store to the living quarters of the Schrocks.

Mose knocked once. After a moment, Gloria Schrock answered it. "Sheriff Kramer, Detective Reynolds, I am mighty glad you are here."

Mose held out a hand and clasped Mrs. Schrock's. "We got here as soon as we could. Where's Aaron, Gloria?"

"He's sitting at the kitchen table."

Mose walked in, and Luke followed. When they got to the table, Aaron Schrock looked up at them with blank eyes. "I suppose you are going to arrest me?"

Mose pulled out a pair of handcuffs. "I'm afraid I have no choice, Aaron."

Luke knew that was true. Even if Aaron couldn't have saved Perry, he didn't even try. And hiding a body was a criminal offense.

As Mose clipped the handcuffs around Aaron's wrists, he recited the Miranda oath. "You have the right to remain silent. Anything you say or do can and will be held against you in a court of law. You have the right to speak to an attorney. If you cannot afford an attorney . . ."

As Mose Mirandized Aaron, Luke watched tears silently fall down Gloria Schrock's cheeks.

"I don't know what to say or do," she murmured.

"You don't have to do anything," Luke reassured her. "Jacob is outside, ma'am. I'll send him inside when we leave." He stood quietly by her side while Mose gripped Aaron's elbow, pulled him to his feet, then escorted him outside.

With Aaron's bigger-than-life personality gone, the kitchen seemed darker and smaller.

"What's next?" Gloria asked after she gingerly took a seat.

"You'll need to call back that lawyer," he replied, doing his best to keep his voice even and without too much emotion. "I'm afraid your husband is going to need his services."

She shook her head. "No, Detective Reynolds. I mean, what happens to me now? My family is broken up. My husband is in jail. And my son? My son might never recover from this."

Luke had arrested dozens of people, some in the most horrifying of situations. He'd thought he'd seen it all.

But not once had anyone asked how to put their lives back together.

After a moment of thought, he replied. "You go on the best you can. You wake up, get through a day, and then you try to sleep."

"And then?"

"And then you do it again the next day." He paused, then said, "It's going to be tough, but I have a feeling Jacob will recover."

Looking more determined, Gloria nodded. "I think he will. He's a strong boy."

"Yes, he is. He did the right thing, calling Mose. And you did the right thing when you encouraged him to make the call." Luke paused, then continued. "Though it had to have been painful, there's something to be said for doing the right thing."

Looking up at him, tears welling in her light blue eyes, she nodded, "I do believe that's so. A person can't live a lifetime covering up lies. They'll eat up a person's heart and soul. My poor Aaron . . ." Her face crumbled. "Jacob will get through this. But right this minute? I don't know how I'll survive."

Her pain broke his heart, but he couldn't deny that she had some very dark times ahead of her. "I am sorry, Mrs. Schrock."

When Luke finally headed out to the cruiser, he found Jacob standing near the entrance of the store. His arms were crossed over his white shirt and he was staring at the car.

It was running, standing idle while Mose waited for Luke to join them.

Luke cleared his throat. "I'm heading out, Jacob. Mose or I will call you later."

Jacob looked at him like he hardly remembered who Luke

was. "My father is handcuffed in the back of Sheriff Kramer's car," he said, his voice hoarse with emotion. "I can hardly believe it."

Luke knew there was nothing to say and no way to ease the boy's pain. "Go inside and take care of your mother. She needs you."

Jacob's lips parted, as if he was going to protest the directive. But in the end, he simply turned away and started into the house.

All of a sudden, Luke felt older than his twenty-nine years. Without a word, he opened the cruiser's passenger-side door and got in. Neither man looked his way, each seemed to wrapped up in his own thoughts.

That suited Luke just fine. He buckled up and stared straight ahead as Mose backed out of the driveway, then drove slowly back to the sheriff's office.

After eight very hard weeks, the case was closed.

Ironically, however, there was no sense of accomplishment. Only the greatest feeling of loss.

Chapter 24

"No one ever said doing the right thing was easy. But if everyone involved had done the right thing from the beginning? . . . my life would have been a great deal easier. It's true."

MOSE KRAMER

Two hours had passed since Sheriff Kramer had broken the news about Aaron Schrock. Once he left, Deborah's father had been even more full of venom and anger, her mother subdued and depressed.

"This is why you should never see Jacob again, Deborah," her mother said from her spot on the worn couch in their living room.

From her own chair by the fireplace, Deborah didn't agree. "Jacob isn't the one we should be upset with."

"It was his father who caused our pain."

"But Jacob is innocent."

Standing up, her father glared at her. "Deborah, you heard what Sheriff Kramer said. Jacob fought with Perry. If he had never fought with Perry in the first place, his father would have never followed him out to the field and tried to clean up Jacob's mess."

Deborah raised a brow. "And if Frannie had never walked out to meet Perry, and if the two of them hadn't argued, if she hadn't been crying . . . then she would have never run into Jacob. And he would have never gone out to the field," she finished. "Do you want me to stay away from Frannie, too?"

Her father looked taken aback. "I don't know."

"What about Lydia?" Deborah said as she got to her feet. "If she had never broken up with Perry, then Perry would never have had a reason to meet Frannie out in that field. Perhaps *Lydia Plank* is the problem, Daed. You want me to stay away from her, too?"

He looked chagrined. "Now you are pulling at straws."

"*Nee*, Daed," she countered. "You are refusing to accept the truth. Jacob and Perry were both fighting. Together. The fight was as much Perry's fault as Jacob's."

"Jacob went out there to do Perry harm."

"Jacob went out there to try to talk some sense into Perry," she countered, her temper rising. "Just like you tried to do, over and over and over. Just like Mamm did years ago. Just like I tried to do, time and again. But he didn't listen, Daed. And then we all gave up on him." Her voice hoarse with pent-up emotion, she said, "Perry never listened and we gave up trying."

"Perry was a good boy . . ."

"Perry was a good boy for a while, but he was also impulsive and willful and stubborn. Yes, he had many good qualities, but he had many bad qualities, too. Just as we all do."

Lowering her voice, she continued. "Daed, I can't condone Mr. Schrock's actions. And I am upset that my brother is gone. I loved him. But you need to finally stop looking for excuses for Perry's misdeeds. And you need to stop blaming everyone else for his faults. He had a great many faults, Daed. I'm sorry, but he wasn't perfect. He wasn't perfect and he never, ever tried to be."

For a moment, Deborah was sure she'd broken through her father's grief and stubbornness. She was sure he was going to turn to her and apologize.

To say she was right about a lot of things.

But instead, he shook his head. "I don't want to talk about this anymore. We won't mention it again." With sure steps, he crossed the room and sat in the rocking chair by the window. "Now, you will go help your mother with supper."

Wearily, her mother stood up; whether she was going to the kitchen or to her bedroom, Deborah had no idea.

But Deborah had had enough. "Do you actually think I'm going to go cook a meal now?" she asked incredulously. "What is wrong with you? I'm going to go see Jacob."

"You will not."

"Daed, I'm not going to do this any longer. I'm not going to stay here, trying to pretend I'm content when everything is so wrong. I'm not going to continue to live my life circling, hoping and waiting that somehow everything will suddenly get better."

"But, daughter, where is your loyalty?"

"Where is your loyalty to me? All my life you've asked me to overlook Perry's problems and his transgressions. You've asked me to ignore my pain in order to try to save face. I won't do it anymore. No longer."

"But your mother . . ." They both looked to the couch where her mother had been sitting. It was empty now. Deborah's mother had gotten up and left the room without either she or her father realizing it.

"I can't take care of Mamm without taking care of myself

too, father. And right now, that means I've got to go see Jacob. I have to."

She walked out the door before she was tempted to say anything more. Before she reminded her father that while Jacob's father might have killed Perry, her brother had stolen from others, had lied to many, and had even sold drugs to people in the community.

She'd hated living in shame because of what her brother had done. She certainly wasn't going to make Jacob live that way.

Outside, the clouds had come, blanketing the fading sun. The waning sunlight barely slid through the foliage as she walked down the worn path to the Schrocks' home.

When she got to there, the windows were dark. She stood at the door, hesitating. Was it okay to knock? She wasn't sure.

But then she noticed a dim light shining from the corner of the front porch of the store. Curious, she walked up the narrow walkway to investigate.

She found Jacob sitting alone on one of the rocking chairs on the front porch. He started when she came around the corner. "Deborah? Is that you?"

"*Jah.* I came the back way."

"Alone? The sun just set. Deb, you need to take care. That's no place to walk in the dark."

In the dim shadows, she let herself smile. It was so like him to put his concerns about her safety over his worries. "I was careful," she said as she walked up the front steps and onto the porch.

He stood up. "So . . . is everything okay? Do you need something?"

Even with all that was going on, Jacob was still worried about her. "I'm all right." Studying his face, she saw lines of worry etched around his mouth and eyes. In the span of two days, he looked like he'd aged ten years. "Actually, I came to see how you are."

He looked down at his feet. "I . . . ah. Have you heard from Mose?"

"Yes. He stopped by the house a few hours ago. I know about your father, Jacob. I'm sorry. I wanted to come to see how you are doing." When he still looked at her blankly, she added, "I can't imagine what you must be feeling."

"You aren't blaming me?"

"I'm sad that your father felt he had no choice but to do what he did . . . but I don't blame you, Jacob." She truly didn't, she realized with a bit of surprise.

Unlike her father's bitterness, her heart went out to Jacob and his parents. She knew what it was like to be disappointed and hurt by a family member's actions. She knew what it was like to feel completely hopeless and helpless. The Schrocks needed her prayers, not her anger.

Jacob's brown eyes skimmed her own, seeming to search for something more than he believed was possible. After a moment, he sighed. "I can't tell you how happy I am to hear that. To be honest, I've been sitting here, thinking about my father and Perry." He shrugged. "Thinking about everything. I've even been thinking about how awful I've been to you at times. Deborah, I'm sorry. I've had a lot I needed to learn about myself."

"Let's stop saying we're sorry to each other. It isn't necessary."

A new awareness flickered in his gaze. "Would you like to sit here with me?"

"I'd rather sit with you than anywhere else."

He chuckled, the noise sounding like a burst of joy in the

still evening air. "You are a constant surprise, Deborah. Just a few weeks ago, I would never have imagined you could be so tough. And until you just showed up, I never thought I'd ever laugh again."

"Then it's time you believed in yourself and the future, don't you think?" she asked lightly as she sat down in the chair next to him.

"Maybe so."

They rocked in the ancient chairs side by side, the darkness of the evening surrounding them. With only the quiet glow of the lantern illuminating the area, it was impossible to see the parking lot or even the winding road beyond.

It felt like they were the only two people in Crittenden County.

"Do you sit out here a lot at night?" Deborah asked.

"Hardly ever."

"If I lived here I probably would come out here every chance I got."

"My *mamm* used to say that. When I was little, I remember my parents coming out here fairly often. But now the evenings seemed to be taken over by bills and plans and invoices."

"That's what happens, I suppose. We all get too busy to enjoy what is in front of our noses."

"Deborah, to be honest, I don't know if I've ever taken the time to be thankful for my blessings."

"I doubt you are the first man to not take the time to give thanks for what he had. It's human nature to always be searching and hoping, I think."

"I don't know what to do, Deborah. My mother's inside crying. And my *daed*? I feel bad for him, but I'm ashamed of his actions, too. I'm struggling with what he did . . . and how he almost let me get charged with Perry's murder. Now I've got the store to manage and a future to try to work out." He rubbed the back of his neck. "It's a lot, you know?"

She wasn't about to start giving him advice. His problems and worries were big and not lightly solved. "One day you'll know what to do," she said finally.

"That's it?" his tone was incredulous. "That's your advice?"

"You don't need my advice. You only need my support." Privately, she knew she could offer him her love, too. But maybe that wasn't in the cards for them. Maybe God had different plans.

She was just about to attempt to say something about giving himself time to grieve and heal when they heard a chattering of voices from the parking lot. "I wonder who that is?"

"No telling." His hands clenched on his rocking chair's arms, but she noticed he was taking care not to show any more emotion.

"Is it okay if we join you? Or is this a private party?"

With a laugh, Deborah got to her feet and raced down the steps as Walker, Lydia, Frannie, and Beth came into view. In the background were Micah Overholt and Kevin Yoder. "Look at all of you! Why on earth did you decide to come to the store this evening?"

Frannie gave her a quick hug. "I'd like to say we spend most evenings wandering around in the dark, but that would be a lie," she said with a laugh. "We came out here to see you, Jacob," she said as she bounded up the steps.

"I can't believe you all are here," he said.

His voice was wooden-sounding. Deborah knew he was desperately trying not to expect too much. She didn't blame him, either. It was a difficult thing, getting used to friendship and support.

"Only you would be surprised to see us, Jacob," Walker said. "Of course we were going to find you this evening. You need us more than ever."

Deborah walked back up the stairs and took a chance. Coming to his side, she grabbed his elbow. "They're reaching out to you, Jacob," she whispered. "Now it's your turn to reach right back."

After sharing a meaningful look with her, he smiled. "I do need you," he finally said.

Their friends bounded up the stairs, Beth and Micah holding baskets. "I hope you need what we brought, too," Beth said. "Food!"

"And Cokes," Micah said with a grin.

"I can't believe you all. It's one of the worst nights of my life, and you all are throwing a party."

"That's because you've got it all wrong, Jacob," Frannie said. "It might have been one of the worst days of your life, but that doesn't mean you have to suffer through it all alone. We're here for you. No matter what."

"I . . ." he cleared his throat. "I mean . . ."

"Nah . . ." Walker slapped him on the shoulder. "Now, don't get all mushy, Jacob. We don't want a speech. Just tell us that it's time to eat."

He grinned. "It's time to eat."

"Thank goodness," Beth said. "I'm starving."

The laughter that floated around them felt like a healing cloak. A reminder that even on the darkness of evenings, the light of hope can still be found.

Chapter 25

"It wasn't too hard to forgive Perry for his transgressions. God reminded me that I had many sins of my own. We all do."

JACOB SCHROCK

Though he'd told Mose he would arrive at the office before ten that morning, Luke couldn't help but stop by Frannie's first. He was used to spending so much time together, he'd felt a little left out when she'd told him that she couldn't talk to him on the phone last night.

When she'd admitted that she and her other friends were going to visit Jacob and offer their support, Luke had been floored. The way everyone in her circle hadn't even hesitated to be there for Jacob was inspiring. And humbling.

But he also felt left out. He wasn't a part of their group, and not because he was a policeman, either. He sensed it was a deeper acknowledgment that he wasn't a part of their community.

Though he was a confident man, he suddenly felt a little awkward. Was he destined to always be on the outskirts of her circle of friends? And . . . did Frannie resent him for arresting Aaron Schrock?

Wondering about all these things, he knocked on her front door.

Less than a minute later, she opened it, her wary expression turning to a big smile when she saw who it was. "Luke, why did you knock? You know you could have walked around to the kitchen door. It's always open for you."

Feeling strangely gratified by her words, he stepped inside and gently pressed his lips to her cheek. "Knocking seemed the right thing to do this morning."

After touching her palm to her cheek, as if she was hoping to hold his kiss close, she looked at him curiously. "And why is that?"

He followed her back to the kitchen. There, he sat on top of his usual wooden stool at the counter as he watched her open a cabinet, pull out a large coffee mug, and pour him a cup of the dark brew. "I wasn't sure after last night how you would feel about me."

"Because I went to see Jacob?" When he nodded, she set the cup of coffee in front of him, then turned to the refrigerator and pulled out two sticks of butter. "Were you jealous? Luke, Jacob is my friend. That's all."

"I know that," he said, picking up the cup of coffee and blowing softly on it. After taking an exploratory sip and finding it as excellent as always, he said, "I know there's nothing romantic between the two of you. But I also know that you are close. I've been worried you might be upset with me."

"Because you arrested his father?"

"Well . . . Yeah."

"Luke, you are a police detective. You were only doing your job."

"But still, it's got to make you uncomfortable . . ." He ached to say a whole lot more, but was reluctant to make the jar of worms he'd just opened up any worse. "I thought maybe you were feeling torn. You know, caught in the middle."

After putting a large mason jar filled with flour on the counter, she walked back to stand in front of him. "I don't feel caught in the middle at all, Luke. My loyalty is to you. I'm proud of you and the work you do. It ain't easy, choosing to be the person to uphold the law, you know."

Once again, Frannie was speaking with her confident authority. It was so familiar, he couldn't help but smile. He relaxed enough to take another sip. "I can't tell you how glad I am to hear that."

"Then you should know that I feel loyal to Jacob, too. It isn't his fault that his father took his vengeance out on Perry. Jacob's going to have to live with that for the rest of his life."

Luke ached to confide in Frannie, to tell him how Aaron had kept saying how he killed Perry in order to help Jacob. But of course he couldn't share that confidential information.

Instead, he concentrated on what he could share with her, his feelings. "I was jealous last night."

"You were?"

To his amazement, she didn't look sad about that fact. Instead, she looked pleased. That spunky part of Frannie was why he was so attracted to her. Sure, he loved the way she looked for the best in people. And the way she wasn't shy about speaking her mind, if she thought it needed to be spoken.

But she was also strong enough to stand up to his personality. She kept him in line and on his toes.

Pulling her toward him, he wrapped his hands around her waist. "I didn't even ask. How many guests do you have today?"

"Three rooms are filled. Two couples and one single lady. They should be appearing downstairs fairly soon."

"How soon?"

Playfully, she slapped the hand that had curved a little more tightly around her waist. "Sooner than you would like, Luke. I told them I made raspberry jam-filled muffins this morning, you know. They won't tarry long."

He dropped his hands and hopped off the stool. "Can I have one to go?"

"You haven't already eaten?"

"Oh, I ate some eggs and bacon at the Marion Inn. But the cook there doesn't make your muffins, Frannie."

"No one does," she said. But her eyes were sparkling.

Which made him pressed another kiss to her cheek when she handed him three muffins on a plate, covered with a pressed gingham napkin. "Frannie, you're the best."

She grinned. "I know. Enjoy the treat."

Heading out the back door, he said, "I'll call you later. Bye, Fran."

He was almost out the door when her voice stopped him in midstride. "Luke? Do you feel better now?"

"Yeah," he admitted. "I feel a lot better. Thanks, Frannie."

When he got in his truck, he knew he'd keep the memory of her understanding smile in his mind all day long.

Dressed in a gray dress and black apron, with a black bonnet covering her *kapp*, Gloria Schrock looked like she was ready to take on the world. "Jacob, I want you to stay here at the store while I go to the sheriff's office," she said.

But Jacob wasn't fooled for an instant. Her eyes were puffy and her skin was pale. She was, like him, barely holding it together. "Mamm, I'd rather you let me go. Or better yet, why don't we close up the store and go together?"

"I think it's better if I go on my own today. Besides, I'll be meeting Mr. Meyer there, and he'll want to talk about payment and such."

All of that sounded like even more reason for his mother not to go to the sheriff's office on her own. "I can do those things. You know I've been helping with the books a lot."

"*Jah*, but I handle the finances." Her voice cracked.

The sound broke his heart. He'd been raised to look out for his mother. And today of all days, he ached to save her from further pain. "Mamm, I don't think Daed wants you to go to the sheriff's office. He isn't going to want you to see him that way. "

"I don't think anything I do is up to your father anymore," she said quietly. "And, Jacob, please stay here. I want the store to be open for business. Even if no one stops by today, I want everyone to know that I'm not about to fold up shop and hide. At least, not yet."

Straightening her shoulders, she raised her chin slightly so she could look at him eye to eye. "Son, I need for us to be in control of something, even if it's only keeping the store open."

Remembering how good it felt to have his friends' support the evening before, Jacob backed down. He wasn't sure how the community would react once the whole truth came out, but he was willing to support his mother's wishes. "All right. But if you need something, send word, would you?"

"I will." Tears filled her eyes. "Jacob," she said, her voice cracking again. "I know you are worried about your father, and about me, too. But we will all be all right. God will give us strength."

"I know," he said, but the moment she left, he exhaled a ragged breath. The Lord was certainly giving them strength. But He was also putting a lot of obstacles in their lives at the moment.

He'd never been one to question why things happened, but at the moment, he couldn't help but wonder why God had led both he and his father to be embroiled in such anger and hate.

Though his father had killed Perry, Jacob knew that it had been his own anger that had spurred it. If he had learned long ago to control his emotions where Perry was concerned, then he wouldn't have held so much in.

And wouldn't have been so angry with Perry back on that dreaded night.

So when would you have finally stood up for yourself? A weak, suggestive voice inside his head murmured. Back when you were waltzing in late for school?

Or . . . the day you both skipped school and went hunting instead?

Jacob wished he couldn't remember that day. The episode had been so disturbing, he'd worked hard to try to erase it from memory. But of course that couldn't happen.

The two of them had been alone in the woods, small-gauge shotguns in their hands. Looking for rabbits.

Jacob had slaughtered hogs before. He'd killed chickens, and helped his father dress a deer more than once or twice. But he'd had a soft spot of rabbits.

He'd never been able to eat rabbit stew, no matter how well his mother made the meal. And so he'd continued to hesitate when a rabbit crossed their path.

Perry, of course, had never hesitated. By the end of their four hours, he had collected five hares.

"You're the worst hunter I've ever seen in my life," Perry scoffed.

"I'm just having a bad day. That's all."

"I think you're chicken. I think you're afraid to hurt the little rabbit." He'd changed his voice to a child's, slurring the words slightly. "Is that what's wrong, Jacob? You don't want to hurt the bunnies?"

"Perry, you were with me when I landed the buck last Thanksgiving. I'm obviously not afraid to shoot my shotgun."

"But today you've hardly done more than hold that gun."

"You've gotten plenty of rabbits. If I'd really wanted to shoot a rabbit, I would have." He started walking, hoping Perry would let the subject drop.

But Perry never let things drop that he didn't want to. "Prove it," he whispered.

Jacob turned his way. "Prove it how?"

Perry pointed. And sure enough, there in the distance was a pair of rabbits. It was obvious that they'd known they'd been spotted. They were frozen in their spots like rabbits often were. Their brown fur blended in well with the bark of the oak tree behind them. So well, a person with weaker eyesight might not even have spied them.

"They're yours," Perry said generously. "Shoot them."

"We have enough."

"Do it. Do it or I'll know you're chicken."

Jacob lifted the eyepiece to his eye and pulled the trigger. Through the finder, the rabbit flinched then went still as Jacob's shotgun shell had found its mark. The rabbit's companion paused for a half-second, then ran through the brush.

Lowering the rifle, he glared at Perry. "Happy?"

"Whatever," Perry said, and started walking.

Jacob realized that Perry hadn't even expected him to go get *the hare. And he didn't want to. He ached to leave it on the ground, ached to turn around and pretend it had never happened.*

But he couldn't even do that.

With a pounding heart, he walked over to the dead rabbit, picked it up by its hind legs, and carried it home. And then he forced himself to skin and gut it and give it to his mother to cook.

Jacob recalled that he couldn't eat the stew, and that he had promised himself to never speak of it again—because, he'd realized then, that there were worse things than being called chicken.

And that was being called a killer.

The front door of the store opened, thankfully blocking out the rest of the memories. "May I help you?" he asked the man he didn't recognize.

"You got any fresh bread?"

"*Jah*, sure." He escorted the man to the bakery section and showed him the fresh loaves that had been delivered from the bakery on the other side of Marion.

After, a few more customers came in, not the usual crowd, but continually steady. More than enough to keep his mind off of the memories and the guilt.

The store was empty when the bell at the front door chimed again. Looking up, he smiled, "Hey, Deborah."

"Hello."

"Did you come here to check up on me or to work?"

She paused, a secret smile on her lips. "Maybe a little bit of both."

"That wasn't necessary. It's pretty quiet in here. I don't need the help. I'm fine."

Looking at him carefully, she shook her head. "No, you need the help."

"Why is that?"

"You don't have either of your father's kittens out for show."

"I fed them this morning, but they seemed happy enough in their cage."

"Your father wants them out for sale. Go get them, Jacob."

"I don't want the kittens out."

"I know. Do it anyway."

With a jerk, he turned and tromped back to the storage room. Predictably, the kittens were nestled together, looking completely at peace. When he picked up the cage, they sprang apart, like lovers caught in a compromising position. "Sorry, cats," he said as he carried them forward.

"Deb, I don't know if anyone's going to want either of these cats."

"Someone might. Next time I work, I'm going to suggest people get them as a pair. It would be a shame to divide them up, don'tcha think?"

"I don't know how you're going to get anyone to buy the pair. Most folks only want one pet at a time."

Her eyes sparkled. "Not if we offer them as a buy one get one free."

"A two for one deal, hmm?"

"I think that would be a bargain." Looking at the cats, now glaring at them both like prospective dinners, Deborah chuckled. "My advice is we aim for a quick sale."

He laughed. "I can't believe we're standing here, worrying about these stupid cats." To his dismay, in a split second, his laughter turned into tears.

Ashamed and furious, he attempted to wipe off his cheeks and his eyes, but he couldn't seem stop the flood. "Sorry," he blurted. "Oh my gosh. I don't know why I'm doing this."

"Have you cried yet?"

For what? He wanted to ask. For his mistakes? For Perry's death? For his father's lies? For the future they were all now destined to have? A life with a father in jail? "No," he finally said. "I haven't cried."

"Then it's time, I think."

"I'm fine." But two more traitorous tears rushed down his cheeks.

He was just attempting to apologize yet again when two arms reached around him and held him close. Deborah was tiny, her head barely reaching his shoulder. And her bones and frame were slim. She shouldn't have been able to support him at all.

But somehow she did. Somehow, being in her arms—being held close and comforted—felt right. He leaned closer and let the tears fall.

She rubbed her hand in between his shoulder blades. "It's okay, Jacob," she murmured.

But it wasn't. He should be tougher, stronger. Not a coward. "I . . . I . . ." he sputtered. Somehow he couldn't seem to catch his breath for long enough to form words.

"I know," she whispered. "I know you're upset. You have every right to be."

With effort he raised his head. "I'm better now."

She smiled and shook her head. "*Nee.* I don't think so." Straightening, she said, "And I don't think the two of us standing this way is good."

He was just about to agree, to say that he completely agreed that they shouldn't be holding each other in the middle of the store, when she pulled him to the counter.

"Deborah?"

To his surprise, she hopped up on the counter just like she

was a child. And then she held open her arms. "Come here, Jacob."

Next thing he knew, he was walking into her arms all over again. Resting his head on her slim shoulder. And though his tears had subsided, the need to feel the comfort of Deborah was stronger than ever.

And so he stayed where he was, nestled in the comfort of her arms. Once again blocking out the pain. Concentrating only on the moment.

Chapter 26

"It would be difficult for me to pinpoint exactly when Perry started down the wrong path. That's because a lot of paths don't seem all that wrong at first, you know? Sometimes they seem like the right way."

MOSE KRAMER

"I just talked to county. The bus is going to pick up Aaron Schrock within the hour."

The bus, of course, was from the county jail. It was standard procedure to take all of the accused there while they awaited bail. And because the district attorney had set the bail fairly high, Luke doubted Aaron would be getting let out anytime soon.

Taking a seat across from Mose, Luke kicked his leg out. It was still stiff, but it didn't continuously ache like it used to. Not even when the rain had begun to fall again.

"I wish it would stop raining."

His friend shrugged off his complaint in his usual relaxed way. "Wishes and dreams, you know. The weathermen say it's here to stay for a while. Maybe through the weekend."

"Just my luck."

"You upset? What's wrong, Luke? You got a hot date?"

"Maybe." He had planned to see Frannie later, but that wasn't what had him restless. "I guess I'm having a hard time believing it's over."

Mose picked up the eight-inch pile of folders and papers from the corner of his desk. "I've got lots of other cases and work to take care of. I'm glad it's over. Most of all, I'm glad we found the right person. I sure wasn't happy when I thought our culprit was Jacob."

"I liked his dad, too."

"Me too." Mose shrugged. "Aaron's been a good friend to me for a long time. But you know as well as I, Luke, that sometimes it's a fine line between a man doing something honorable and contemptible. When Aaron made that choice, he crossed the line."

"I agree." He felt weak for even admitting his feelings. What kind of officer even thought about regrets? "Sorry. Don't know why I'm talking like this."

"You're not saying anything I haven't thought as well. Aaron getting arrested is going to shake things up around here."

Slowly getting to his feet, Luke walked over to Mose. "When I first got to Crittenden County, I thought you needed my help."

"I did. I called you. Don't you recall?"

"No, what I mean is, I thought you needed my help because I was a better detective."

Mose raised his brows. "Luke, you are—"

"I'm not. I learned a lot from working by your side, Mose. You taught me a lot about trusting your instincts, and to stop looking at cases from a distance. You taught me to take things personal, and to remember why we do things. To help others. I'm grateful to you for that."

"You're welcome, though I think you're giving me too much credit."

That was vintage Mose, wasn't it? Always humble. Never wanting the spotlight or the accolades. "No, Mose, I don't think I can ever give you too much credit."

Whatever Mose would have said next was a mystery, because the bus from the county jail drove up. Frowning, he stood up and walked to the front door.

"There are some days I'm glad I'm not doing my job alone. Today's one of those days," Mose said as he went to greet the van driver.

Luke felt the same way. He turned toward the back hall to go fetch Aaron. At least he could spare Mose from having to escort his friend to the county jail.

"Walker? Where are you?"

"I'm in the back hallway, Grandma," Walker replied. "I'll be right there."

But before he could get to his feet, his grandma had popped her head in. After her eagle eyes spied him sitting on his father's old bench, sore and dirty and exhausted, she bustled forward. "Walker, you look tuckered out."

That would be an understatement. "I am. I think I walked more than that pair of horses. I know I stepped in every single hole and patch of mud in that field."

"You might have." Her lips twitched. "I fear the horses are taking advantage of you."

"Is that even possible?"

"I fear that it is. Horses are smart animals. They can spy an easy target from a hundred yards away. You aren't used to telling them what to do—they most likely figured that out right quick."

Walker would have been ashamed of his uselessness . . . if he weren't so tired. "Plowing fields is a lot harder than it looks, Mommi."

"Most things are."

Very aware of how sweaty he was, he shifted. "I'm going to go shower in just a minute. I was just resting." He pushed back a lock of his hair with two fingers on his right hand, which weren't blistered.

Right away his grandmother noticed. Taking hold of both of his hands, she turned them palm up and then winced at the sight. "Oh, Walker! Your hands are in terrible shape. When did this happen?"

He looked at the scabs that had formed on top of his old blisters and the quarter-sized sore that had formed on his left palm. "When I was trying to guide the horses." And when he'd chopped wood for hours. And had to mend a couple of fences. And mucked-out stalls.

"You should have said something."

"There was no need. I'm fine."

"You are definitely not fine." With a clicking motion, she looped her fingers around his wrist and pulled him out of the doorway and into the kitchen. When they got to the sink, she ran the faucet. When she deemed the temperature warm enough, she scooted him closer. "Wash."

He was in no hurry to put the soap on the open wounds, but he knew she was right to want his hands clean. "I was going to go wash upstairs."

"And I'm sure you still will. But now we can talk, too."

As Grandma Francis guided his hands under the faucet, she squirted some soap on her hands, then gently rubbed his own.

Just as if he was still a child.

He closed his eyes, letting her smooth fingers remove the grime from his palms. As always, his grandmother's touch was gentle and strong. So much like the woman herself.

"Walker, are you positive this life is what you want?"

"I'm positive that I want Lydia in my life."

She turned off the faucet and folded his hands into a fluffy kitchen towel. "I know you love her. But I fear you might be taking on more than you are ready for."

"I'll get the hang of farming, Grandma. My skin just needs to get a little tougher." Okay, a lot tougher.

"I'm not just talking about farming."

"I went to church with you yesterday at the Yoders."

She opened up the towel and inspected one of his hands with a frown. "I know," she said. She then examined his other hand, tsking over the torn skin.

"Did I do something wrong at the service?"

"Not at all. I'm not judging you, Walker. I am merely asking questions."

"Lydia said I did all right. And I kind of enjoyed being there. Even though, you know, I hardly understood a word of it."

Her lips twitched. "You wouldn't be the first man to think the three-hour service felt long, Walker." Wryly, she added, "Some might even say understanding all the words don't help. It's still a long sit."

"But being there, it also felt right. I was peaceful, sitting there. Watching other men and women deep in their faith. It made me want to deepen my faith, too. And that is for me, Grandma. It has nothing to do with Lydia."

"That is a relief to hear." Going back to the faucet, she filled a glass with cool well water, then handed it to him. "Drink," she ordered. While he did, she asked, "Have you talked to your father about all this?"

"A little." When the glass was empty, he set it on the counter.

"And?"

"And I think he's as confused as anybody." He was tempted to stop talking, but then decided to reveal all that he was thinking. It seemed like the right thing to do. "I'm afraid he thinks he's made a mistake with me."

"How so?"

"I think my dad's been so happy with his life, he's wondering how I can want something that he worked so hard to get away from."

"Hmm. Well, he'll get over those doubts, I imagine. You are doing much the same thing as he did. Breaking away from your parents takes a lot of strength. If he isn't proud that you've become your own man, he will be."

"What about Grandpa? Does he think I'm being foolish?"

"Foolish? Not at all! He's proud of you, Walker. As am I."

"And you think I'll do okay? I mean, after I learn to plow a field decently?"

"I think you'll do just fine, Walker." After glancing at the clock over the oven, she said, "But for now, you'd better run upstairs to the shower and get the rest of you cleaned up. I do believe you are about to have a caller."

"What? Who?"

She pointed to a buggy and horse riding up the driveway. The buggy was black of course. But the horse was silver. "Lydia's here."

"Grandma, I smell like dirt."

She chuckled. "Oh no, son. I promise, you smell much worse than that! Go shower."

"I'll be quick."

"Don't be too quick. You're going to need a lot of soap, I fear. I'm sure Lydia and I will have a nice visit until you come back downstairs. Go on now, Walker."

His grandmother's advice was so good, it almost didn't hurt to climb the stairs, two at a time.

Chapter 27

"*Deborah used to follow us everywhere when we were in school. One time I asked Perry why she followed him around so much. Perry grinned and said he wasn't the one she was following.*"

JACOB SCHROCK

In her arms, Jacob must have cried for a solid fifteen minutes, his shoulders shaking with the force of his emotion. Never had Deborah felt so needed or loved.

It had taken an incredible amount of trust for him to let down his guard enough to cry in front of her. Through it all, she'd patted his back and murmured reassurances. She didn't know if what she'd said even registered, but she'd meant every word. Together, they would get through this. She was sure of it.

Now Jacob was looking at her like he wished he was anywhere else on earth. His cheeks were red and his gaze wary. "I can't believe I did that. I'm so sorry."

Deborah ached to tell him that she was glad he cried. But she knew there was no way a man like him was going to take that the way she'd meant it. "It's okay," she said instead.

"I bet you want to leave now."

"Why on earth would I want to leave?"

"Because I'm so weak. Crying in front of you."

"I've never thought you were stronger," she said. "It takes a strong to man to admit when he's weak."

"You think?"

"I don't think I've ever thought you were stronger than right at this minute," she said honestly. So he wouldn't get anymore embarrassed, she said, "How about I stay and work at the store with you?"

"There's no reason for you to do that. It's pretty dead here."

"Maybe there's another reason I'd want to stay. Maybe I'm not ready to be away from you yet."

He blinked, then slowly smiled. "You know what? You're pretty amazing, Deborah."

"You think so?"

"I know so. I can't think of another woman on earth who wouldn't hate me if she were in your position."

He was wrong, of course. What had happened to their families wasn't their fault. Both of them were victims of their relatives' poor judgment.

She didn't think she was the only woman to realize that, either. Jacob was a good man. He wasn't perfect by any means, but he had a good heart, and he worked hard, and loved his family, too.

He also just happened to be handsome. To her, he'd always been the most handsome man in the world.

Afraid to tell him that, she kept things easy and light. "It just shows you that I'm a mighty special person, Jacob. It's time you realized that."

He looked at her, really looked at her. His gaze warm and tender. "Maybe I have. Finally."

"What have you realized?"

"I've realized that you've been in my life for so long for a reason," he said quietly. "I think God put us together to give each other support. I think maybe we're meant to be together. I don't know if anyone else in the world could understand the pain we're both going through."

"So what's going to happen to us? I hope we'll stay together."

Pressing his lips to her brow, he smiled softly. "I hope we will." After a moment, he said, "Who knows what will happen with the store. I can't imagine that my mom will want to keep running it. It wouldn't be the same without my *daed*, anyway. But this store is as much a part of my life as it was a part of my parents'. It's going to be really hard to see it closed."

"Maybe you can keep it running."

"Me?"

"Why is that so hard to imagine? You've been pretty much running the store for the past few years."

Hope shone in his eyes . . . as well as a good bit of doubt. "Do you really think anyone is even going to want to shop here again?"

"Jacob, perhaps people aren't staying away from you because they're upset about what your father did. Maybe they're trying to give you some space. I promise, things will turn around in time. They always do."

He shrugged. "At this point, I don't even know what to say or do. Or who to worry about."

"Then let's just worry about today. I think that's enough. Let's get through today and then we'll worry about tomorrow tomorrow."

"It's not that easy."

"Sure it is."

Running his fingertips over her cheek, he looked at her in wonder. "Have I told you that I don't deserve you?"

"I promise, you do, Jacob. If I know anything, it's that we deserve each other." He'd just enfolded her in his arms when the door opened and a group of four ladies walked in.

They were English tourists, obviously in town for the day.

Stepping away from her, Jacob looked like he'd never been so happy to have customers. "May I help you?"

"We just wanted to come look around. People have told us that you can't come to Crittenden County without stopping by Schrock's Variety. My friend Jean said this place wasn't to be missed."

Deborah smiled warmly. "Is that so? And where are you from?"

"St. Louis," another replied. Stepping forward in her olive green jogging suit, she added, "I'm so glad there's not a crowd here. Tuesday's going to be bad, you know."

"Why Tuesday?"

"A busload from the retirement home is coming here on Tuesday."

"A busload? Truly?"

The woman laughed. "I wouldn't kid about that. Your store has become a destination, young man."

As the ladies spread out and began shopping in earnest, Deborah covered her mouth with her hands. When she could contain her laughter, she dropped her hands and smiled at Jacob. "See? Everything's going to be all right. We'll get through today . . ."

"And then we'll get through Tuesday."

"And then before you know it, we'll look forward to another day. It's going to be okay, Jacob," she said quietly. "It really is."

"I think you're right. And I think you'd best stay here by my side, too. These ladies look like trouble," he joked when one of them came a little closer.

"Don't worry, Jacob. I'm not going anywhere." After all this time, during the worst of their sorrows . . . once again, they were able to find a sliver of light.

Epilogue

"We are not put on this earth to see through one another, but to see one another through."

LAVINA MILLER

Years ago, back when Mose had been a willful teenager, he used to walk through the Millers' land to get to Schrock's Variety. Taking the narrow trail through the dense woods and across the rocky fields had been the shortest route by far.

Walking through the farm had also held a tiny bit of danger: Mr. Miller didn't care for trespassers.

And that, of course, had been one of the reasons Mose had always trespassed. Sometimes it was fun to do things he wasn't supposed to.

Now, as he walked in the midst of a procession across a neatly mowed field, he had a curious sense of déjà vu. Even though they'd been invited to come on the property, it still felt a little bit dangerous. After all, they were all walking toward a place that many wished never existed.

"I'm kind of surprised the Millers are doing this. From what I know of them, it seems out of character," Luke said to him as they walked along.

As he glanced at the thicket of bushes to their right, framed by dark woods, Mose nodded. "I'm surprised, too, if you want to know the truth. But it's a fitting thing, I think. It's always a blessing to have something good come out of the bad."

And boy, had they had their fair share of bad episodes here.

For the last six months, it had seemed like a cloud had fallen over their area. Drug peddling had been a real problem, and suspecting that one of their own had been a dealer had been a difficult thing to deal with. And to prove.

Then there was the sense of loss and confusion that had fallen over all of them when Perry had gone missing. It wasn't easy to admit out loud that you were happy a person was gone . . . so happy that you didn't care what had happened to him.

But none of that guilt lit a candle to the shock waves that had reverberated through the community when Perry's body was found in the well. Not only had the young man not been missed . . . but his body had been lying in wait among them for months. Just waiting for someone to discover.

Now, too many secrets had been revealed for even Mose to count. People's lives had been shuffled and ruined and changed. Other folks had grown and matured and become better.

Strange, that.

"Looks like Walker Anderson has decided his future," Luke said as he pointed out Walker and Lydia Plank walking a few feet in front of them.

"Looks like it." Walker was dressed in a deep blue shirt, black trousers, and a straw hat. He was dressed Amish, and the clothes suited him. Beside him, his girlfriend, Lydia, was wearing a green dress the color of the meadow they were walking in. They were a handsome pair.

Of course, Walker hadn't yet professed his faith in the church. He had at least a year of education before that. Most likely the bishop was currently walking him through his Pennsylvania Dutch and rules of the *Ordnung* first.

"I saw Lydia's folks at Mary King's the other day," Luke said. "They're pleased as punch about their daughter's choice."

"I bet. Walker's an upstanding man. Always has been."

Walking on the other side of Luke was Frannie Eicher. She was currently chatting with her best friend, Beth Byler. And though Luke was talking with Mose and Frannie was chatting with Beth, Mose noticed that every few minutes Luke would look Frannie's way. Just like he was making sure she was still there.

Mose couldn't help but notice that Frannie had made a switch in her way of dressing, too. She was now dressing Mennonite. Mose privately thought the long–sleeved flowered dress made her auburn hair look right pretty. Of course the smile she often shot Luke's way was attractive, too.

Just to needle Luke a bit, he said, "Have you talked to Mr. Eicher recently?"

"He came over to Frannie's for dinner two nights ago."

"And?"

"And he still doesn't have much to say to me." Luke frowned. "You'd think by now he'd have warmed up at least a little bit. He's got to realize that I'd do just about anything for Frannie. I really love her."

Ah, love. "Don't worry, Luke. He'll come around. It just takes time."

"How long, do you reckon?"

"A couple of years. Maybe a bit more," he quipped, though he was only half joking. John Paul Eicher was a standoffish man and always had been.

Luke chuckled low. "If he talks to me before I die, I'll consider it a good sign."

There was one more couple Mose couldn't help but look out for as they continued the last few yards of their journey. Pointing at Jacob and Deborah Schrock, who were walking near the very front, Mose said, "Now there's a couple who don't seem to have any more hurdles to overcome. They married quickly, too." Mose had heard through the area's gossip mill that Jacob and Deborah had asked their bishop to marry them in a quiet ceremony.

Luckily, both of their families hadn't objected to the short courtship. Now they were living behind Schrock's Variety. Jacob was running the store, Deborah by his side.

Luke shook his head slowly. "They are a good match, but I sure didn't seem that one coming. At first I thought they hated each other. Even Frannie said she was taken off guard. I guess Deborah and Jacob took everyone by surprise."

Mose almost agreed, but he thought about Deborah's brother, Perry. For all his selfish ways, Perry had always seemed to know that Deborah and Jacob were meant to be together. More than once Perry had insinuated that he knew something about the two of them that no one else did.

Perhaps Perry had seen hope shining bright in a place where the rest of them had only seen darkness.

Now that was a fitting thought, Mose reflected as they all came to stop.

Gathering in a half circle, the group of thirty stood in front of Mr. and Mrs. Miller. Behind them was the well where Perry's body had been discovered, the rocks surrounding it where Abby Anderson had once been sitting, and the patch of ground where Jacob and Perry had fought.

Now the well had been filled with cement, securely closed for all time. A handsome plaque made of granite had been placed on the top of it. At the foot of the well were hundreds and hundreds of daffodils. Their bright yellow blooms, fluttering softly in the breeze among the bright green grasses, were beautiful.

"I'm glad you all could come out here today," Mrs. Miller said when everyone around them quieted. "For the last few months, we have been trying to figure out what to do with this place."

"At first, we thought we'd tear down the well and cover the rest of it up," Mr. Miller said. "But that didn't seem right."

His wife continued, her proud, thoughtful expression framed by her neatly parted black hair under a newly pressed white *kapp*. "We thought we ought to do something to remember this place. To honor it, not just attempt to forget about it."

She cleared her throat. "Then I got to thinking about how God takes each of us by the hand and molds our bodies to his liking." Looking out at the crowd, she met several peoples' gazes and nodded slightly. "In turn, God gives each of us special people in our lives to mold us, too. So, instead of trying to forget what we lost here, we thought perhaps we could try to remember everything that's been found."

Mr. Miller took a step forward and raised his voice. "Here, we've renewed friendships, and discovered more about ourselves than we knew existed. We've found that we can be tougher than we thought and more compassionate than we dreamed possible. But perhaps we've found what's most important . . . that each of us can grow into something beautiful from the harshest of circumstances. And bloom." He rubbed the back of his neck. "Which is why Lavina had me plant all these daffodils."

"Three hundred," Mrs. Miller said with a smile.

After a pause, the crowd began to laugh. Then Mr. and Mrs. Borntrager clapped. Gloria Schrock joined in. Then Jacob and Deborah. And Lydia and Walker. And the rest.

Finally, they were all clapping together. For the moment, and for Perry, and for the future. For what had never been, and for what would always be.

There, in Crittenden County. On an outlying field on the Millers' farm—where, until recently, no one had ever been actually invited to walk on.

When the clapping stopped, little Becky Plank's voice rose high and pure. "Mrs. Miller, you never told us what the plaque says."

"Indeed, you are right, child." Lavina Miller smiled brightly. "It is only one word. But it's the right word, I think. Fitting." After a pause, she continued. "It says 'Hope'."

Mose grinned. The Millers had chosen well. *Hope* was really all they had ever needed. For now. For the future.

Because, for a time, hope had been all they'd ever really had.

Dear Reader,

One afternoon two years ago, I was sitting at my desk, looking at pictures of Crittenden County, Kentucky, when an image formed in my head: a group of Amish circled around a well, staring at a body. Soon, the characters came to life, and a pretty good story began to form.

That was the easy part.

I don't usually write mysteries, so I had a lot of work to do and questions to ask while writing this series. Thank goodness for Heather Webber, my critique partner. She writes mysteries, and helped me so much with pacing and structuring the central mystery. A certain police detective in Denver very patiently listened to my somewhat creepy questions about dead bodies, collecting evidence, and other police procedures. Judy, one of my reader friends, told me all about working in a small-town sheriff's office. Thank you, Judy! I'm also indebted to several folks in Crittenden County who took time to talk to me about the area. Most of all, I have my editor to thank for asking me to try a little harder to make this series everything I dreamed it could be.

By the time *Found* was finished, I knew I had once again fallen in love with the characters. I'll miss Frannie and her bossy nature and her Yellow Bird Inn. I'll miss Mose and his stories about everyone and anyone in town. I'll miss Aaron and his animals, Walker and Lydia, and even Mary King's restaurant. But most of all, I'll miss the days I spent envisioning beautiful, rural Kentucky.

Thank you for reading the series, and for taking this trip to Kentucky with me. As always, I'm grateful for your letters, your emails, and your friendship on Facebook. Thanks for visiting with me at book signings, and for asking your librarians to carry my books.

The next series will be set in Berlin, Ohio. Hopefully, I'll see you there!

With blessings,

Shelley Shepard Gray

P.S. I love to hear from readers. Please find me on Facebook, on my website, or you can write me at:

Shelley Shepard Gray
10663 Loveland Madeira Rd. #167
Loveland, OH 45140

Questions for Discussion

1. This verse from Psalm 35 guided me while writing this book: *"Those who look to Him for help will be radiant with joy; no shadow of shame will darken their faces."* How do you think prayer will help Deborah and Jacob? When have you needed to look to the Lord for help?

2. The idea of grieving for a loved one, and for the past, was an integral theme in *Found*. Mr. and Mrs. Borntrager in particular have a difficult time moving forward. What do you think they need to do for their grief to be eased?

3. I really related to the Amish proverb, *"It is better to look ahead and prepare than to look back with regret."* Is there a time in your life when you needed to follow this advice?

4. Mr. Schrock certainly is flawed, and he definitely made his share of mistakes. But I find as humans, we're all more complicated than the outside appears. How has this proved true in your experience?

5.   How do you imagine the future looks for Deborah and Jacob?

6.   What do you think would have happened if Perry hadn't died? Do you think he was close to returning to his roots . . . or close to leaving Crittenden County for good?

7.   How would the series have been different if Perry had been without any faults?

8.   I debated for quite a while about what word should be on the Millers' plaque. Do you think "Hope" was the right word? Or, do you have a better word in mind?

Turn the page for an exciting preview of
Shelley Shepard Gray's next book,

Daybreak

These shall wake the yawning maid;
She the door shall open—
Finding dew on garden glade
And the morning broken.

FROM "NIGHT AND DAY," BY ROBERT LOUIS STEVENSON

January
Berlin, OH

The moment Viola Keim entered the main parlor of the Mennonite retirement home where she worked, she heard her favorite resident calling her name.

"Viola, come here quick," Mr. Swartz ordered. "I received another letter from Edward this mornin'."

After straightening her black apron over her purple dress and smoothing a wayward strand of hair under her white *kapp*, Viola grabbed a carafe of coffee, and did as he bid. She tried to summon a smile. Atle Swartz adored his son. Nothing could make his day like a letter from Edward.

Unfortunately, Viola could think of a dozen other things she'd rather do than listen to more news from the wayward Ed Swartz. She privately thought Ed sounded like a jerk.

Mr. Swartz's eyebrows clamped together as he glared at

her. "What's wrong with your feet? You're walking so slow, you'd think they were cobbled together."

"I'm holding a pot of coffee, Mr. Swartz," she retorted. "I've no desire to spill it on the carpet or myself. Or you," she said with a small smile as she filled his coffee cup. "It would be a real shame if I stained the carpet. Or burned someone," she said with a wink.

"You haven't burned me yet, Viola."

"There's still time. I've only been working here six months," she teased.

"Feels longer."

It did, indeed. Six short months ago, after a series of interviews, she'd gotten the job as an assistant at the Daybreak Retirement Home. Right from the start she'd hit it off with the seventy-four-year-old gentleman. He was a spry man, with lots of energy and a biting wit. Somehow, he'd taken to teasing her, and she'd learned to give as good as she got.

Now she looked forward to visiting with him every day.

Though, truth be told, she didn't think he belonged there. He was too young to be in a retirement home. In her opinion, all Atle Swartz needed was someone to look out for him every once in a while. To do a little cleaning, and to make sure he had his coffee and supper.

Actually, what he really needed was his son. After all, it was a child's duty to look after his parents in their declining years. Not be off gallivanting in South America.

Not that it was any of her business.

Taking a seat beside him, she poured herself a cup of coffee as well and pretended she was eager to hear every word the illustrious Ed Swartz wrote. "I can't wait to hear what he has to say," she lied. "What a wonderful-*gut* way to start my day."

When Atle narrowed his eyes over the brim of his cup,

she felt her cheeks heat. Perhaps she had laid things on a bit thick. "Is the coffee all right?"

"*Jah*. It is fine . . ." Carefully, he unfolded the letter smoothly on the table in front of him. "Viola, are you certain you want to hear the letter? I'm beginning to get the feeling you don't enjoy my son's letters all that much."

Now she felt terrible. Sharing his only child's letters were the highlight of Atle's day, and she was ruining it by letting her personal feelings get in the way. "Of course I want to hear it, Mr. Swartz. You know I enjoy sitting with you." Now that was the God's honest truth.

Two men sitting on a nearby couch cackled.

"You'd best watch it, Viola," one of them called out, his smile broad over a graying beard. "Atle's going to read every single word of Ed's letter. Might even read it twice, just to make sure you didn't miss a single thing. You won't be able to attend to anyone else for at least an hour."

"I guess I'll simply have to hope that you won't need me anytime soon, Mr. Miller," she said sweetly, smiling when the men chuckled again.

The camaraderie she'd found with the residents of the home brought joy to her heart. She loved working with the elderly Mennonite folks in the area, loved feeling like she was making a difference in their lives.

"Girly, you ready to listen?" Two raps on the table with his knuckles brought her back to the present.

"Of course," she replied mildly. Truly, one day she was going to tell him that she was twenty-two years old. Too old to be called "Girly." "Ah, what does Edward have to say this time?"

After casting a sideways glance her way, he cleared his throat and began. "Dear Daed, greetings from Nicaragua. It's cold here, but my heart is warm from all the good works we've been doing with the children in the area. . . ."

As Mr. Swartz continued to read about Ed and his mission work, Viola tried to imagine what would possess a man to leave everything he knew and loved to attend to people so far away. Though, of course, he was doing many good things with the Christian Aid Ministries, there was much in Holmes County, Ohio, that he could focus on.

Most especially, his wonderful father.

As Atle continued to read, stopping every now and then to repeat what his son said—just to make sure Viola didn't miss a single word—she felt her attention drift. Edward's stories, while impressive and heartfelt, simply didn't mean that much to her. Not when she had plenty of concerns right here in Berlin.

She couldn't imagine walking away from her family, it was so tight-knit and demanding. Though her family was New Order Amish, not Mennonite like the residents here, she found that her traditions and values weren't much different than the folks she helped.

That said, she was so grateful for the many blessings God had graced her with. She'd grown up in a beautiful white house, part of the newest addition to their already sprawling property that had first been built in the 1920's. She was close to her grandparents, who lived in the *Dawdi Haus* behind them, and close to her parents, and to the few aunts and uncles who hadn't moved far away.

She'd always gotten along fine with her brother, Roman, and her twin sister, Elsie, as well.

Of course, things would likely start changing soon. After all, she and her siblings were all of marriageable age. One day, she and Roman would get married and move on.

But no matter what happened, she intended to live close and continue to help Elsie. Her sister was surely always going to need a lot of help. Born with a degenerative eye disease, Elsie would likely need at least one of them to look out for her for the rest of her life.

Just imagining the idea of leaving Elsie in the care of strangers made her heart clench.

Thank goodness neither she nor Roman were like Ed Swartz!

" . . . and so, Daed, I must let you go. The children are about to open their shoe boxes and I don't want to miss a minute."

That caught her attention. "Shoe boxes?" she blurted. "Why in the world does he need to hurry to open a shoe box?"

"It was Christmas, Viola," Atle said with more than a touch of exaggerated patience. "Weren't you listening?"

Oh!

"There's only one right answer, Viola!" Mr. Miller called out. "Otherwise, you'll be hearing that there letter again, mark my words."

After giving her heckler a disapproving frown, she got to her feet. "Of course I was listening, Mr. Swartz. Once again, your son, Edward, seems to be having a mighty fulfilling and charitable life. I was just caught off guard by the mention of the shoe boxes. That's all."

But Atle didn't buy her words for even a minute. "It was Christmas, Girly. This was his Christmas letter. Those boxes were from us! Our shoe box ministry! Don'tcha remember?"

"Sorry. I had forgotten."

"I didn't."

With more patience than her parents would have ever

guessed she had, she smiled tightly. "I'm sorry, Mr. Swartz. It's simply that, uh, I thought he would have been talking about something else by now. It is the end of January, you know."

"He's far away. All the way in Nicaragua," he said slowly. Pulling out the country's name like she had trouble understanding things. "The letters take a long time to get here."

Feeling her cheeks heat all over again, she tucked her chin. "Oh. *Jah*. I mean, yes, of course. Thank you for reading it to me."

"But don't you want to talk about the letter? I'm sure you have questions . . ."

The only question she ever had was "why." As in why did Ed never ask his father how he was doing? As in why didn't he ever come back to visit? Why didn't he care enough to stay close to home?

But, of course, it was best to keep those things to herself. She didn't want to hurt Mr. Swartz's feelings for the world. "The letter was so thoughtful, so detailed . . . I um, I don't have a single question. And I had better deliver more of this coffee before it all runs cold. You know that Mrs. Decker expects me to visit with several people this morning. Have a good day, now."

The spark in his blue eyes faded. "You're certain you can't stay for a bit longer? I have some more news to share."

Oh, he was lonely. It broke her heart. "I'm so sorry, I can't stay today." She just wasn't up to hearing one more story about his perfect child. "I've got quite a bit to do before I leave."

"Well, all right, then. Have a good day, Viola."

"You too, Mr. Swartz."

After topping off his cup, and refilling the other two men's mugs, she rushed out of the room and went to the kitchen, where she put coffee and snacks on a tray for the ladies in the craft room. Balancing too much on the white wooden tray, she hurried out of the kitchen, turned left, and then headed toward the back of the building.

When two cups started to wobble, she abruptly stopped and set them to rights. Then rushed forward, and promptly ran into a man leaving the head office.

When their bodies collided, the plastic bowls of snack mix fell to the ground. And the coffee carafe began to wobble.

"Watch out!" she said as she tried to gain control of the tray.

Two capable-looking hands reached out and pulled the tray from her. "Careful," he murmured, his voice deep and steady and strong-sounding. Almost as steady and strong as his hands looked. "You almost ended up wearing that coffee."

Feeling a true mixture of relief and embarrassment, she looked up into the speaker's eyes.

And noticed that his dark blue eyes were tinged with gold. Much like a certain older gentleman's. "Oh!" she gasped.

"What?"

"You . . . you look much like one of our residents."

"Atle Swartz?"

"Yes. Are you a relation?"

"You could say that. I'm Edward Swartz."

If his unusual eyes hadn't given him away, his tan and square jaw would have. The man looked like a carbon copy of his father. Well, a younger, spryer, tanner version of him.

"You finally came back?" she blurted. Before she could stop herself.

"Finally?"

She bit her lip as Mrs. Decker came out of her office. "Is everything all right, Viola?"

"Oh, *jah*."

Mrs. Decker stared at the tray the man was holding. "Any reason Ed here is holding the coffee tray?"

"*Nee*." With a jerk, she pulled the tray from his hands. "*Danke*. Um. Excuse me, I have work to do."

"Hey, I'll be happy to help you," he said after the administrator turned to the right and walked down the hall. Leaving the two of them alone again. "That tray is fairly heavy."

"I can manage just fine." Unable to stop herself, she raised a brow. "Besides, don't you think it's time you went to see your father?"

She turned without waiting for an answer.

But still, her cheeks burned with shame for her behavior. And for the fact that as much as she didn't like him . . . she couldn't help but notice he was as handsome as she'd imagined.

Ed Swartz stood in the middle of the black-and-white-tiled hallway, more than a little perturbed. First she almost spilled coffee on him, then acted like he was about to mug her when he helped her with the tray . . .

Then had reprimanded him. Like he was a wayward child.

What was her problem? Was she just in a bad mood, or had she really gotten upset that he'd knocked into her?

Hmm. Maybe he was simply used to the kindness of the people he worked with in Nicaragua. The people there had so little, they were thankful for the smallest amount of care.

"Can I help you, young man?"

An elderly lady wearing polyester tan slacks, white tennis

shoes, and a bright blue sweater pointed to the sign-in sheet. "If you're visiting, you've got to sign in. It's the rules."

"Sorry. I guess I got distracted." After signing his name, he said, "Can you tell me where I might find Atle Swartz?"

A wave of emotion transformed her face. "Are you his son?"

"Yes, ma'am. Edward."

"All the way from your mission trip? Praise God!"

She darted around the welcome desk, squeezed his arm, and practically dragged him to their left. "Your father is going to be so happy to see you!"

He doubted his father's happiness would hold a candle to his own. He'd missed his father terribly during his two-year absence.

But his steps slowed when he caught sight of him, sitting in his wheelchair in front of the gas-lit fireplace. His father looked older, frailer.

"Daed?"

His father's head popped up. Stared at him like he'd risen from the dead. "Edward? Edward!"

As Ed crossed the room and wrapped his father in a hug, he realized nothing else needed to be said. For now, they were together, and nothing else mattered. With effort, he pushed all thoughts of the woman with the pretty brown eyes from his mind.

In the grand scheme of things, she didn't matter to him at all.

Peter Keim pulled another cardboard box off a shelf, looked at his mother, and groaned. "Mamm, every time I turn around, I'm finding another box of yours. Why do you have so much stuff?" And more to the point, how come he hadn't seen any of it before?

It was like his mother had hidden a secret life up in the rafters of their home, and it had all gathered dust and begun to slowly rot. When a spider crept out from under the box's top flap, he grimaced. "We should throw this all out."

From the other side of the attic, his mother looked at the four boxes, two trunks, and six or seven large wicker baskets that were filled to overflowing. She looked a bit surprised to see everything, but even in the dim light of the attic, Peter noticed a faint gleam of anticipation too. "Oh, Peter, settle down. It's not so much stuff. Not really so much for a woman's whole life. I am fairly old, you know."

Peter sighed. His mother had been talking like that for months now, which was exasperating, since she was only sixty-two and enjoying exceptionally good health. As far as the family was concerned, the matriarch of their family had decades to go before she went around and proclaimed she was old.

"Well, all this cleaning is making me feel old." Opening up one of the five green plastic garbage bags he'd brought up to the attic, he crouched down next to one of the trunks. "This women's work is wearing me out."

As he knew she would, his daughter Elsie found fault with that. "Father, you mustn't talk like that. Cleaning is most definitely not women's work. Besides, you know Mamm with her asthma can't be up here in all this dust."

He did love how prim and proper his daughter was. "I'm just teasing, Elsie. I don't mind helping with the attic. Besides, it's a whole lot warmer up here in the attic than outside in the fields."

She rubbed her arms. "I'm tired of winter and it's only January."

"Patience, Elsie," his mother cautioned. "Everything comes in its own time. Even spring."

Getting back on track, Peter brushed aside yet another traveling insect and pushed the box he'd just taken down a little more toward the center of the attic. "I can't wait to see what you have in here. This doesn't look like it's been touched since you moved in."

Before his eyes, his mother stiffened. "I had forgotten that box was in here."

"Then it's time we found out all your secrets," Elsie teased from her chair near the window. "*Mommi*, you know what's going to have to happen, don't you? You're going to have to tell us all the stories that go with the items in the box."

For some reason, his mother looked even more perturbed. "I doubt you'd be interested, Elsie. There's nothing out of the ordinary inside. Nothing that you haven't heard about at least a dozen times. You know, dear, perhaps you should go downstairs with your father. I'll finish up here on my own."

"I'm not going to let you be up here by yourself, Mamm," he said. "Stop worrying so much."

"And I'm not going to leave you either, *Mommi*. There might be something inside that you've forgotten about. . . . A deep, dark secret . . ."

His mom laughed. "I think not. My life isn't filled with secrets. That's not what the Lord intended."

Peter felt his smile falter as his mother's pious remarks floated over him. For all his life, both of his parents had set themselves up as pillars of the community. And as models for their six children to follow.

But their markers were so high, their children never felt they could meet their parents' high standards. It was one of the reasons his brothers Jacob and Aden moved to Indiana, and his little sister Sara had moved all the way to New York.

Even though he was the middle child, not the eldest son, he was the one who'd elected to live with them. But, of course, that made the most sense. He was used to keeping the peace—a quality that was definitely needed in his parents' company.

But even he was finding it difficult to hear their criticisms day after day.

Well, at least that was the reason he gave for his own private behavior.

Pushing his dark thoughts away, he pulled open the flaps of the box and pulled an armful of the contents out. On top was an embroidered sampler.

"What does it say, Daed?" Elsie asked, reminding him that with her eye disease, it was getting harder and harder for her to see most anything.

"It says, 'Start and End the Day with Prayer.' "

Elsie smiled. "That sounds like *Mommi*."

Indeed it did. Lovina Keim was the epitome of a dutiful Amish wife. She'd borne six children, had organized charity events for the community, kept a bountiful garden, quilted well, and even had a lovely voice.

She was a handsome woman, with dark brown eyes that her children and grandchildren had all inherited. She was a hard worker and never asked anyone to do anything she wasn't prepared to do herself.

However, she was also critical and judgmental. It was next to impossible to live up to such high standards.

Elsie moved closer, kneeling next to him. "What else is inside?"

Peter looked at his mother, who seemed frozen, her eyes fastened on the box.

Slowly, he pulled out a heavily embroidered linen tablecloth, a pair of crystal candlesticks. They were very fine. And while some Amish women did buy some pretty tableware every now and then, these items were a bit extravagant. "Mother, where did these come from?" He held up one of the heavy crystal candlesticks.

That seemed to set her back to motion. Busily smoothing out the rough fabric of a quilt, his mother glanced away. "I'm not sure where those came from. I've forgotten."

Peter had never known his mother to forget a thing. "Come on, now. You must have an idea."

"I do not. If I knew, I would tell you, Peter." Standing up, his mother shook her head. "I'm getting tired. I no longer care to look in these boxes." Her voice turning pinched, she continued, "Elsie, please walk with me back to my rooms?"

Obediently, Elsie moved to stand up, but Peter held her back with a hand on her arm. "*Nee*, stay, Elsie. Now that we've started digging in here, I'd like to see what else is inside." Something was propelling him forward. Maybe it was his mother's unfamiliar hesitancy.

Perhaps it was his own selfish wants—a part of him enjoyed seeing her discomfort. It gave her a taste of what he'd felt much of his life. With purposeful motions, he pulled out another sampler of a Psalm, the stitching uneven and childlike. A cloth doll. An old packet of flower seeds.

And then a framed photograph, wrapped in plastic bubble wrap. The Amish didn't accept photographs, believing that copying their image was a graven sin. "Mamm, what in the world?"

"Peter, don't unwrap that."

His mother's voice was like steel, but Peter ignored the command. He was forty-two years old, not fourteen. And now he was curious.

"Who is this, Mother?" he asked as pulled the plastic away, finding himself staring at a photograph of a beautiful young woman. Her hair was dark and smooth, her eyes the same brown, coffee-with-cream color that looked back at him in the mirror.

A vague thread of apprehension coursed through him.

"Who is it?" Elsie asked.

"It's a woman, a woman of about your age," he said patiently, ignoring the tension reverberating from his mother. "She's mighty pretty, with brown, wide-set eyes and hair. Why, she could be your twin, Elsie."

Elsie gazed at the photograph, but the three of them knew it was only for show. Her eyesight had gotten much worse over the last two years. "She is pretty," she allowed. "Though we all know I already have a twin. I'm glad this girl isn't one, too. I have no need for one more!"

"Since she's an Englisher, she couldn't be your twin. Ain't so, Mamm?" He chuckled, raising his eyes to share a smile with his mother. Then stilled.

His mother looked like a deer caught in the headlights of an oncoming vehicle. Her face was pale, twin splotches of color decorated her cheeks. And her eyes . . .

They were the exact ones in the photograph.

Suddenly, he knew. "Mother, this is you, isn't it? This is you in a cap and gown. At your high school graduation."

His mom averted her eyes.

Elsie gasped. "*Mommi?* What were you doing, dressed up like an *Englischer?*"

Though his mother said nothing, Peter realized he didn't need an explanation. The item in his hands was clear enough. Slowly, he got to his feet, his knees creaking with the effort. "Your grandmother wasn't dressed up as an *Englischer*, Elsie," he said quietly. "For some reason, she wasn't Amish here. She was English."

Bitterness coursed through him as he thought of the many, many times she'd belittled all of them because they weren't perfect enough. Weren't devout enough. Didn't obey the *Ordnung* to the letter.

In a flash, he recalled the stories she'd spun about growing up in a perfect Amish home in the fifties. The way her criticisms had driven his siblings Jacob and Aden and Sara away.

The way her perfection had made his other brother, Sam, try too hard, had made his youngest sister, Lorene, feel terrible about herself.

The way her iron will had even pulled apart his God-given, easy-going nature, even causing him to do things he shouldn't.

And she'd done all of this on top of a heap of lies.

He thought of all the times she'd even been critical of his sweet wife, Marie. The way she'd criticized meals and housekeeping and sewing.

Appalled, he stared at his mother. Really looked at her, as if for the very first time. "Talk to me, Mamm. Were you raised English?"

"*Jah.*"

"Were you ever going to tell us the truth?"

For a few seconds, time seemed to stand still. The dust particles in the air froze. Then Lovina Keim's face turned colder. "*Nee.*" Slowly, she walked to the narrow, steep steps and began descending.

Still holding the photograph in his hands, Peter let her walk down by herself.

"Daed, what does this mean?" Elsie asked.

It meant everything.

"I don't know," he whispered. But, of course, he could withhold the truth as well as his mother. "Let's go downstairs, too, Elsie."

Slipping the photograph under his arm, he helped guide Elsie down the stairs.

When she was in her room, and he was sure the rest of the house was silent, he strode to his bedroom, opened up the door to his bedside table, and pushed aside the neat stack of books.

Behind the well-worn hardbacks, he found what he was looking for.

And though it wouldn't solve his problems, it would help him not care. Even if it was just for a little while.